LATIN AMERICA

LATIN AMERICA

The Writer's Journey

·

GREG PRICE

HAMISH HAMILTON · LONDON

HAMISH HAMILTON LTD

Published by the Penguin Group
27 Wrights Lane, London W8 5TZ, England
Viking Penguin Inc., 375 Hudson Street, New York, New York 10014, USA
Penguin Books Australia Ltd, Ringwood, Victoria, Australia
Penguin Books Canada Ltd, 2801 John Street, Markham, Ontario, Canada L3R 1B4
Penguin Books (NZ) Ltd, 182–190 Wairau Road, Auckland 10, New Zealand

Penguin Books Ltd, Registered Offices: Harmondsworth, Middlesex, England

First Published 1990
1 3 5 7 9 10 8 6 4 2

Filmset and Printed in Great Britain by
Butler & Tanner Ltd, Frome, Somerset.

A CIP catalogue record for this book is available from the British Library

ISBN 0–241–12952–4

For Joyce and Kenneth Price

Contents

Acknowledgements

This book owes a very great deal to the constant advice and suggestions offered by Steve Gregory of the Department of Spanish Studies at the University of New South Wales. Thanks to Dr Robert Wilson of the English Department at the University of Alberta, who encouraged me to embark on this project. Thanks also to Aida Tomescu Tassa for her patience and empathy, not to mention her critical scrutiny of the prefaces to the interviews. Without the generous assistance of Gavin Millar and Carmel Fitzsimmons the Augusto Roa Bastos and Jorge Amado interviews could not have taken place; many thanks also to Maud Millar. The contacts provided by Peg Job were crucial for the Mexican interviews. Vital logistical support came from Elizabeth Britton. The Ana Miranda and Octavio Paz interviews were made possible by a travel grant from the Literature Board of the Australia Council.

Introduction

Literature in Latin America has evolved as part of a great debate stretching from Buenos Aires to Mexico City. This book attempts to capture the main currents of that debate. In Latin America the great, old questions are being asked again with freshness, excitement and urgency and it is this profound questioning that has given rise to a literature that is unparalleled both in the scope of its literary and social concerns and in its innovation.

Latin America has a certain cultural cohesiveness. The faces of the modern nations may be distinct but the factors that went into their making are largely held in common. These common factors can be sensed throughout this book, as can the important regional differences. With the exception of Brazil, there is the possession of a common language; books have travelled easily across frontiers. Writers have keenly read each other's work and responded with the partisan emotions of enthusiasm or anger that only members of the same community can feel. That community has sometimes been a purely literary one, at others it has been quite tangible, based on friendships formed during shared years overseas, sometimes in exile. Latin American writing has had some of the closeness of an expatriate community.

When these friendships have broken down it has often been for political reasons. Heated political debate is understandable, given that writers in Latin America are looked on, in a real sense, as the voices of large sectors of the population. Such prominence is unenviable and has its dangers; writers are often the ones who step into the shoes of the media or the politicians when dissent has been repressed. Their political engagement is, I think, one of the things that comes through most clearly in the interviews. This is true even of those writers whose work draws on the bizarre and the fantastic; realism has proved to be inadequate to capture the realities of life in a continent where 'reality' has always been a questionable notion. At one of the world's greatest cultural crossroads the ground is constantly shifting and literary innovation is a sort of necessary lightness of foot.

In preparing this book I wanted to focus on writers whose work has been translated into English – not because they are necessarily the 'best' but simply because their voices are likely to be familiar.* However, where a writer was less well known but had important views to contribute I did not hesitate to make an approach: Luis Alfredo Arango, for instance, has only published one novel but is in a position to give some unique insights into the role of the writer in Central America. With a project of this scale it was inevitable that some important figures would, for one reason or another, not be available; that was the case with Gabriel García Márquez and Carlos Fuentes. In terms of political balance it would have been interesting to hear the views of some of the Nicaraguan writers who were prominent in government. Despite two trips to Nicaragua, however, what seemed to be bureaucratic hurdles prevented me from speaking to any of them, though I wonder if this response wasn't a measure of the wariness generated by the war. Other writers might have been included, but the book is intended to be not a collection of literary stars but a window on to the central issues and the forces of creation in what is arguably the world's most productive literary community.

Most of the interviews were made during a journey of several months that began in Buenos Aires and meandered northwards. The interviews are presented by country, reflecting the order

* The Select Bibliography (pp. 276ff) is a list of some relevant titles available in English translation. The dates in the text refer to a work's first publication in Spanish or Portuguese.

in which they were made, which allows certain ideas to develop gradually. A year after returning to Australia I made another trip, via Mexico, to Europe and there completed the series.

The interviews were generally conducted in Spanish on the assumption that even the writers who speak very good English would be more comfortable in their own language. Manuel Puig, however, spoke in English, as did Márcio Souza and João Ubaldo Ribeiro. Ignácio de Loyola Brandão and Lygia Fagundes Telles spoke in Portuguese. I hope that no misrepresentations have crept into the translations of the interviews, as that would be a very poor way to repay the generosity with which the writers gave me their time.

URUGUAY

·

Mario Benedetti

Uruguay was for many years known as the Latin American Switzerland, not only because of its size – it is one of the smallest nations in South America – but because it seemed an ideal republic, isolated from the economic and social problems faced by much of the rest of the continent. It seemed to be a well-functioning democracy. The wealth from its agriculture supported a large middle class, mostly employed in government jobs with retirement at fifty. The capital, Montevideo, was a quiet, charming city whose lifestyle reflected the fact that at one time it had been governed by the French. Uruguay and neighbouring Argentina are the most European of the Latin American nations.

Mario Benedetti's early work presented Uruguay as a rather hollow society, imbued with bureaucratic complacency, where strong emotions or conflict of any sort were avoided. In the novel *La tregua* (1960) the inability of the protagonist to make any commitment leads to tragedy. Uruguayans are portrayed as people unwilling to leave their armchairs or desks to confront reality. The elements in Uruguayan society that were to emerge and rip this comfortable reality to shreds in the period before and after the military coup of 1973 were prophetically implied in *El país de la cola de paja* (1960).

From the 1950s the agricultural exports that had been the source of Uruguay's prosperity began to slip in value. In the 1960s inflation began to get out of hand and in the resulting hard times Benedetti's work became more political and he was involved in the founding of a political party. This experiment was cut short by the military, who, disturbed by popular protests, governed through the 1970s and early 1980s. The military instituted tactics of terror and torture on such a scale that a very large percentage of the middle class was driven away. Benedetti was among those who left. In the years that followed he found his inspiration in the lives of middle-class Uruguayans scattered throughout Europe and Latin America.

Trauma, alienation and sadness are emotions that surface in the writing of these years, though the sadness is lit up by a very humane irony. Even when dealing with painful themes Benedetti has always had the strength to smile. Wit functions as a way to distance the narrative, leaving room for works of meditative clarity. Benedetti's writing is characterized by a straightforward concern and honesty in the face of first apathy, then horror, then the loneliness and dismay of exile. The sanity, calm and lack of bitterness with which he writes mark one of the dictators' defeats.

In political terms Benedetti would belong to the left, although the division into left and right can be misleading, because very few Latin American intellectuals are doctrinaire. It is not always easy to judge how far writers have really moved apart since the debate over issues like civil rights in Cuba split the literary community.

The dictators who chased Benedetti from Uruguay, Peru and Argentina probably weren't interested in the answer to this question. Following some difficult years Benedetti settled in Cuba, and then moved to Spain. He has now returned to Uruguay and we met in Montevideo. He spoke with the same quiet wit that has won him so many readers.

GP You wrote in one of your essays that 'for the dictatorships of the Southern Cone, culture is subversion' and of the dictators you said that 'their projects always include cultural genocide'.

MB Well, that's not really saying anything new. Culture in general always bothers dictatorships, and writing in particular bothers them, because writers work with ideas. That's not to say that painters and musicians don't express ideas, merely that they are more clearly defined in writing. Also, in the Southern

Cone the great majority of intellectuals, writers and artists have been against dictatorships. In Uruguay, even though there were writers who stayed in the country – some because they wanted to, others because they couldn't leave or were imprisoned (including some who died in prison) – you could count on the fingers of one hand the number of writers who collaborated with the dictators. Despite our political and aesthetic differences – and we do argue a lot – as far as the dictatorship was concerned, we were united.

GP You also wrote that there are 'vast zones of critical silence in Latin America'. Would you say that writers are automatically social critics? Are they always mixed up in social and political matters here?

MB There is no obligation to be a social critic but if writers want to play that role they can only do so where there is freedom of expression. That never exists under a dictatorship, which is why so many writers emigrate and there are 'zones of critical silence'. I think I wrote that for a seminar about criticism in Latin America. At the time I was living in Caracas because Uruguay had become one of those zones.

GP To what extent would you say that Cuba was a 'zone of critical silence'? There's very little self-criticism in Cuba.

MB Oh, yes, there is. I lived there for eight years, so I know the country well. It's just that the criticism isn't evident from overseas. In the factories, in the cultural organizations, there are always sections that promote and analyse internal criticism. There's much more of that than in the capitalist countries. In Uruguay, where would you find a factory where the workers and the management get together to discuss the problems of the way the factory works, bureaucratic difficulties and so on?

GP What about the writers who have been exiled?

MB You mean the writers who exiled themselves, which is a different thing entirely. They left; that's their own affair. Cabrera Infante left. So did Severo Sarduy and Heberto Padilla, but no one expelled them. Padilla was in jail for twenty days and not a hair on his head was touched. It's true there were great international repercussions. There was a great outcry on behalf of a writer who was a prisoner for twenty days, on charges not related to his writing. The charges were of espionage and there was proof to support them. He was interrogated but not on account of his writing. On the other hand Mauricio Rosencof, one of Uruguay's leading playwrights, was imprisoned for ten years and the same people who made such a fuss over Padilla didn't stir at all. Rosencof was tortured. They almost broke him physically. No one came out on behalf of Julio Castro, who disappeared without a trace, nor for Ibero Gutiérrez, a young poet whom they tortured and killed. But Yes, they protested over Padilla and his twenty days in prison.*

I'd say that Cuba is the most free of the socialist countries. What's happening in Russia now, with *perestroika*, has been going on in Cuba for a long time. In art, for example, there are no problems over form. Socialist realism is not the official style, though you are free to write that way if you want to. You can go to art galleries and find abstract painting, pop art, figurative art or anything else.

GP How influential is the writer in social and political matters?

MB We don't delude ourselves that what we write or say will have much influence on politicians. Politicians in general don't pay any attention to us. But sometimes what you write may help a particular citizen or group of citizens to see certain aspects of their country more clearly. If what I write helps one fellow Latin American, I'm happy. If it helps more than one, all the better, but I'd say that helping one person should be a big enough reward for a writer.

GP To what extent does ideology affect the literary value of a work? You've written about the dislike some people had for Jorge Luis Borges, because of his political views, and how this led them to dislike his writing too.

MB The case of Borges, being an extreme one, is easier to judge clearly. Borges is a great writer, a man who has changed literary language. He was a very reactionary man and at times

* This interview was recorded in 1988.

he supported the worst causes. That wasn't always obvious, because he had a very peculiar sense of humour. He would come out with an aberration and you wouldn't know if he was joking. Sometimes it was obviously a joke; for instance, he suggested solving the problem between Argentina and Britain by donating the Falklands to Bolivia, so that it would finally have an outlet to the sea. On the other hand, when he said that the great mistake of the US had been to teach Negroes how to write, he was probably serious; and no ambiguity is possible when you accept a decoration from General Pinochet.

He wrote a lot during the rule of the Argentinian dictator Videla, praising him as a gentleman. Then in his final years he had a change of attitude. He started to make statements against the Argentinian dictatorship (not against Pinochet, but at least against the Argentinians). I think something must have happened to someone close to him or his family. He suddenly changed his mind. He became convinced that the military were torturing people, which previously he wouldn't admit.

GP Perhaps it was just that, for various reasons, he was very isolated from the real world.

MB Not that isolated. Borges was always very sharp; being misinformed wasn't one of his sins. But returning to your question, it is logical that someone's ideology should influence what they write. At times, as with Borges, the writing betrays almost nothing of the writer's ideology. With Vargas Llosa, to take another example, you find that until his most recent novels the writing was to the left of the writer: he moved towards the right but his work remained quite leftist. In the last two or three books, though, the writing has followed the path of the writer. There are also writers with a clearly defined ideology who write non-political work. I'm thinking of Julio Cortázar, who was very politically involved and who supported Nicaragua and Cuba. His position as an anti-imperialist was clearly defined yet, with a few exceptions, his books are not political. There are all kinds of variations.

GP So you'd say that Borges' writing loses no value as a result of his political views?

MB It would have been much better had Borges been more progressive. I'd say that an appropriate social background enhances a work of literature, but that doesn't in any way mean that Borges was a bad writer. He's an excellent writer and I think it's a shame he was never awarded the Nobel Prize.

GP Do you think that Vargas Llosa's ideological changes have affected the literary quality of his last few books?

MB I think the quality of his work has declined. His most recent novels don't reach the heights of *The Green House*, *Conversation in the Cathedral* or *The Time of the Hero*, which are very important novels. When a writer's work is very political, as Vargas Llosa's is, it is easy for changes in the writer's views to affect its literary value, whereas Borges wasn't very political. He was reactionary and conservative but, deep down, politics didn't mean much to him.

In the case of Vargas Llosa, the change is more notable in the themes than in the style. He treats his themes in a less objective way, I think. Apart from any ideological objections, I find them less satisfying as works of fiction.

GP Could we talk a little about your exile under the dictatorship?

MB In the early 1970s, before the coup, as well as being a writer, I was prominent in a left-wing political movement. I was receiving about three death threats a week. It was very dangerous and everyone advised me to go, so I left. I spent three years in Argentina but then I began to receive death threats again. It was even more dangerous than in Uruguay – at least twenty bodies were appearing every day in the rubbish dumps of Buenos Aires. I left for Peru, but after six months they sent me back to Argentina. I hadn't been politically active in either country. In Argentina I had to keep a very low profile because the death threats were still effective. Eventually I left for Cuba, where while working for the publishing house Casa de las Américas I had founded and directed the Centre for Literary Research. I became part of the committee that ran La Casa and kept working on literary research. I spent a couple of years there and then left for Spain. Even now, although I've returned to Uruguay, I spend three or four months a year in Spain.

GP You've written a lot about the problems the exile has to face, which you called the seven plagues of exile, but you've also said that the writer in exile has to seek new ways to write.

MB I've always been a little limited in my range of themes. I've always written about middle-class Montevideans, because that's the social level I know and can write about comfortably. I'm still writing about middle-class Montevideans, though the characters are scattered all over the world. In a country of less than three million inhabitants it's estimated that there were half a million or even 800,000 political exiles. I travelled a lot during the twelve years I spent in exile and in every country I visited I was in contact with other Uruguayan exiles. So I kept writing about Uruguayans, although I had to write in different ways because each place was different – the language, traditions, history, climate. For example, Sweden was the European country that gave Latin Americans the best treatment. However, this didn't mean that it was easy to adapt to the climate: in winter dawn is at eleven in the morning and dusk is at three in the afternoon. That keeps even the Swedish confined to their houses, which made it very difficult for the exiles to communicate with the people of the country. In my most recent book, *Geografía*, there are a number of stories where these problems appear.

GP You've also said that writers in exile have to keep creating so that when they return they can bring with them some of the culture that the country has lost. You're not just talking about high culture. It seems that writers here write for everyone.

MB In general, Latin American writers write for everyone, or at least everyone who is literate. In Uruguay there is a very low level of illiteracy, although Uruguay today isn't the same as it was before the dictatorship. The economic situation is much worse, so readers find it much more difficult to buy books. Far fewer books are now sold than in the years before the dictatorship. Ten young people may pool their money to buy one book and then share it.

GP That says something about the importance literature still has here.

MB Yes, it's still important. But during those twelve years the young people lost contact with literature because hardly any books were published and many were banned. In a sense, culture is a habit and many people have lost that habit. Uruguay was always one of the most culture-conscious nations in Latin America. Of course there are other factors. In all parts of the world television now takes up much of the time that might once have been spent reading.

GP In Europe it seems that writing is aimed at a more specialized group than it is here.

MB It is a more hermetic and esoteric literature. It's very rare for Latin American writers to be locked up in themselves. The Cuban writer José Lezama Lima is an exception; his work is extremely difficult. With Borges, the literary universe is very complicated but the writing itself is simple, transparent. It's the vision, the *Weltanschauung* that's complex; the writing is simple enough to be accessible to anyone.

Europeans are obsessed with language. There are exceptions in Latin America – João Guimarães Rosa, for example, the great Brazilian novelist, who is rather like James Joyce in the difficulty of his language.

GP What value do you see in literature that is principally an investigation of language?

MB The word is an important element in literature, though not the only one. Even for writers who have political preoccupations and who want to convey a social or political message, I think the literary element of their work has to be given priority. No matter how strong or revolutionary the content, if the form is clumsy, it will work against the message. The worst thing a work with a social message can do is to bore its readers, because that will prevent the message getting through. The better the container, the further the message will travel.

GP I've sometimes wondered if literature, in itself, isn't a trivial subject. What do you think of works that confine themselves to literary matters?

MB It's difficult to generalize. There are cases when writing can seem excessively abstract, up in the air, unconnected with life or anything else. Yet it may be saying something important. Also, as Sartre said, turning your back on reality is a form of commitment. There are no uncommitted writers. It's just that different writers are involved with different matters. Turning your back on reality doesn't mean that you are not committed to it, but rather that you have a commitment against it.

GP You've said that the sort of people writers are likely to meet at a dinner party are not their real readers. Do you have a mental picture of the people you write for?

MB This is a very complicated matter because one reader is so different from another, even when they are both on the same social level. There are differences in interpretive ability. Some have more intuition than others, or more intelligence, or a fuller cultural background. Some will get more of the cultural references, yet those working by intuition may reach a more profound understanding. I wouldn't say I write for anyone in particular. What I can say is that I don't write for critics or other writers. I just write the way it comes to me and on whatever themes spring to mind.

Every writer has their own language. If the language that comes naturally to you is complex and you try to write simply, then it will sound false. One of the problems writers face in finding their own identity is finding their own language. That means finding the style most appropriate to your thoughts and feelings. In my case, I have an obsession with clarity and simplicity.

GP When you write about exiles who have undergone torture have you done journalistic research? Do you do interviews?

MB I was never tortured because I was never a prisoner, except briefly in Peru. But many people close to me were tortured, so I've heard a lot of first-hand accounts, even though people who've suffered in this way generally don't like talking about it. They don't want to remember, which is understandable. However, there have been times when close friends have told me how it was. In general, though, I've written about torture through imagination. I imagine how I would feel if I were tortured. Torture is also present in those who escape it because it affects the way you think. It makes you dwell on what will happen if you're taken prisoner. I've written a play called *Pedro y el Capitán*, which is about torture, although torture isn't shown on stage. There are four acts consisting of dialogues between the prisoner and the 'good' interrogator. In each act the prisoner has suffered more gravely than in the previous one. When I wrote it I felt that I'd imagined everything. Then a performance was arranged at the Galpón theatre in Mexico. Many of the members of the theatre company had undergone torture. When I read the play to them for the first time they found it unsettling because of the dialogues I'd imagined were so similar to the real ones they'd had with their torturers. Imagination can also be a way of arriving at reality.

GP You once said that you'd abandoned the novel for poetry because you'd discovered that you expressed yourself better through images than through plot.

MB No, what I said was that, of the various genres I'd worked in, the most important for me had been poetry. From time to time I publish a novel – the last one was published in 1982 and I'm working on one now, but the genre in which I work most is poetry. I've published fifteen or sixteen books of poetry, I think, while I've published five novels and five books of short stories.

GP You've also published books of essays. You've written plays . . .

MB . . . and literary criticism; fifty-five works in total.

GP Why do you work in so many genres?

MB It's just the way things occur to me. A theme comes with the genre it is best suited to. If I have a theme for a novel, I don't try to turn it into a poem. I'm not going to try to turn a play into a short story, although sometimes that can happen.

I started to write *Pedro y el Capitán* as a novel. When I'd written a few pages I realized it was a subject that had dramatic rather than narrative possibilities. I've also written an experimental novel in verse. The protagonist lives through different ages in the space of one day – when he wakes up he's eight years old; as the day goes on he gets older, until he's thirty-five at the end. I'd thought of this as a fantasy novel but when I'd written about a hundred pages of prose I wasn't happy. I realized the concept was not fantastic; it was poetic. So I thought, if it's a poetic idea, why not write it in verse? It's one of the few novels in verse.

GP Your writing seems a little more European than that of some other Latin American writers. Of course, you could say that Uruguay and Argentina were the most European of the Latin American nations.

MB Yes, though there is European influence throughout Latin America. Further north, US influence is stronger, though Faulkner, Hemingway and Thomas Wolfe are all well known here. I've written a work of criticism on Faulkner. In general, the countries of the Río de la Plata have closer ties with European literature, above all with the urban novel; not so much with the rural one.

GP In Uruguay the mixture of races is much less evident than elsewhere.

MB Yes, because there are no Indians. Some were exterminated by the Spanish and the rest by the Creoles. Only 2 or 3 per cent of the population are Negroes and most of them live in one of the suburbs of Montevideo.

GP When you started writing you were very preoccupied with personal and ethical issues. Later your work became more political. In the poetry you seem to have been trying to link the two concerns.

MB In the last two collections, *Preguntas al azar* and *Yesterday y mañana*, the poetry has been less political and more reflective. I've returned to the reflective manner of my first books, though with more maturity. The political and social aspects are still there but as a background. Times change and your situation changes. I've always been very affected by the problems around me, whether they've been to do with the political situation or the difficulties of exile. Now it is time to reflect a little. Political issues are much more serious when you are organizing a political movement. There is no time to reflect and so you sometimes make mistakes. When I was politically prominent I was busy practically twenty-four hours a day – I never had time to think. Now I've decided not to play that role.

GP You've left politics for good?

MB I still work with the Frente Amplio and I was active in the National Commission for the Referendum. I write political pieces for magazines, but I'm not trying to run an organization any more. I never had a vocation for that anyway. Even though you may be concerned about the social, political or economic situation of the country, you need time to think about it. You need time to reflect on personal matters too. As you get older you even have to think about death.

GP What led to your political commitment?

MB Three things. The first was a trip to the United States in the 1950s. That was the only time they let me in – I haven't been able to get a visa since. I was quite naïve at the time, but I was very disturbed by the situation there – the way the Negroes and the Puerto Ricans had to live, for example. Those five months were my first lesson in anti-imperialism. Then there was the Cuban revolution, which was a very important event for many Latin American intellectuals. We hadn't thought that any country could successfully stand up to the United States, yet here was Cuba, a tiny country, going ahead and doing it. It made us a little ashamed. It changed our frame of reference. Instead of looking so much to Europe, we began to pay attention to Latin America. We realized we ought to be uniting and standing up to the US. Finally there was the situation of my own country. The two other factors had made me more mature and when things became serious here, I had to face up to my responsibilities, firstly as an intellectual and then as a politician.

GP What hopes do you have for Uruguay in the near future?

MB I'm not optimistic, because there will have to be quite a radical change of political direction before Uruguay's problems can be solved. The governing party is the most conservative of our three parties and that doesn't look like changing at the next elections. The present economic policy is not very different from that of the dictatorship. They are privatizing the public sector. They are going along with the IMF, paying the foreign debt, doing exactly what the IMF and the United States wants. If we are to get out of this crisis, we need to be bolder than that.

GP Do you think that Uruguay's constitution is adequate to enable it to solve its problems?

MB It's not a progressive constitution but before we start thinking about writing a more advanced constitution we should at least carry out the directives of the one we've got. We're not even doing that at the moment. Conservative though it is, the constitution no longer suits the government. They are violating it every day. They are still spending 43 per cent of the federal budget on the repressive forces – the police and the army – in a country that was always proud of spending more on culture and education than on the armed forces and the police. The universities are now getting 3.4 per cent of the budget. Even the dictatorship gave them more than that.

Eduardo Galeano

Eduardo Galeano's fiction grows out of concerns he first expressed in non-fiction. Galeano started his career as a journalist, editing a daily newspaper in his native Montevideo at a precocious age, and journalism is a strong influence in his work *The Open Veins of Latin America* (1971). This book is a hybrid, part history, part travel writing, part autobiography, though the tone is generally polemical, driven by an anger that will use any available means to make a point. In some senses it is a tract, a gust of indignation that owes a great deal to dependency theory, a school of thought that has had a lot of influence among Latin American intellectuals. Dependency theory holds that underdevelopment is no accident. It is the result of a world trade system that unfairly favours the developed nations, while perversely maintaining Latin America as a source of cheap natural resources, cheap labour and a convenient place to offload anything from old technology to bank loans.

The Open Veins of Latin America is the story of a looting that began when the Spaniards landed, sword in hand, and has continued in sometimes subtler but equally rapacious forms up to the present day, with effects that permeate the political, social and even literary life of the continent. The book is disturbing and challenging, crossing genre boundaries, becoming almost fictional at times, but the style is always driven by a crusading obsession.

Galeano's other books are also works of synthesis. *Days and Nights of Love and War* (1978) grows out of the repression Uruguay suffered under its dictators during the 1970s. It is autobiographical but uses the language of fiction to talk about social issues that go far beyond personal experience. *Vagamundo* (1973) shows similar concerns but is clearly fiction; it uses some of the forms of myth. In writing *Memory of Fire* (1982–6) Galeano seems to weave all the strands of his previous work together into a kind of fictionalized history. *Memory of Fire* is an account of hundreds of moments, history told as a succession of glimpses, rewritten with the brevity and punch of lyric poetry, with an overview of impressive erudition and scholarship.

Scholarship is something that might weigh down a work of literature, but in Galeano's case everything is told vividly and concretely, introducing implied narratives into what you might have thought of as completely intractable material. It is the willingness to tackle non-literary themes such as economics, power politics or international relations and transform them into moving and illuminating narrative that makes the *Memory of Fire* an important contribution to literature.

Eduardo Galeano lived in exile for many years but returned to Montevideo with the return of democracy in March 1985. I found him at home in a Montevideo suburb, a genial though unsmiling man who sat in a front room crowded with the art and artefacts gathered on his travels, an appropriate setting for one of the great synthetic minds of the continent.

GP Tell me about your background. Did you come from a middle-class family?

EG It was part of the ruined aristocracy. The family had come down quite a bit in the world. One part of the family had been rural landowners, the others had been in business.

I went to an English school, or rather one where they taught English. That's where I learnt the little English I know. I only did two years of secondary school, then I started work. I had no systematic education except for those first years and even then the teaching wasn't good. Really, the little that I know results from my own curiosity and the goodwill of my friends.

When I was fourteen I began publishing cartoons and a few articles. Then, with time, I began to realize that people

understood me better through words than images. I was
unhappy about this. I think that, deep down, I would have
preferred it to be the other way round. I was a sort of frustrated
painter who ended up writing articles and books.

The visual arts are very powerful and vigorous in Latin
America. They have tremendous expressive force, both on a
professional level and a popular one. Just look around you –
the work in this room is very beautiful, though nearly all of it
is by anonymous painters. There is great creativity in the plastic
arts. Unfortunately I never felt that I could express myself
through my drawings and the bad paintings that I did. I realized
I could achieve more with words, even though there is always
a gap between the wish to say something and the capacity to
do so. That gap seems inevitable: words never exactly correspond to the wish for communication that they grow out of.
However, it's out of the tension between the wish to speak and
the ability to speak that something worthwhile is written. There
is both a tremendous impotence in human communication and
a tremendous power. You never know if you're going to find
a way to make yourself understood, though you feel compelled
to try.

When I write it is to give others an embrace. Writing is my
way of feeling that I'm giving this embrace. The need to
communicate generates a great energy and often you feel that
you have managed to say almost what you wanted to say –
that's a source of great happiness.

GP You began writing fairly traditional fiction but then
you changed completely. It is difficult to know whether your
later work should be classified as fiction or as something else.
Presumably *The Open Veins of Latin America* began as a work
of non-fiction?

EG Yes, of course. I hadn't really taken literature very
seriously. It was a kind of parallel activity for me, of secondary
importance. Until I was about thirty I was a journalist first and
foremost. I was the editor of a number of publications, including a daily newspaper which I took over when I was twenty-
three, and magazines both here and in Argentina. It made me

feel very much in contact with people and events. Literature was just a kind of by-product – I'd written some books of short stories and a novel, but it wasn't my main concern. *The Open Veins of Latin America* was written more as journalist than as a writer. I was about to turn thirty and, to mark a change in my life, I was drawing together experiences, emotions and ideas from my work. After that I began to develop as a writer. My identity had been very divided – between the journalist, the writer, the latent poet and the social and political militant. After writing the book I began to feel the need to bring all these pieces together, to be more integrated.

GP In your most recent work, *Memory of Fire*, you've created a synthesis of all these things. It's partly journalistic, partly poetic . . .

EG *The Open Veins* is a forerunner in terms of the theme, and *Days and Nights of Love and War* gave me some of the technique. I began to invent, as a way of expressing myself, when writing *Days and Nights*. It was something I hadn't done in the other books, or at least not in a way that was really mine.

GP Yet *Days and Nights of Love and War* looks auto-biographical, while in *Memory of Fire* the author almost disappears.

EG Well, there are two levels of autobiography. *Days and Nights* is a completely autobiographical work. Everything in it really happened to me. *Memory of Fire* is autobiographical in the deeper sense of a writer immersing himself in the history of his continent and trying to recognize himself in it. You are continually finding reasons for acceptance or rejection when reading. You get worked up and this enables you to write about past events as if they were occurring now. It's as if you are participating in the history you're writing. The book is not an objective history but a subjective one. It makes no apologies for being subjective but rather proposes indignation, love, anger or desire as legitimate ways to interpret reality.

GP Latin American writers often play with time in their works. With this last work you've almost annihilated it. Everything is synchronic.

EG It is synchronic because the idea was to blur the frontier between the past and the present. The book began as a project to rub out dividing lines, including those between the different literary genres – the lines that say, 'This is an essay. Poetry goes as far as this point. This is where the novel begins. That's a short story. That's autobiographical. That's non-fiction.' The book is an enemy of these sorts of boundaries. It is a synthesis of all the genres, an attempt to recover the essential unity of the human message.

It is also an enemy of the dividing line between reason and the emotions, because *Memory of Fire* speaks a language that is '*sentipensante*', to use a beautiful word invented by the fishermen of the Colombian coast – it means thinking and feeling at the same time, with no difference between the world of the emotions and the world of ideas. There are other distinctions it tries to blur, for example that between spoken and written language. It's a book written to be read aloud. It tries to recover the collective voice by making no clear distinction between the individual and the collective voice. They are mixed up all the time.

There is also the frontier that separates specialized works from those accessible to the general public, the people that intellectuals condescendingly refer to as 'the common man'. I wanted to recover writing as a democratic activity. When you want to convey something you use language that people understand. That doesn't imply any deterioration in the quality of the language you use. As a writer you are part of a collectivity and it is just a matter of expressing this, rather than letting your style be generated by some intellectual order. That doesn't mean you decide to use a particular kind of language just because that is what people understand. If it were like that, your hand would obey without enthusiasm. The writing would have no life. No, it is much simpler: no one gives any orders. The hand doesn't have to obey the conscience, the head or the heart. You just express yourself in the language you normally speak.

GP You must have read an enormous amount to write *Memory of Fire*. How did you select what to read?

EG The book wasn't the result of a plan, at least not to begin with. It grew out of my natural curiosity. I am very curious about everything. For example, I'm the worst person you could ever pick to deliver a love-letter because I'd always open it. Curiosity has always guided my reading and when the idea of writing the trilogy came to me I had already accumulated a lot of knowledge of Latin America and the history of the continent. Then I began to read with the project in mind. An enormous amount of primary material lies behind each fragment in the book – I've listed my most important sources at the end of each volume and they come to about 1,200 works. My later reading was more clearly directed in the sense that there were certain things I had to find out, but it was still a matter of jumping in at the deep end and reading anthropology, history, the social sciences, travel writing or whatever came into my hands. You never know where you may find a hidden pearl. I was swimming, looking for shells and opening them patiently. That meant exploring libraries in search of something that would be revealing – a fact or a story that would illuminate the larger reality.

GP In *Memory of Fire*, it is as if you have realized your ambition to be a painter – each piece in the book is like a painting. Everything is very visual.

EG Yes, *I'm* very visual. Proust said he perceived the world through his sense of smell. The world was an aroma for him; life was an aroma. For me above all it's a colour, a form. Before being able to express an idea, an emotion or an experience in writing, I need to see it. If I don't see it, I can't write it. The reader also sees it, because in a way the reader reproduces the process the writer goes through.

I close my eyes and I see images, forms, colours. What I write is a description of what I see and what I see is a kind of incarnation of what I feel and think.

GP So did the process of writing *Memory of Fire* involve

reading something, forgetting it for a while and then rewriting it from memory?

EG Exactly. The theme, the episode that had electricity, the revealing fragment that illuminated the larger story, the moment where the human condition revealed itself through insignificant details often went unnoticed when I was reading. I initially passed over many things but used them later because they stayed in my memory. Something inside me tells me later that something is juicy, that it's worth telling.

GP Do you worry whether your text corresponds exactly to what you found in the source material?

EG No, not at all, because the sources cease to have any importance, or rather they are important only in a certain sense. *Memory of Fire* is unclassifiable, but let's call it a history book, at least in terms of its themes. It's important that the documentary basis is respected, so that no lies are told. What appears in the book really happened; I didn't invent it. What I do is to give the facts life. Information is lifeless and my part is to resurrect it through poetry.

Every vignette rests on some documentary foundation but it is realized freely. The only way to reflect life is through freedom. A way of writing that puts you in a cage, that makes you a prisoner of the facts in your possession, will annihilate your creative energy. The only way that the text can really breathe is to write freely, so I adopted a very heterodox way of writing. The freedom with which I handled the material horrified sociologists, economists and anthropologists. Still, what I wrote is real. It's just that by using poetic licence people can come to terms with the facts; they receive them freely.

The aim of all this was to achieve a kind of confidential contact with the reader. The book is history told as a story to a very dear friend. You are telling him things that you feel might help him, because they've helped you. You want to give him a sense of the human adventure, to tell him that we are here for a reason.

As you know, there are two levels of discourse, the spoken

and the written. At times the separation seems quite pathetic. It comes close to schizophrenia. Literature has always suffered because of this division between real language (the one you normally use to communicate with) and another language that's imported or imposed. I want my language to be unified because I want to be a whole person, not some schizophrenic whose culture drags him in different directions. I don't want to be drawn and quartered by my culture.

GP You have always been very open about where you stand on social and political issues, even in your writing. Many writers prefer not to let their convictions show so clearly in their works.

EG Well, another of the barriers that I want to help to overcome through my writing is between public and private life. *Days and Nights of Love and War* was written with this intention. I wanted to show the degree to which the wars of the heart are the same as the wars in the street, that what happens inside you is the same as what happens outside. Everything is shuffled together like a pack of cards. This is a century that has begun to see the necessity of doing away with the traditional division between the internal and external world, which is a lie based on bourgeois hypocrisy. The bourgeoisie accepts two levels of discourse, just as it accepts other double standards. Traditionally there is one morality for acting and another for speaking. There is one attitude towards what goes on inside and another for what happens outside. There is always a contradiction.

GP Would you call yourself a Marxist?

EG I was brought up a Catholic. My early childhood was rigorously Catholic. Later, during my adolescence, I was influenced by Marxism. I am a result of those two streams, the Catholic and the Marxist. Both marked me very deeply, yet Marxists view me with suspicion because I'm unclassifiable. By nature I am very anti-dogmatic. I couldn't adapt myself to any particular religion and for some people Marxism is a kind of religion.

GP Presumably being a Marxist and a journalist involves a conflict: journalism is supposed to seem objective and not reveal whatever ideology may be at work behind it.

EG I don't believe in objectivity in writing. I don't think anyone is objective. Writers always transmit their own conception of things, even if they seem to be as cool as a computer. In my case it's all quite open and intentional. I'm not capable of seeing things from a distance and so I have no choice but to take part. I am condemned to take sides. Anyway, as I said, there is no objectivity. There is no human message that is not impregnated with subjectivity.

You can have an *objective* – in the sense of something directed beyond yourself – that is realized in the influence the printed word has over the conscience, memory and imagination of the reader. That involves the writer in a certain responsibility. There is no such thing as an innocent writer. No one can truly say, 'I write only for myself. I don't care about anything else.' You are always responsible for your acts and words are acts. They become acts in the process of dissemination. If you talked only to yourself and the four walls or wrote love-letters to yourself, then perhaps you could speak of having a certain innocence or neutrality. However, this seems so much like masturbation that you couldn't recommend it. You'd die of boredom.

GP How does ideology influence the way you write?

EG Well, I don't follow any ideological line. Our conception of things, our set of values, which is what you could call ideology, results from the way we accept or reject the world and the way we feel things ought to be changed. I don't feel that the function of the writer is to either applaud the world or vomit on it. There are points of agreement and disagreement. Writers act upon reality by having an effect on the conscience of the reader. We are helping to change things. They say that no book has changed the world but neither has any spectacular event. The great processes of change in history are just that, *processes*, not events. Change is the result of innumerable factors.

GP Have your ideas on politics or history changed through writing?

EG They start to link up. The essential unity of the human message begins to emerge. Also, if they are well written, they cease to be political or historical or sentimental or intimate and become simply human messages, or human adventures in communication.

In *Memory of Fire* I tried to choose historical episodes that were revealing, that help you to see. Sometimes they are just little things. There was a child, the son of a friend of mine, who hadn't seen the ocean. When he was six or seven he asked his father to show it to him. His father agreed. On the day they went, as they got close, crossing the sand dunes, they could hear the ocean and the breakers against the rocks. There was the strong smell of the sea, a salty wind, and the child could feel they were getting closer until, suddenly, the sea was there, sparkling in the sun. It was so beautiful that the child could say nothing. Then he asked his father, 'Help me to see.' I think literature does that. When it is true it helps you to see.

GP *Memory of Fire* strikes me as a sort of encyclopaedia – you could almost be a Latin-American Diderot.

EG My aim was that the book should open itself to every possible reading, so that you could read it as an encyclopaedia, a history book, a work of poetry, a novel, an epic, a love story, a cookbook, or whatever. Above all I wanted it to be a book that could be read aloud, as I said before. I think that the teaching of literature lost a lot when teachers stopped having their students read aloud. Some used to make their students learn passages by heart. At the time it seemed ridiculous but I have gradually come round to the point of view of a fine Spanish critic, José María Valverde, who maintains that it is very important to recover the oral quality of the text.

Memory of Fire is the result of a complex creative process. Every section is the product of fifteen or twenty drafts; if a draft didn't sound good musically, I started again. The book was an attempt to recover the musicality of words, so that the story could be told as a sort of poem, beside an open hearth, to someone who couldn't read, just as stories were told long ago.

GP Isn't it also part of a movement in Latin America to try to create a way of seeing that is specific to this continent?

EG It's a matter of writing from our own point of view, which is different from the one we inherited. The book is an anti-history in that sense. It is the recovery of our history from another point of view. It is a collection of myths and real experiences that aim to help create a new way of looking at things. We are in the early stages of something important in Latin America. A number of writers are working to create a new culture, one that isn't an enemy of the people, which promotes creation and not consumption, which helps Latin Americans to cease spitting in the mirror. The dominant culture here has always taught us to underestimate ourselves; it has always domesticated us, making us incapable of action and convincing us that it is impossible to be what we really are. The recovery of our history, the recovery of a sense of horror and wonder, has the objective of helping to break through the structure of impotence that has stopped us thinking with our own minds, feeling with our own hearts and standing on our own feet.

All the time that I was working my way along the paths of Latin American history, I felt that this story was mine. I had a sense of something that involved much more than just the place where you were born, the colour of your skin, your personal, family or national background. In telling the story of others you find yourself telling your own story. You recognize yourself in these stories about other people when you realize that it could all have happened to you. The reader senses this deep identi-fication, which sometimes leads to rage.

The complexity of the work arises from an awareness that it is necessary to create new answers, which in turn generate new questions. The questions work against a consumer culture that manipulates us and trains us to fear. I feel that we have to reply to that culture in a vigorous way. When you think of how things used to be, it's clear that quite a lot of progress has been made — we are now aware of the need not only to create but to create in our own way and to start to see things with our own eyes. Throughout Latin America we are prisoners of forms of education that de-educate us and means of communication that stop us communicating. That is what we are fighting against.

PERU

·

Mario Vargas Llosa

In the late 1960s the consensus that had prevailed among Latin American intellectuals since the Cuban revolution began to break up. The credibility of the left took a severe blow from the Soviet invasion of Czechoslovakia in 1968 and then in 1971 there was fierce debate over civil rights in Cuba.

Mario Vargas Llosa was one of the writers who protested vigorously at the Soviet Union's treatment of its intellectuals. He was further disillusioned by the advent of a left-wing military dictatorship in his native Peru in the early 1970s and was equally unhappy when other military factions moved the government towards the right. Vargas Llosa maintained that even if many of the government's goals were admirable and supported by large sectors of the population, the dictators doomed themselves to failure by stifling criticism. In the late 1970s Vargas Llosa's political evolution began to affect his literary position; he called for a new concreteness and simplicity, which was remarkable in a writer whose early style had been very complex and challenging.

Vargas Llosa had seemed to conceive of the world as a labyrinth peopled by social victims. His novels enforced a kind of sympathy for the characters – the readers wandered as they did, uncertain, in stories with multiple narrators where key facts had to be pieced together. Vargas Llosa has always considered his work to be realist, albeit experimental. That is true of *Conversation in the Cathedral* (1969), which traces the pathways of political corruption, or the book he travelled to the Peruvian rainforest to research, *The Green House* (1966). Though in *The Green House* situations are captured with dream-like ellipsis, the thrust of his work is towards a critical social realism, written with implicit awareness of what Graham Greene put very well: the disturbed or dangerous individual is in many ways quite harmless without the collusion and perhaps corruption of society.

There is a swing away from this attitude in *Who Killed Palomino Molero?* (1986), a much later work written as a kind of detective story. It begins with a murder and ends by discounting many of the larger social factors that could have been involved.

Vargas Llosa's ties with the left had been unequivocally broken in the *The Real Life of Alejandro Mayta* (1984), which portrays the Peruvian left as hopelessly muddled and dangerously misguided. In the later novels the bewildered voice of the social victim is replaced by a sophisticated narrator who makes his way though the Peruvian landscape with the guile and resources of an investigative journalist or a detective.

Vargas Llosa is a man with an aristocratic charm who seems rather far removed from the gritty world of his novels. When I arrived in Lima, Vargas Llosa was about to stand as a Conservative presidential candidate. His house was well guarded, as he is an obvious target for the Sendero Luminoso, the Maoist guerrillas who control large areas of Peru. Lima, once a rich colonial capital, is now in a state of decay and national bankruptcy threatens to overwhelm the fragile democracy that returned in the early 1980s.

GP Your early novels were extremely complex, so complex that you seemed to be trying to compete with reality. Recently, your novels have been much more narrowly focused. They are less like enormous labyrinths and more like mystery stories. Why the change?

MVL Firstly, I don't think writers are always conscious of the changes that may occur in their work. That is certainly true in my case, where everyday experience has been the raw material, fundamental to everything I have written. Our personal development, the way we live, the way we think, is naturally reflected in what we write. Even though my work is not strictly autobiographical, almost all my novels make use of my personal experiences. They are based on situations I have lived through, people I have known, things I have read, or very vivid experiences that have stayed in my memory. So in that sense my work has reflected the evolution of the way I feel and live.

I am aware of certain changes. I think that when I was young I unconsciously associated complexity with difficulty. I think all writers, when they start, tend to do this. In trying to portray a dense and complex world you feel you must use difficult techniques and impenetrable language. Then, with time, you discover that perhaps the most difficult thing to achieve in literature, as an aesthetic ideal, is simplicity. It is much more difficult to portray a complex world using a simple structure and transparent language than through the labyrinth.

So, even though I'm always very aware of the complexity of the world, in my recent novels I have tried to achieve clarity and transparency in the language and structure. I have had to force myself at times, because, like all Latin Americans, I have a predilection for baroque structures and luxuriant language. My novel *Who Killed Palomino Molero?* was one of the most difficult things I have written, yet the language is extremely simple. It is almost a long short story, where what you see is just the tip of an iceberg. The story is not told but merely suggested to the reader. However, all this does not mean that I cannot change back. Tomorrow I might return to writing very involved and complicated novels. One thing that I have learnt in my life as a writer is that nothing is laid down beforehand.

GP In your more recent novels the protagonists face problems of interpretation just as much as the reader does. Previously, it was much more difficult for the reader – I sometimes found it hard to follow what was happening in your early novels.

MVL In some works this complexity could be justified not just on aesthetic grounds but because of the subject matter, as in *Conversation in the Cathedral*, where I was trying to show a whole society in movement, with all its involved and inter-connected mechanisms. I wanted to show how the different levels of society determined and modified each other. Life was also determined by a very corrupt, underhand dictatorial system. Using a complicated and labyrinthine structure to portray this very dirty, involved world had a certain justification, wouldn't you say?

In other cases it was more of a luxury, a kind of brilliant intellectual game, as in *The Green House*, where there is a kind of delight in form itself. Form is a character in the story. At the time I wrote *The Green House* I was very influenced by the novels of William Faulkner, which I admire greatly for their technical brilliance.

GP When you write now, do you have the ideas you want to present more clearly worked out than you used to?

MVL I don't know about that. When I start a novel, despite having a lot of background material, not to mention plans and outlines, my vision of the novel is very confused, very primary. I discover a novel as I work, and this has not changed for me. It is still a great search, an exploration, although it always begins with certain ideas, images and plans. A novel is something that is constructed as I write. That is as true of *Palomino Molero* as of *The Green House*.

GP Yet the more recent novel seems to have a more clearly rhetorical structure, like a well-thought-out argument.

MVL *Palomino Molero* is a novel that was born of an image – the image of a soldier tortured in the desert. Starting from that image, I then had the idea of showing, by means of a police investigation, all the mental and imaginative processes involved. However, I wanted everything to be revealed almost by accident. I intended the novel to be very deceptive. It appears to be a police story but it is trying to reveal the mechanisms of the human imagination, both on an individual and on a collective level.

Of course there is also the political aspect, but above all I was interested in the imagination, in how it constantly constructs a kind of counterpoint to reality in order to defend itself from that reality, to counteract everything it finds intolerable or irritating or inadequate.

This is a constant theme in my work, though it has been treated in many different ways. If you think about *The Green House*, you will see that it was really something imaginary. It lived in people's imaginations, and the full story is never revealed in that novel. *Palomino Molero* is more or less the same in that respect, though the processes dealt with are very different. In *Palomino Molero* you are faced with a tragedy. What really happened? It is difficult to say, but the story does show how people react when confronted with certain facts and how, through these reactions, you can discover the deficiencies and limitations of a world.

GP *Palomino Molero* seems to argue that people put political constructions on events that have a purely personal or psychological significance. The novel also seems to be concerned with how what might be called the imagination of the left reacts when confronted with certain kinds of events in Peru. It is a kind of *reductio ad absurdum* of an attitude that is expressed very succinctly in *The War at the End of the World*, where one of the characters says that chance does not exist: there is always, behind even the most puzzling outward circumstances, a hidden rationality.

MVL What you have quoted is really the definition of all dogmatic philosophies of history. My position is directly opposed to that.

GP Yet there is a very clear formal order in your novels, especially the recent ones.

MVL The construction is very rational and very clearly thought-out, but the stories themselves are not so rational. There is always an element that is spontaneous or unfinished, which leaves room for the imagination. There is a liberty which breaks through the plans I make, though the form remains strict and rational. In that sense I feel I have followed Flaubert. Structurally, his work is very compact and coherent. I like to read novels written like that, and that is the way I try to write. But reality is much more chaotic and unpredictable than the forms we use to express it. The disorderly world is there within the clear, symmetrical structures of my work.

I redo things many times. I rewrite. I cut. It takes a great deal of work to discover the form necessary for each novel. I only find it after a lot of revision. I have never begun a novel with a very clear idea of it. I remember how struck I was when Julio Cortázar told me that he had written *Hopscotch* practically without correcting it and without knowing, each day, what he was going to write. He'd just sit down at the typewriter and write. For me that would be unthinkable.

GP In your book about the writing of *The Green House* you say that it grew out of two different novels.

MVL To begin with there were two novels, each quite distinct. One was about Piura in northern Peru and one was about the jungle. Later the two were combined.

GP As in *Aunt Julia and the Scriptwriter*? At the end of that novel all the writer's radio serials become mixed up.

MVL They get confused in his mind. I think that in my work there are always parallel worlds that interact. There is one reality that is purely imaginary and another that is, let's say, historical. The two are constantly confronting each other and getting mixed up. Sometimes, as in the case of *Aunt Julia and the Scriptwriter*, there is one world that is lived and another that is invented – the world of the scriptwriter's stories.

In *The Storyteller* there is also this contrast between an objective and a purely imaginary world – that of a storyteller, who is the narrator of the novel. These two worlds, though they belong to different levels of reality, are really complementary. They both have the same source, which is human nature. Human beings invent stories and project them, they try to fill the gaps between events by means of the imagination. The human totality is created not just by history but by the imagination.

GP Yes, but in the case of the scriptwriter the two separate worlds become a nightmare. They drive him mad.

MVL Exactly. His is a pathological case. But when you live a lot in the world of the imagination you sometimes feel threatened by the scriptwriter's nightmare – that everything is going to get mixed up. It happens to me sometimes when I am writing. When I began *The War at the End of the World* I suffered from a sort of anxiety because it was difficult to keep so many characters separate.

GP I was wondering if the scriptwriter was a study of what might happen to a writer without an ideology. He is not guided by any beliefs, he simply writes stories. He does not know what he is saying. When something occurs to him, he just writes it down.

MVL That's right. He is a spontaneous narrator involved in a narrative industry.

GP In your early novels there are many narrators. You see the world through many different eyes, the eyes of the characters. Recently you seem to be more controlled and more distant from the characters.

MVL I don't agree. For one thing, the writer is never the narrator of a story. He always invents and hides behind a narrator. For me, that's an axiom. The narrator may be visible or invisible. He may be a character in the story. Sometimes he even takes the author's name, but he is never the author. There is always a kind of personality split: you give the task of narrating to the narrator. The principal character of a novel is always the narrator.

GP Sometimes in *The Green House* it's not easy to tell who is narrating, whereas in *The War at the End of the World* you always know who is doing what. You see the characters from the outside and the story is told in the third person.

MVL There is an omniscient narrator, although there are also episodes narrated through the eyes of the characters.

GP Does this mean you now have more confidence in what you are saying? Does it indicate an ideological change?

MVL No. *The War at the End of the World* is a historical novel – the action takes place at the end of the last century. I was interested in making the form reflect the period in which the novel was set. There is a certain symbiosis between the form and the period. I didn't want to impose a contemporary or avant-garde form on a story about the past. There are some liberties taken with narrative time and they reflect a certain modernity, but as a rule I tried to maintain a temporal distance. That is evident not only in the structure but also in the language. In the passages about the adventures of the counsellor, the narration has an epic tone reminiscent of some nineteenth-century novels. That also keeps the characters at an almost mythic distance. The narrator is never close to the counsellor. He is always seen from a distance, just as he was seen by the faithful who followed him. In that respect the form found its justification in the subject matter of the story.

GP Why did you decide to write a historical novel set in Brazil?

MVL I was very struck by the story of the rebellion in Canudos and the story of The Counsellor.* I was also very impressed by the person through whom I found out about all this – the great Brazilian writer Euclydes da Cunha, who wrote *Revolt in the Backlands* in 1902. He was there at the front as a journalist with the Fourth Army, but because he was a fanatical Republican, he saw only what his ideology ordered him to see. He wrote frenzied articles calling on the government to repress the revolt, claiming that the rebellion was organized by exiles in conjunction with the British monarchy, that the rebels were English soldiers in disguise who used weapons only the British had. Ideology completely prevailed over reality for him, as it did for the journalist in my book. The extraordinary thing is that da Cunha was also one of the first Brazilians to react critically to what had happened and this drove him to write *Revolt in the Backlands* in an attempt to find out what had really occurred and what had caused this great misunderstanding in Brazil.

I was very affected by this story and by the way it showed that intelligence and education are not enough when it comes to understanding reality. On the contrary, they are the sources

* Antonio Conselheiro, a Messianic figure who tried to set up a secessionist community in Canudos in north-eastern Brazil at the turn of the century.

of the worst kind of misunderstanding and the worst kind of confusion if they are accompanied by a dogmatic attitude towards the world. Ironically, it's often those who are supposed to be the most lucid observers, the intellectuals, who fall victim to this sort of thing. This has been a constant problem in Latin America and is still very much a part of our reality today. At the moment in Peru the Shining Path guerrillas, Maoist fundamentalists, also have a vision of reality that is based on ideological convictions, which turns it into something completely abstract and schematic. Yet is has gained credibility, become a way of seeing, feeling and living, even for some people with a sophisticated cultural background. I found this reflected in the story of Canudos.

GP In an essay in *Contra viento y marea* published in 1978 you said that the writer needs to use language that is more concrete and which really communicates.

MVL I meant that it is necessary to get away from stereotypes. In literature stereotypes can provide a way of narrating. For example, in *Aunt Julia and the Scriptwriter* Pedro Camacho moves in a world of stereotypes and clichés, which is fine for the world of the imagination and unreality. However, in politics it is very dangerous, because in politics unreality means prejudice. If you move in an unreal world you destroy yourself. Your mind is distorted and what's more you distort the minds of other people. You make them confuse reality with unreality and that can have catastrophic results. This is something that very often happens on the left – in Latin America at least. As a rule when the left tries to transform reality it is very ineffectual and inefficient, because its approach to reality is based more on stereotypes and rhetoric than on ideas.

GP Do you now distrust language rather more?

MVL Language has its limitations and you discover that as you write. This marvellous living thing, language, has certain limits and you can't transcend or go beyond them. This is something that all writers have discovered, especially the great stylists. Reflected in all Flaubert's correspondence is a fight with language. In his case it was truly dramatic: the way he'd look for the right word, pushing himself to the point of anguish and despair in search of the perfect correspondence between word and object that, of course, can never be found. It doesn't exist. Words and things are never the same.

GP To what extent does the method of the writer in *The Real Life of Alejandro Mayta* reflect your own method as a writer?

MVL It reflects it quite accurately. Like the narrator in that story I always do 'field work', not so that I can reconstruct the story in a way that is faithful to reality, but rather, as the narrator of the novel says, in order to be able to lie while knowing what you're talking about. On the basis of a concrete objective reality I start to imagine and invent. That is my way of working.

I always need to familiarize myself with the context. If it's the jungle, for instance, I need to know about the vegetation, the animals, the heat, the colours, the smells, the kind of people who live there and the way they speak. Everything is based on real events. I try to read as much as possible, to become infected, impregnated with the atmosphere of the world I'm writing about. This familiarization is what I find stimulating, it's what lets the imagination loose.

For example, when I wrote *The War at the End of the World* I tried to read everything that had been written about Canudos. I read works by sociologists and historians and journalists. I went to the regions. I visited the towns where The Counsellor had been. I returned with a lot of cards to catalogue and a lot of documents, though not to follow faithfully. I didn't respect the real story, I changed many things, but this is the way I manage to stimulate the imagination. It's a realist methodology, a little like Pedro Camacho putting on disguises in order to feel more closely identified with his characters.

GP It's not really accurate to call this lying, is it? It's more like a game based on reality.

MVL No, it is a lie, because reality is transformed into something different, which is then presented as if it were real. If a novel is successful, we feel it is truthful, something that has been experienced. We believe in its reality. In fact, we tend to perceive reality as we read it, because the world we live in is so chaotic. It doesn't have a clear, coherent structure. Novels give us that order (as do philosophies, of course); we expect a novel to order and organize the world for us, yet the order that a novel gives us is a fiction. It's something imposed on the world, but it helps us to understand the world better, even though the world is never the way it is in novels.

Novels serve to create a sensitivity towards the world. A good novel educates you. It helps you to perceive the great complexity and diversity of the world. Moreover I believe Oscar Wilde's statement is true: life imitates art. We tend to organize life in accordance with the imaginary models of art, literature and philosophy.

GP In an essay in *Contra viento y marea* you wrote that the Peruvian dictatorship of the 1970s failed because there was no free press: the lack of fertile debate and criticism played a big part in the regime's failure to carry out its reforms. In *Alejandro Mayta* many people are spoken to and many viewpoints are sought in order to arrive at a final truth; does this make it a pluralist novel?

MVL I didn't plan it that way, but that is a credible interpretation.

GP Yet the narrator accuses himself of wearing glasses, just like the myopic journalist in *The War at the End of the World*. It's as if the writer always has to work to take these glasses off, and listening to different viewpoints is necessary, almost indispensable.

MVL It is fundamental to the true knowledge of reality, the only knowledge possible.

GP How do you feel, knowing that you are unpopular with a lot of people because of your statements on political issues?

MVL You can never be popular with everybody. If you are popular with some people you are unpopular with others. You have to resign yourself to that. There is no way to reach unanimity – except when you die. The dead reach unanimity but the living never do.

GP There used to be a community of writers in Latin America, during the years of the 'boom'.

MVL Yes, we were quite a closely knit group. As time went on we grew apart for personal and political reasons, but that always happens. It doesn't just occur amongst writers. It is almost inevitable. Life draws people apart. It is constantly remaking relationships, unmaking some and making others.

GP Why do you choose to spend part of the year in England?

MVL Despite all its problems, England is a very civilized country, where there is a great respect for your private life. You can isolate yourself easily. The emotional distance between people in England is something that many Latin Americans find dreadful, but that is precisely what I like. During the months I'm in London I live quite a solitary life. I only see who I want to see. I have a lot of free time which is something I never have in my own country. My privacy is always invaded here. I'm always being asked to do things, life can sometimes be quite exhausting.

I also like the English character and the way the English live. England is a marvellous country for the theatre, which I love. Also, my children are studying there. It makes for a very interesting contrast, living between Lima and London. They are like night and day.

GP The free exchange of ideas we've been talking about owes a lot to England and has found an expression there in the form of parliamentary democracy.

MVL Yes, when I said that it was a civilized country I was thinking about that. It is the only country that has given common sense such great political importance. In Latin America common sense is rather looked down upon. A politician who says that you need to have common sense is liable to be scorned. The respected politician is the one who gets delirious. Delirium is a great political virtue in the Latin world. The great leaders have to be great dreamers – they have to separate themselves from reality. In England you are supposed to keep your feet firmly on the ground, to be pragmatic.

Then there is the tolerance of the English, which I admire very much because we don't have it. It is taking us a long time to learn to coexist in diversity. It's difficult for us because we come from a tradition of intolerance. We each believe that the truth is our personal possession and we act on that, even if it means hurting others. That's why our history is so bloody and violent, why there has been so much persecution and repression. In England there is a real political and social pluralism. There is a great respect for institutions, for the law. The law is considered quite reasonable – people move easily and naturally within legal bounds. They don't feel, as we do, an almost insuperable division between the law and life.

These are all things that I like about England. Of course, I'm not so naïve as to think that England is a country without its problems; far from it. There is a lot to criticize as well. But as far as its way of life is concerned, and its general orientation, I feel it has reached an admirable level of civilization.

GP You've written critically about Nicaragua. To what extent can you demand that a country like Nicaragua reach political pluralism in a short time? Isn't that asking a bit much. After all, it took the English centuries.

MVL No, I don't agree. A country can be poor and free at the same time. It can be tolerant. It's not true that only rich countries can be free and democratic. That is an ethnocentric prejudice I've encountered a lot in Europe.

In Latin America there are poor countries where there is a great deal of tolerance. Costa Rica is an admirable example: it's a poor country, but it's a very tolerant one. It's pluralistic. There is real freedom. It has a very democratic tradition. These ways of thinking are taking hold in other Latin American countries despite poverty. Venezuela, for example, has had quite an open system for the last twenty-five years. Of course, these things are perfected with time, and with prosperity, but it's wrong to think that you have to reach a high degree of development before you can be free and tolerant.

GP Do you have hopes for Peru?

MVL Yes, I have hopes, moderate ones, because the country

is in a very difficult situation. There is a lot of violence and instability. I have greater hopes for other countries in Latin America, yet there are grounds for optimism, as a great many Peruvians wish that we should live in peace, without killing each other, and that, after all, is the basis of a democracy.

CHILE

.

José Donoso

The sight of a nanny wheeling a young child through the park in one of Santiago's more genteel areas makes Chile seem rather like a nineteenth-century society. Labour conditions under the government of Pinochet were certainly rather Dickensian. While central Santiago is a showcase of relative prosperity, it is ringed by a mock suburbia where orderly rows of little makeshift houses sit in the dust like a memory of the world from which many of the residents have slipped.

Chile is an enigma. For many years one of the most literate of the Latin American nations, it had a relatively large middle class, yet power, influence and wealth were concentrated to an almost feudal extent. Although the country was nominally democratic, for much of the century the poor were effectively disenfranchised. The social hierarchy has always had a sort of Hispanic rigidity in Chile, their sense of order and propriety makes Chileans rather dour and correct, though perhaps their dourness is in part inherited from the stoical indigenous tribes who survived in sufficient numbers to leave their mark on the majority of the population.

José Donoso's work has always drawn on an awareness of the divisions in Chilean society and of the psychological cost of those divisions. Wife is divided from husband, parent from child and master from servant. Donoso portrays a world driven by the anguish of rejection, where etiquette can be as cold as poverty. Human warmth is usually gained illicitly and some-times at terrible cost.

Donoso began publishing in the 1950s, initially writing realistic fiction, though his awareness of the underside of

Chilean life moved him towards a tortured language and a
fictional landscape churned up by the violence of his characters'
emotions. Realism changed to metaphor and parable while his
obsessions seemed to demand more and more the language of
the grotesque. *The Obscene Bird of Night* (1970), perhaps his
greatest novel, reads like a long nightmare.

Donoso's work is too complex to invite simple social parallels, but his later novels do seem less like upwellings of the
unconscious and more like social allegories. In *A House in the
Country* (1978) a large group of children are abandoned by
their parents to the care of a head servant who seems to mirror
the military dictators.

José Donoso left Chile in the 1960s and lived abroad for
many years, which has prompted him to explore the dilemmas
of the expatriate. He was considered one of the main authors
(with Vargas Llosa, García Márquez and Julio Cortázar) of the
Latin American 'boom' of the 1960s, the years when the
strength of Latin American fiction began to be fully appreciated, though, as he points out, the notion of the 'boom' was a
false one. Latin American writing had been strong for a very
long time before it was noticed.

Now quite old, with silvery hair and beard, he talked in a
distracted way: quite a prickly individual, as I was to find
out, and still keen to attack anything he considered a literary
stereotype.

GP Did you grow up in an upper-class atmosphere similar to
some of the stories in your book *Charleston*?

JD There is no upper class in Chile. I was part of what you
would call a comfortable middle class.

GP But did you have servants and maids?

JD Everyone has them. Having servants isn't a sign of class
in Chile. Even my maids have maids.

GP That makes Santiago sound a little like Freud's Vienna
in the last century...

JD I wish it were, because Vienna was a very enlightened
city at that time. Freud wasn't the only one at work; there

was Schoenberg and Mahler, not to mention Schnitzler and Hoffmann; Strauss too. In Chile there wouldn't have been anything even vaguely similar to that.

GP I was thinking about the sort of clients Freud had – he might not have noticed much difference between the middle-class women of his Vienna and the middle-class women of Santiago.

JD That's true, but this is a very provincial society, very remote. It's a long way from the sources of culture. Everything takes a long time to get here and when things do arrive they often have little to do with our society. Chile is essentially provincial.

GP But in terms of the roles people would play in this society, and their psychology ... I remember reading about rich whites in the southern United States who had been cared for during most of their infancy by black nurses. When they began to grow up they had to reject their nurses because of their race, which caused psychological problems. Racial distinctions aren't quite so strong here, but there is great discrimination between the classes. Does this cause an identity crisis for Chilean children brought up by a nurse? Who would they identify with, their nurse or their real mother?

JD Well, the mother and the nurse have quite distinct roles. The mother takes care of one part of the child, then there's a darker side that the maid or nurse takes care of. If, with time, you are capable of synthesizing the dark and light sides, 'You're a man my son,' as Kipling said. Some of us manage it. However, I don't think that this is something that preoccupies us much, at least not consciously.

It is true that the maids in our house put us in contact with a different world – the world of 'the people'. We didn't know much about that world. We were protected. We lived in gardens or saw the world from cars. The servants were very alien to us, though we found ourselves developing bonds of affection, with the cook, for example, or with the maid who brought us up, or with the gardener. These emotional bonds

taught us much more about 'the people' than any other experience, though we always knew them in a state of dependence.

GP You spoke about a light and dark side developing in
relation to these roles. Is it this that generates the opposition
between light and dark in *The Obscene Bird of Night*? That
opposition is central to the novel.

JD That's true. The novel is my 'negative' experience of
Chile, which I wanted to leave behind. I didn't want to have
anything more to do with this kind of problem. It was repulsive.
It was like a skin I wanted to discard.

GP Returning to Freud, to what extent is the novel a
psychoanalytical investigation of this atmosphere?

JD A novel is never a psychoanalytical investigation. When
it begins to be a psychoanalytical investigation it stops being a
novel. My intention was to tell a story, to create a world – of
dreams, perhaps, but their Freudian aspects are unconscious.
The novel wasn't related from a Freudian standpoint. It may
have incorporated certain Freudian influences, but they were
linked to so many other things. Freud is no more important in
understanding this novel than, say, Baudelaire. Things cross-
fertilize without us being aware of it and then something
completely new is created.

GP The world of *The Obscene Bird of Night* is dream-like in
a number of ways. People are transformed into other people.
There are no barriers between one person and another. The
visual element of the novel is much less important than the
verbal. There is a very strong element of the grotesque, another
dream-like quality. All this makes me think that the novel must
have come out of a crisis.

JD It partly came out of an illness that I had. I was given an
overdose of morphine in hospital and I was out of my mind
for about twenty days – I had a high. I had a lot of dreams and
a great many things came out of my unconscious into my
conscious mind.

GP And this helped you to solve the problems you'd been
having in writing the novel?

JD Yes. For quite a few years I'd been stuck. I was going

round in circles and couldn't find a way to make it work. After the time in hospital I was able to do what I really wanted to do.

GP A bit like T. S. Eliot having a nervous breakdown before writing 'The Waste Land'?

JD Yes, but what happens with me is that after *finishing* each novel I have a nervous breakdown, or at least some form of psychosomatic illness.

GP Is that due to a crisis of confidence?

JD No, it is the result of an existential crisis. Who am I? What am I? Have I written the truth? Have I written my truth? It occurs with novels that I've finished rather than ones I'm still working on. I've abandoned many in an embryonic state. They may make me uneasy or neurotic, but that's something I can take in my stride. The crisis is something much deeper. It goes right down to the level where the unconscious is linked to the body. I may get an ulcer or have vascular problems that verge on hemiplegia. Once I passed out when I was leaving evening mass. On finishing a novel I always have to face things like that.

GP How do you get over it?

JD By holding on to life as hard as I can. It's just a matter of hoping against hope.

GP We've spoken of Freud and of Chile being a society with nineteenth-century characteristics. Because there is such a strong division between the classes here, in many ways it could be a classic case-study for a Marxist.

JD Marx was read at an early stage in Chile and unions were formed along Marxist lines. We've lived through the results of Marxist politics in Chile.

GP You often seem to be preoccupied with the psychological damage caused by class divisions and the rejections that are involved.

JD Yes, this is my specific concern when I write about class in Chile. It's not that I try to write from a social viewpoint, but I think that this psychological damage produces the divisions you see here.

GP Your work is often about personal rejection or the breaking down of relationships – all sorts of rejections in a family context as well as a social one. In *This Sunday* the head of the house sleeps with his maid but rejects her as a person. At the same time he won't sleep with his wife. Then the maid, who is quite old, sleeps with a younger man who is attracted to the wife. The wife feels sexually attracted to the younger man but feels he is like a son to her. Relationships like these contribute to the atmosphere of the grotesque in your work.

JD They don't seem grotesque to me. They seem perfectly normal. They are experiences close to my own. It's all almost autobiographical.

GP Did some of the images in *The Obscene Bird of Night* that I would call grotesque grow out of these kinds of human relationships?

JD The images were the form I had of expressing myself. Images have a reality for me that experience often lacks. It's only through images that I can make sense of experience.

GP In *The Obscene Bird of Night* many characters sleep with the retarded girl Iris by wearing the same mask. Is the mask a way of bringing together the things that have been separated through the rejections in the novel?

JD I wonder. It's not something I've given much thought. After all, writers are much more ingenuous than journalists or critics. We write with much more naïvety.

GP I can't recall any instances of reconciliation in your work.

JD No, because my work is an expression of rage. There is so much rancour that breaches aren't closed easily.

GP In *The Obscene Bird of Night* the rich Jerónimo rejects the grotesque side of his life, as represented by the poor, abandoned old women, the ex-domestic servants. Yet what he rejects pursues him and extracts its vengeance.

JD I don't think hell is grotesque. It has other qualities. I see the grotesque as being a way of surviving, a way of existence. It's also a form of aesthetic expression. The idiom of the grotesque is just as valid as any other way of writing.

Writers don't *choose* a way of writing – it just comes to you. It's rare that someone chooses a theme. A theme gradually imposes itself on you, just as images and experiences do. These are things that gradually make themselves your master. Only a hack chooses. Only a hack says 'I'm going to write a novel about this subject and develop it in this particular way.' Writers who are more than hacks are much less organized. The images that appear in their work, the worlds they create, the way in which they write – all this comes out of the unconscious at moments when you least expect it.

GP I can believe that very easily of *The Obscene Bird of Night*, but I find it harder to understand how you could write *A House in the Country* in that way. The book is an allegory, and seems to have been well-planned. The structure and the message seem to be the product of a critical intelligence.

JD Of course, but a novel isn't merely a message. It is also a world of flesh and blood. Even if the message, the form and the plot are clear, the flesh is unclear. For example, a character may suddenly grow out of all proportion and say, 'I want it this way.' The novel begins to impose itself on you even when you have a plan clearly worked out.

Of course I couldn't have written *A House in the Country* without having made a lot of notes. They remained as a sort of skeleton, which isn't evident.

GP Did you intend *A House in the Country* to be an image of Chilean society?

JD To an extent, yes, but it's not a blueprint.

GP It's interesting that you used the structure of the family as a model for the structure of the society.

JD I was raised on the English tradition of the novel – I read a lot of English novels, and I still do. The central image of the nineteenth-century English novel is the family, the family with its hierarchy and all its good and bad aspects. I think that has something to do with the way I write.

GP In several of your novels you seem to be drawing parallels between social and psychological structures. To what extent is the social rebellion of the children in *A House in the*

Country or of Maya in *This Sunday* like the rebellion of the senses or the unconscious?

JD To the extent that neither is very much determined by rules.

GP In your novels, the lower-class characters appear to be more elemental than the upper class ones. The upper classes seem to be more intellectual, colder, like Alvaro who has no sexual relations with his wife. The other character, Maya, is much earthier.

JD In Latin America there is a big rift between the lower and upper classes. The poor don't have a life of their own, or very little. They imitate the ways of the middle class and a lack of education means people abandon their traditional, rural world. They enter an urban society without any idea of what they're doing, they don't know how to survive. They lose what they had in the country and in exchange they might get a Volkswagen or a little house that will collapse with the first earth tremor.

GP So they are left with only the most basic or primitive elements of their culture?

JD Not even that. It's all wiped out. They are ashamed of their rural customs and want to forget about them. They end up being lumpen.

GP In that case it does make sense to compare the social struggle with a psychological one, because the lower class is, in a Freudian sense, the unconscious. The poor are the instincts.

JD Yes, because that's all that's left to them. Their folklore and their customs have all gone.

GP Many of your characters would not be the sort of people who read your books. The maid in *This Sunday*, for instance, would read a different kind of novel.

JD Not necessarily. She'd be reading the novels that are talked about in Santiago, those that are talked about on television. She might be reading Bertolucci's *Open City*, or Milan Kundera, for example.

GP In your recent novel *La desesperanza* (1986) the central figure is an artist, a singer, but he is ineffectual politically. How can writers overcome this limitation?

JD Why do they have to overcome it?

GP Well, I'd have thought you would have some kind of social programme.

JD No, not at all. Novels with a social programme really irritate me. They're all a load of shit!

GP So you don't aim to be didactic in any way?

JD No: not pedagogical nor didactic nor programmatic nor political nor sociological. None of that.

GP But *La desesperanza* seems to show the left in Chile as being so divided that it is incapable of doing anything. That makes it a kind of social criticism.

JD There may be social criticism in it, but it is not a novel of social criticism.

GP So *La desesperanza* isn't about despair of political change?

JD This is an area where writers don't have to justify themselves. It irritates me. Why the devil do I have to explain what I write? I write what I write. I write the way things are. I write because I like writing and because something is expressed in what I write, but not to preach in any way. I begin my novels without a very clear idea of what I'm going to say. Writing is a kind of existential discovery of what I'm going to say.

GP Does the title come at the end?

JD No, always at the beginning, with the exception of the novel that I'm working on now.

GP Could you tell me a little about it?

JD That's difficult. I don't want to destroy it by talking about it, but it is a novel with elements of fantasy, very Chilean and very true to the Chilean reality. It's about the coal mines. I can't say more than that at the moment.

GP Have you ever been influenced by surrealism?

JD I've never had a liking for surrealism, but the critics write studies of me as a surrealist; that's their problem.

GP *El jardín de al lado* is an exploration of the difficulties of living outside your own country. Did the book have anything to do with your reasons for returning to Chile?

JD Well, I'd travelled a lot. There is a moment to leave and there is a moment to come back.

GP Why did you leave?

JD I was bored with the country. It was so far from all the sources of culture.

GP Did you find it easier writing in Mexico?

JD No. It wasn't a matter of making things easier. In literature it's more a case of looking for a fight, for stimulation. In Chile there was a very impoverished literary movement known as Criollismo. It called for realistic fiction that would give a detailed account of the customs of the people in the provinces. I was expected to continue writing in this tradition but I rebelled. I read a lot of James Joyce and Virginia Woolf, not to mention European writers like Proust and Kafka, because Chilean writing wasn't able to provide a satisfactory model for writing. I found Baudelaire much more interesting than any Chilean poet. So I left Chile in search of a world where the books I was reading had more validity.

GP Yet you kept on writing about Chile and Chileans.

JD The writers of my generation, of the 'boom' years, all left their countries but continued to write about them. Ernesto Sábato was an exception, but Onetti, Fuentes, Vargas Llosa, Cortázar and García Márquez were living in places like Paris or London and writing about their countries of origin. I think this distancing was a very important aspect of the Latin American novel at that time.

Isabel Allende

Isabel Allende's first novel *The House of the Spirits* (1982) has some of the qualities of a popular romance – a number of passionate and striking men and women romp across the pages of a long, larger-than-life novel, written with a quirky humour that has helped to make it a best-seller in a number of countries. On another level it is a social allegory that traces Chile's progress over the course of this century.

The central male character is Estebán Trueba, who builds himself a kind of feudal domain as a landowner and stands for the group that has generally made the decisions in Chile. Opposed to his sternness and ruthlessness is his wife Clara, who is sensitive to the extent of being clairvoyant. The novel owes much to techniques developed in the Caribbean region among novelists such as Alejo Carpentier, who suggested that what is fantastic in Europe is not necessarily so in Latin America. The geography, the exuberance of nature and the often bizarre twists of history introduce an element of the wonderful and terrible that is real, not fictional. In this novel, however, the marvellous tends to be a possession of women, and magic becomes a metaphorical counterweight to brutality.

Of Love and Shadows (1984) takes up where *The House of the Spirits* left off and is much more matter-of-fact. The magic is lost at the beginning of the novel when the extra-sensory talents of a young girl make her a victim of the military. It seems that the pre-coup world with its possibility of whimsy has been erased. It is perhaps in defiance of this loss that Isabel Allende sets a love story in the unpromising terrain of a mass murder.

The book ends with the heroine having to flee the country, something that Isabel Allende herself had to do.

The House of the Spirits is so remarkable that one tends to forget that it is a first novel. In *Eva Luna* (1987), Isabel Allende perhaps finds her true voice: the book has a relative leanness and mental toughness absent in the first two. While it draws inspiration from the soap operas that are so popular in Latin America, it does not retain their sentimentality. It has a wonderful, irreverent humour, and humour is the deadly enemy of soap. Its political message is conveyed through farce. The magical elements of *The House of the Spirits* have been replaced by the power of the word, represented by the storyteller Eva Luna, an orphan whose picaresque misfortunes provide a wealth of anecdotes and glimpses of Venezuela, Isabel Allende's adopted country. She is currently living near San Francisco.

GP When I was reading Eva Luna I couldn't help thinking of the sixteenth-century Spanish picaresque novel, *Lazarillo de Tormes*, which follows the adventures and tribulations of a poor boy. In some ways you are reworking that story in *Eva Luna*, but with a female protagonist.

IA Yes, a number of people have said that, but I didn't set out to write a picaresque novel. It was only after it was finished that people drew my attention to the parallels. I have to confess, that I had never read a picaresque novel. I was educated in English schools where I learnt nothing about Spanish literature. I was brought up reading Chaucer and Milton but nothing from the Golden Age of Spanish literature, so when they started talking to me about the picaresque novel I had to find out what a picaresque novel was.

GP One of the features of the picaresque form is that the protagonist doesn't change within. Everything is seen from the outside. Even though *Lazarillo de Tormes* is told in the first person, it's not the narrator himself or any development of his character that is important. To an extent, this is also the case in *Eva Luna*, isn't it?

IA Now that you point that out, it occurs to me that none

of the principal female characters of the three novels, Alba, Irene and Eva, talk about themselves. They are just windows on to what happens. I don't know why it should be that way.

GP It's interesting because, being educated in the English tradition, you would have been familiar with the nineteenth-century novel, where characterization is so important, as are ethical and psychological questions. In the Spanish tradition action and the external world are much more important.

IA The world is more important than the person. I feel that important and extraordinary things happen *around* me; nothing that happens to *me* could have the same weight. It would be very difficult for me to write my memoirs.

Literature that is centred on the writer leaves me cold. Those interminable books where the writer tells you about the torment of writing – if it's such a torment why not do something else? Take up woodwork. I don't want the dancer, ready to dance *Swan Lake*, to come on stage and start telling me about her training, her diet and how difficult it is to dance. Get on with it! I want a book to appear the way a magician pulls a rabbit out of a hat. Don't tell me how it's done.

GP Could we talk about the magical elements that appear in *The House of the Spirits*?

IA In that book and the two others there are elements that could be called magical but they are generally symbolic: they stand for something else. The spirits of the title represent the passions, the obsessions and the dreams of the family. Estebán Trueba, who appears to be the most practical and the only rational member of the family, is really the one most driven by obsessions. Once taken by an idea, he is capable of pursuing that particular dream or nightmare to its most extreme consequences. Clara is the person who controls the spirits. She is the least obsessed and the most free, the most tolerant spirit in the house, the most emotionally healthy.

The spirits are also memories – memories of the past, of the people who have died, those who Clara puts in her notebook and who will later be part of the story she writes. The spirits are the past, which is always with us and in our memory. I feel that you have to be careful about calling the spirits the souls of the dead because it is all symbolic. The fact that Clara is clairvoyant and can move objects around the table has an ironic edge; she herself jokes about it. My grandmother was like that. She was always experimenting with a three-legged table, calling up spirits, moving objects around and communicating by telepathy. She was wonderful and she left me, as a sort of inheritance, the idea that nothing is the way it seems. Everything has a second or third face and our poetic task is to find the hidden dimensions of things and events. That means, first of all, finding a sense of humour. What is humour but the ability to see behind things? We all see certain aspects of people but when we get a glimpse from behind it makes us laugh, because no one has seen them that way before.

Seeing behind things is a source of great understanding of the world and of great tolerance for people's weaknesses. It is a source of love, because you realize that people are never completely bad or good. We all have elements of bad and good. You can understand what made people the way they are, though this doesn't mean you don't intervene in the world. I can understand why someone might torture, but that doesn't mean I'll be tolerant of it. I'll fight it with all the energy and rage in the world. At the same time I'm able to comprehend the forces at work. These are the spirits.

GP I find it intriguing that you have written about Chile using the style of magic realism, which is associated more with the tropics than with the nations of the far south, yet when you come to write about the tropics in *Eva Luna*, you move away from the genre. Why is that?

IA I don't know; I was concerned with other things in *Eva Luna*. There were different emotions, different things that I wanted to portray. I wanted to surprise the reader; I didn't want it to be clear whether the story was Eva Luna's life or whether it was the life that she had invented for herself. She says, 'I live and write novels in the way that I wish life was,' and then, later, 'I live life like a novel,' so the reader doesn't know exactly what they are reading, especially because the novel is always on the verge of exaggeration and improbability. The reader doesn't know if it's the truth or if she is telling an enormous lie. It might even be one of the serials she writes for television – or maybe she is simply telling the story of a novel she is writing. It's a game with reality. Different doors open on to different aspects of reality. That is the fascination of literature.

Literature is a reinterpretation of the world. You open a door and put yourself in the world where you live, but the rules are different. The first new rule in literature is that things occur in chronological order, whereas in life everything happens simultaneously. While we are speaking here they are dying in Afghanistan, but to express that fact we have to say it in a certain order. There is a chronological order in words that is false and artificial. That's the first artifice of literature, trying to put the world in order, to establish cause and effect, impose rules where there aren't any. In the real world we have to get by without anyone being able to tell us what the rules are. Yet we can't really live with this disorder: we have to try to organize it, and literature is one of the ways we have of doing that. Eva tries to put some order into this fracas that we live in, using literature, but of course what results is just another sort of fracas.

GP Game playing must be a kind of writer's liberation. If you play games you can write more freely, without always having to worry whether what you are saying is true or not.

IA Yes, but it depends on the story you're telling. I couldn't have written *Of Love and Shadows* in that way. It had foundations you couldn't play games with. I wanted to tell a story beginning with the terror in Chile and carrying on from there. And when I wrote *The House of the Spirits* I didn't have enough experience as a writer to be able to play, nor could I just do as I wished with the material. I simply wanted to tell a story.

GP You have talked about putting normal time in doubt, but you don't tend to change the traditional narrative time scale. Your novels have a lot in common with the work of someone like Dickens, for example.

IA Yes. For fifteen or twenty years Latin American writers
have been experimenting with language in order to break up
time, using techniques like the flashback or mixing up frag-
ments of dialogue from different times and places. In *Conversation in the Cathedral*, for example, or *The Real Life of
Alejandro Mayta*, Mario Vargas Llosa does this so brilliantly
that, despite the fragmentation of time, you are never lost. I
am not tempted to experiment with form in this way because
what interests me most is communicating with the reader. I
want the text to be comprehensible. If the content gives your
message, it is not necessary that the form do so too; it could
result in a sort of redundancy on the formal level.

In one of the drafts of *Eva Luna* I tried this technique,
thinking that I could express the idea of disorder better by
breaking with the normal structure of the novel and disrupting
narrative time. I reversed the order of events, cut things up with
scissors and jumbled them together. It worked well because it
looked very original. Perhaps it was even better than the final
draft, from a literary point of view, but I had the feeling it was
terribly artificial. It was like putting too much icing on a cake.
If the cake is good enough, leave it alone. Why put on more
decoration? I found it all overloaded and overworked, so I
went back to the traditional, natural way of telling a story.

At the moment I'm writing short stories for the first time in
my life. I'm doing this because Eva Luna is a storyteller but
her stories don't appear in the novel, or rather bits of them
appear. Only one is told from beginning to end. So I thought,
'I'm going to tell Eva's stories.' I am writing stories that could
have been told by her, so they have to be narrated by a woman
who has her perspective on the world rather than mine. There
couldn't be a story set in Finland, for example, because I've
been there but she hasn't; I've been trying to see the world
through her eyes. I also feel the temptation to play with the
structure of the short story, to experiment, yet I always come
back to the classical style because I want each story to have
something substantial, an original idea; that should be what the
reader remembers, not the way the story was told. No one

ever remembers the way stories are told. They only remember the anecdotes and the characters.

When I wrote Eva Luna I had in mind a narrative form, the television or radio serial, the soap opera, which is such an important genre in Latin America. There's not a family in the continent that doesn't follow one of these serials. A whole culture has grown up around them. This is part of our hunger for stories. If you say, 'Come here, I've got a story to tell you,' I don't know anyone who won't come with big, round eyes. All the indigenous communities of Latin America have the marvellous tradition of the storyteller. It also exists in Asia and Africa. A man will go from town to town telling a story. Every time he comes into a new town he sits down and tells his story. This is how people learn that someone has married, that a distant cousin has gone on a journey, that someone died – it's all in the story. Then people give the storyteller some bananas or a chicken and ask him to add to the story that there's another child in the house, for example, and his name is Ambrosio; so the storyteller goes to a new town and tells his story, adding what he has learnt, always in a certain order.

This still happens in towns where there's no tradition of writing, where there is only an oral tradition. There are many indigenous cultures in Latin America which have very little written language and where the oral tradition is still very important. There is very little written in Quechua, for example, or in the original language of the Aymara or the Guaraní. The Piroroa in the interior of Venezuela grow up hearing stories which are always told in exactly the same way, with the same words in the same order. There is the story a father tells when he goes out with his son to hunt a jaguar. The child has to learn it exactly because it tells how you hunt the jaguar, about the trees, how the air smells, which direction the wind comes from; it tells how to track a jaguar and how to set a trap. The child learns to look at the sky and know what time it is. Stories tell him about the stars and he has to memorize the names of the stars and put them in order. He needs to know the story of the fish, because one day he'll be a fisherman. He needs to know about water and what lives in it.

GP Your novels sometimes arouse a sense of wonder similar to that provoked by these myths, though your characters are not generally indigenous people but city dwellers. It's notable that the characters most in touch with this sense of wonder are women. Why is that?

IA That is because I come from the continent of machismo, where men and women are educated separately. Or rather, that used to be the case. In certain cities and social classes machismo is gradually being overcome. However, when I was young we were brought up separately. The men were mutilated emotionally. Men didn't cry. They were strong, they were protectors, they were ambitious, aggressive; they were *conquistadores* who related to the world in terms of power. That was true even in love. One speaks of 'possessing' a woman, as if one could possess another human being. A woman is said to 'give' herself to a man but a man is never said to give himself to a woman. The terminology makes clear the thinking that is behind it all.

I was brought up this way and it has taken me forty-five years of clear thinking to be able to fight that education. We women were the lowest kind of citizen. We were the poor amongst the poor. The men of the family had everything. We were meant to be of service, whether in the home, or as secretaries or nurses, never bosses or doctors. We were always secondary. They taught us to be silent. What we might have thought or wanted to do interested nobody. A woman ought to be silent in her house, the Bible says. I belong to the generation that rebelled. We fought to change these things. It was and still is a brutal battle in my continent, which leaves a lot of wounds and scars. Yet it's a marvellous battle and you have to fight with joy, because it's not going to end – as Eva Luna says, you have to make war with joy because you are never going to see the results. If she waits to see the results before she can feel happy, she will die waiting. Also, we women are really only the most obvious victims of the system; men are also victims. Their role is a rough one too. It is just as detestable as ours.

GP Love is important in your books not only in the general sense of the word – all the novels are in a sense romantic, love stories.

IA There are two things that I'm obsessively aware of, both in my writing and in my life: love and violence. Violence is generally represented by death, though love appears in many different forms. These two things are always present and though I'd prefer all my stories to have a happy ending, an ending of love, it doesn't always work out that way. Half the time things end awfully; pain and death are also there.

GP It must be difficult to put into the same book, into the same mental space, a lot of horrible things and something as fragile as romantic love. At the end of *Of Love and Shadows* when Irene is at the border checkpoint, she remarks that fear is stronger than love. I imagine that living with atrocities would kill a lot of feelings like love. How can you fit the two things together?

IA I think they naturally fit together. There is a phrase in *The House of the Spirits* that I've often had to explain. Alba is in a prison; they've tortured her, they've mutilated her, they've raped her, and when she's been through this terrible Calvary she is sent to a women's prison camp. They make life very, very hard for her, but she is there with other women. When she finally leaves the camp she says, 'I was happy in this place.' I've had to explain that a lot but it is the truth. In the times and places where the greatest atrocities occur the greatest, feelings also flourish. Alba was a child of aristocrats, a rich, spoilt and deeply solitary girl. She was brought up alone. This was the first time in her life that she'd been involved in a group, where the conditions were the same for everyone. She shares everything she has, but above all she shares her pain and solitude and fear. She feels that these women are a part of her. They are her sisters. When she first arrives at the camp, with her hand infected and emotionally in a very bad way, these women greet her by singing. That is based on fact. In the Chilean prisons they greet each new prisoner by singing the Song of Joy. They greet Alba in this way to tell her, 'We are with you.' When the guards beat on the walls and shout, 'Shut up you whores!' the women answer, 'Shut us up if you can, you bastards!' because they know that they are stronger, that while they are together they are stronger. So in this experience Alba learns to share. She learns to feel an absolute love, a disinterested and total love.

GP *Eva Luna* does not share the intense seriousness of *Of Love and Shadows*. Is this because it is set in Venezuela rather than Chile?

IA The tone of this book is completely different to that of the other two. I wanted the language to have some of the disorder and freedom of the tropics. In the countries of the Caribbean there's a kind of agitation, what we call *despelote* — a mixture of joy and disorder. *Despelote* doesn't have serious consequences, or if it does, they are treated lightly. I wanted the novel to have that lightness so as to give a better picture of the society, whereas *Of Love and Shadows* is very concise, almost journalistic, which is appropriate for a story about real crimes committed in a place like Chile. Chile is a very structured country, very hierarchical. I wanted the language to reflect the fact that the story unfolds in a country under a dictatorship, where society is compartmentalized, confined in a straight jacket. In *Eva Luna* I wanted to let language loose, to fit in with a story that is much freer and easier.

GP Part of the novel is about street children, prostitutes and transvestites. How did you learn about this side of life?

IA Because I'd been a journalist and journalists are always in the street and in contact with people and events. I was trained to listen to people, to observe and be involved. The characters in my books aren't strangers to me or outside my reality. I can enter their world too. I'm often asked why so many poor people appear in my books when I was never poor. Well, I've had a lot of contact with poor people and even though I was lucky enough to be born in a social class that gave me an education and a certain culture, that doesn't make me blind to other realities.

Having said that, in Chile I lived in a sort of perpetual innocence, an extended adolescence, until the day of the military coup. Then I realized the capacity for evil that is in all of us and I suddenly felt driven to make some commitment. I lost my innocence that day and, realizing the way the world was, I felt that if I had the chance to help someone or to change the world in even the slightest way, I was obliged to do it. So I began to work with the opposition to the dictatorship. I didn't need to leave the country to find out what was happening. I stayed in Chile for a year and a half and during that time I knew exactly what was going on. I stayed for as long as I could. When I felt the circle of repression closing around me, fear was greater than any other feeling and I left.

Many people stayed and have continued working and fighting throughout the fifteen years of the dictatorship. I have tried to fight from outside the country and I've never missed an opportunity to speak or to write or to fight against the dictatorship.

GP Tell me about your involvement in the resistance in Chile.

IA On the day of the coup they outlawed practically all political parties, unions and other socially active organizations. The only organization that survived, and indeed grew, was the Catholic Church. I'm not a religious person, and I didn't have any links with the Church, but at that time there was no other way of helping. I was in contact with the priests to give people asylum, to get people out of the country, to help prisoners or those living on the fringes of society who were dying of hunger. Communal meals were started, and special meals for children who ate only what the Church gave them. So that was my work, obtaining food, helping people to flee the country and helping prisoners.

I also got information that was to be smuggled out of the country. We journalists had access to certain kinds of information, such as where the torture centres were and who the torturers were. We gathered information about those who had disappeared, where they were being held and how long they had been held prisoner. All this information was sent out to Amnesty and other organizations in Germany and northern Europe which helped a lot of people. This was very dangerous work, not so much for those who gathered the information as for those who had to smuggle it out. If they caught you at the frontier, it was very serious. For example, one of my mother's uncles was carrying something – he didn't know what, exactly, only that it was inside a gift he'd been given. He was a socialist. Someone betrayed him and he was caught at the frontier carrying a cassette with information on it. He was sent to prison for five years, was tortured and sent from one prison camp to another. They ruined his life. So that was the most dangerous work. Of course it was also dangerous to give people asylum, but we didn't realize that at first. When I found out how risky it was I didn't dare continue. Fear was greater than love: I had to leave the country.

GP How did you find out that they were on to you?

IA Because I lost my job. They threatened me, beat up my children as they left school, tapped my phone, came to my house – a lot of things. It all happened in a week. Someone in the government who cared for me let me know that I had only three days to get out of the country. It was clear that many people were disappearing and they were often taken with their children. Children were being tortured in front of their parents. I couldn't bear the thought of that. I left first, because it was me that they were really interested in – I'd been acting more openly. A month later my husband left with the children.

GP Were you warned because they preferred not to take prisoners who were well known?

IA I have no idea. I had a television programme that was very popular – I wrote scripts and presented them. As my face was on television every week everybody knew me. The programme was a comedy, so people always associated me with jokes. I suppose the dictatorship never took me seriously either. They thought I was crazy. I used to dress like a hippy.

I had a car all painted with flowers in which I took people who needed asylum to the embassies. Everyone in Santiago knew that car and I suppose they thought it was all a joke, because I was associated with very frivolous things, humour and feminism.

GP Feminism is frivolous?

IA No, but my way of treating it was always a little frivolous. I wrote a column in a Chilean newspaper from a feminist point of view, but it was funny. It was called 'Civilize your Caveman'. Now I see it as one of the mistakes of my youth but at the time it was quite popular.

GP Your car painted with flowers appears in *Of Love and Shadows*, Eva Luna writes for television – are there a lot of things in your novels that aren't invented?

IA Yes, and even if I haven't lived through things, they have often happened to people close to me. The first part of *The House of the Spirits* draws heavily on anecdotes that were always told in my family and the characters resemble some members of my family: Estebán Trueba is very like my grandfather; Clara del Valle is very like my grandmother; Jamie and Nicolas are similar to my uncles Paolo and Mario. The Candidate is a homage to Salvador Allende, even though he wasn't personally like that, nor is the character biographically correct. The Poet is a homage to Pablo Neruda, and Pedro Tercero García is a homage to Victor Jara. In the second part of the book, the section on the terror is practically a documentary account of what happened in Chile during the military coup and the period of repression that followed.

Of Love and Shadows is based on a crime that occurred in Chile. In 1973, during the coup, a group of police in the area of Lonquen, a hundred kilometres from Santiago, detained fifteen rural workers. They put them in trucks, carried them off, killed them and then buried them in an abandoned mine. For seven years they simply 'disappeared'. Very many people have disappeared in Chile, in Argentina and in Uruguay, they're still disappearing in El Salvador, in Bolivia and other countries – it's a macabre practice on our continent. In 1980 a person told a priest in confession that he knew where they had hidden the bodies and he authorized the priest to tell the ecclesiastical authorities. The Church mobilized the human-rights organizations and gave the news to several foreign correspondents and lawyers. They went to the mine and opened it before the government could stop them. They came out with the corpses of the fifteen people. Amongst the fifteen was a father and his four sons.

I read about it in Caracas. The foreign journalists had relayed the news to many different countries so it was impossible for the dictatorship to stifle the scandal. It was the first time during the dictatorship that the police were prosecuted. They were tried first in a civil court and found guilty, then a military tribunal also found them guilty. The evidence was crushing. After that they were found guilty of first degree murder. The military saw this verdict as a threat to their authority so the dictatorship decreed an amnesty and the officers concerned were promoted. Today, they're walking around in uniform with their new ranks, perfectly free; and they're murderers.

I wanted to talk about the murderers. I wanted to talk about the 'disappeared' on my continent. However, it's such an enormous problem that you can't speak about the 'disappeared' in general. The problem is too large, too horrible and too painful to comprehend, but if we talk about one person who disappeared, or two, and they have names and faces, then we can relate to the tragedy.

There was a decade of dictatorships in Latin America and it has generated a wave of books, mine among them. My generation of writers is very much marked by the political process and by exile; some of us also by prison. It's impossible for a Latin American writer to ignore the political process because it affects us both personally and collectively.

GP Why is it that truly bad characters almost never appear in your books? You never see the people behind the coup, for example, and there's only one person in *The House of the Spirits* who seems really evil.

IA Because terror doesn't have a face. The most terrifying

thing about political repression is that it doesn't have a face. There is no one with direct responsibility. The victims of torture are blindfolded so they can't see the torturers. Torturers disguise themselves when they go into the street. Dictators wear dark glasses to avoid looking you in the eyes. Terror works because its crimes are committed in secret and with impunity. It can't be open about what it does. So when I write the most important thing is to create in the reader the same fear that I had and still have: the sensation of a terror without a face.

Terror is a presence, it's a black cloth that is always over us, it's part of a horrifying dimension that is even here with us in this room, right now. It's a capacity every one of us has and which is present in the world. From time to time, for a few moments, we are able to forget about it and pretend it doesn't exist; there are even some societies, such as here in the United States that are so spoilt they believe they are somehow protected from it. No one is protected.

ARGENTINA

.

Ernesto Sábato

Argentina has been a crossroads for many European cultures. The Francophile élite of the late nineteenth century built Buenos Aires in the architectural style of Paris. Italian migrants flooded in around the turn of the century in such numbers that about half the citizens of Buenos Aires have Italian forebears; their nostalgia is evident in the enormous opera house, modelled on La Scala. The Argentinians have also been Anglophiles and even today some of the richer families send their children to English-speaking schools. The military were founded on the Prussian model, with instructors and handbooks that predisposed them to intervene in affairs of state. Buenos Aires has been a great, cosmopolitan city and, until the 1960s, was a prosperous one, the focus of the largest economy in South America.

The wealth of that economy was reflected in the cultural life. In Parisian style, lively debate took place in the cafés and bars. Even in tough times there was a bohemian culture. The great Argentinian writer Jorge Luis Borges first became known in the 1920s by dropping off free copies of his poems in restaurants, where they were likely to find an audience. Argentina introduced foreign literature to the rest of the continent through its literary magazines and the important work that was done in translating European classics, which travelled as far north as Mexico and Cuba.

Ernesto Sábato showed his brilliance initially as a physicist. While working at the Curie Laboratories in Paris during the 1930s he became involved with the surrealists and began to devote himself to literature, firstly as a prolific essayist; his first novel, *The Tunnel*, was published in 1948.

The Tunnel is a view of the world through a paranoid mind driven by a relentless, overheated logic. The narrator is a man who has turned his lover into a sort of icon, the object of a ferocious obsession that feeds on both love and insecurity. The novel is an exploration of terrible egotism, which seems to have disturbing parallels with attitudes that might be considered normal; in this sense it is a study of machismo. *The Tunnel* (1948) can be seen as a detective story, a novel focused on an existentialist anti-hero, or even an exploration of a much older, universal phenomenon: the violence that underlies the reverence of a man who turns his lover into a kind of madonna or mother figure.

Sábato's second novel, *On Heroes and Tombs* (1961), also deals with obsession: three men are all drawn in different ways to one woman. Madness again plays a part and in Part Three of the novel, 'Report on the Blind', elements of the grotesque and the fantastic emerge. The style may owe something to Sábato's brush with surrealism and also European romanticism, which has been an important part of Argentina's high culture. Some critics have read it as an allegory of Argentinian society.

Ernesto Sábato has been prominent not only in literature but also in politics. His courageous commentary in magazines has brought him face to face with dictators on a number of occasions, but the even-handedness of his criticisms has won respect on all sides. When democracy returned to Argentina in the early 1980s he was appointed to the commission to investigate the abuse of human rights under the military dictatorship. Many of his political concerns can be seen in his third novel, *Abaddón el exterminador* (1974), written almost as a series of philosophical or political dialogues, with an uncanny prescience of the nightmare years that were to come.

GP Why is it that your work has been translated into English only recently?

ES An English translation of *El tunel* came out in 1951 under the title *The Outsider*, but that edition sold out and the novel was not re-issued until 1988, entitled *The Tunnel*, by Ballantine.

With *On Heroes and Tombs* something rather regrettable happened. In 1962 Heinemann and Alfred Knopf bought the rights but the translation turned out to be so bad that I wouldn't allow publication. This was the start of a quarrel with the publishers that lasted for fifteen years. That's why, even though my books have been translated into many languages, even quite exotic ones like Albanian or Japanese, they haven't appeared in the most important language of our time, English. This has saddened me; after all, a writer writes to be read. Finally, David Godine of Boston published *On Heroes and Tombs*, beautifully translated by Helen Lane. Then Ballantine brought out this work and *The Outsider* in paperback. At the moment my third and last novel *Abaddón el exterminador* is being translated.

GP Do you mean that you don't intend to write or publish any more?

ES That's right. In this third novel I appear as one of the characters; my tomb appears too, by which I meant that I had decided not to publish any more. Perhaps this decision was premonitory, because a few years ago I began to have serious problems with my sight. Specialists have advised me not to read or write, so the most I write these days is a few letters, and even they are done on a typewriter. Because of these problems I've recently returned to the other passion of my adolescence, painting.

GP Would you like to have written more novels?

ES No, as I said, I had decided to write no more after *Abaddón el exterminador*. In any case, I have written more than three novels, but I have burnt all but three. I'm very critical by nature. If I've written just one novel that stands the test of time I'll be happy, it's not the number that counts. By that criterion Agatha Christie would be more important than Malcolm Lowry. In the works I've published I've said all I have to say on life and death, anxiety and hope, alienation and the sense or senselessness of existence.

GP It's clear that even though you are a modern writer you have important roots in the literature of the nineteenth century, notably Russian literature.

ES Yes. Dostoyevsky is a great nineteenth-century writer but also a great precursor of what we would call 'modern literature'. The term is an imprecise one because the centuries don't begin or finish at the same time for everyone. There are people alive today who belong to previous centuries, just as there were people in the last century who inaugurated modern times. Modernity was marked by the discovery of existential philosophy. Dostoyevsky started existential literature and Kierkegaard founded existential philosophy. Nietzsche is another of the great precursors.

It's also true that every writer has roots in the past. There is no such thing as absolute originality. In Herman Melville's story 'Bartleby the Scrivener', you find Kafka prefigured. In George Eliot's *The Mill on the Floss* there is a chapter where a woman is trying on a hat in front of a mirror. If I'm not mistaken, Proust is here in embryo. One of the great modern painters, Balthus, has roots in Lorenzetti, Giotto, Sassetta and Piero della Francesca. There is always a dialectic between renovation and tradition. There is no renovation without tradition.

GP Apart from Dostoyevsky, which other writers are important to you?

ES Depending on my psychological and spiritual state, I might be interested in the German romantics, Proust, Kafka, Faulkner, Strindberg, Thomas Mann, Stendahl . . .

GP Do you consider yourself in any sense a realist writer?

ES The word 'reality' is one of the most controversial ones in philosophy. The great philosophers have based their work on this word, though that hasn't stopped them contradicting each other. For Plato the true reality consisted of abstract ideas, while other philosophers looked for reality in the external world. But if you are thinking of literary 'realism', giving a naturalistic account of society, then, no, I don't have anything to do with it. You need only think of 'Report on the Blind' or *Abaddón el exterminador*, where I turn myself into a great bat, as big as a man.

GP Where, then, would you place yourself?

ES I couldn't properly answer that without first saying something about the crisis of our time. That means taking into account the philosophers of German romanticism and then, later, Kierkegaard. From the seventeenth century onwards you find increasing prestige being given to reason and the sciences, while myth and anything you could call 'magic thought' is increasingly looked down on. Myth is relegated to the museum of the superstitions, and you find an unfortunate identification of the two words 'demystification' and 'demythification'. Myth comes to be seen as a sort of charlatanism or trickery, whereas it is really a profound revelation of the collective unconscious, and for that reason absolutely true. The same goes for dreams – you can say anything you like about a dream except that it is a lie. Myth is related to dreams just as it is related to poetry, in the broader sense of the word. Spurning myth was a very serious matter, because it meant spurning half of the human being – the unconscious part.

Fortunately, man is not inert; sooner or later he rebels. It is misleading to put dates on the great historical movements, but we can speak of a great romantic rebellion which fought to re-establish the value of the unconscious as against the pure values of the intellect. You could see romanticism as a great, complex and subtle movement that has been fighting ever since Greek rationalism decreed the excommunication of the passions in the name of sacred reason, sometimes in the open, sometimes in secret (it's never been really respectable to be a romantic), but it has never completely stopped. Finally, the battle became completely open, breaking out all over Europe. It involved not just the arts but philosophy. Think of men like Pascal and Giambattista Vico. This was the resurgence of magic, according to Haman, that 'magician of the north' for whom poetry was prophecy. What a shock to find dreams and infancy and the 'primitive mentality' being defended. The rediscovery of Shakespeare by the German romantics is like a symbol of the insurrection.

Romanticism was not only a movement in art but a rebellion

of the whole human spirit that ended up attacking the very foundations of rationalist philosophy (thanks to Kierkegaard). The scientists, in their adolescent enthusiasm for reason, continued to see this movement as a backward one, but men of flesh and blood were asking themselves how the chill museums of algebra could be of any use. Of what use were these great mechanisms to subdue nature if they did not lessen man's anguish or give him any help in solving the great dilemmas of life and death? As a result, in addition to the essence of natural things, the existence of man began to be questioned. You find subjectivity being opposed to scientific objectivity. There is a realization that the often tragic knowledge of man's own nature cannot be arrived at through reason alone. The passions are necessary, after all. Nietzsche asked himself if science ought to dominate life and came to the conclusion that life ought to dominate science. For Nietzsche, as for Kierkegaard and Dostoyevsky, life ought to be ruled not by the reasons of the mind but by what Pascal called the reasons of the heart. Existence cannot be contained by any logical schema because it is something contradictory, paradoxical and senseless; it is not governed by the principles of identity and contradiction.

Does all this mean proclaiming the superiority of literature over science? Kierkegaard put his anarchist bombs under the Hegelian cathedral, which was the culmination and glory of Western rationalism. He defended the radical incomprehensibility of the human being against the Hegelian system. Existence causes scandal with its dark, subterranean truths; it is the demon that makes man so often prefer disorder to order, war to peace, sin to virtue and destruction to construction. This strange animal, man, can't be studied like a polyhedron or a chain of syllogisms. His feelings are unique and personal.

So, the abstract Hegelian universe flowed into the concrete universe. As a consequence, the character of the novel is a concrete one. This is especially true of those novels that reject objectivism and liberate themselves from the canons of scientific thought. This is what we might call existential literature, though it appears not in post-war France but in the last century.

I would say that my work belongs to this existential literature. I don't know if my writing is important but I do know
that it belongs to this movement. There is something more
to add. From Husserl and the phenomenologists onwards,
existentialism manages to overcome this absolute subjectivity,
as it is able to describe the relation between the self and the
world. Our time has been, in many senses, the discovery of the
Other and the advent of what we might call intersubjectivity,
even where history is concerned.

GP Is that the case with *On Heroes and Tombs*, where Argentinian history is so important?

ES Yes, but the vision of history is multiple and depends on
the viewpoint of each character. There is no overall authorial
viewpoint, as there would be in a 'scientific' novel. Every
character has his or her own vision of the world and history
and the author ought really to be dispensable. From the different
historical perspectives of the characters comes an unobjective
scheme of social and historical movements. Imagine there's an
accident in the street: each witness gives a version of the facts,
but the accounts are so different that they even give different
colours to the cars involved.

GP This, then, is the 'novel in our time'.

ES Yes, so long as you don't take 'our time' to mean the
mentality that has to do with science and computers. I mean,
on the contrary, a post-scientific mentality.

GP You're not suggesting, I presume, that there should be
no ideas in a novel?

ES No. Man not only feels but thinks. He is neither a thing
nor an animal nor a hermit. Our problems grow out of the
problems of a society, of a family, of a country. Man is a being
preoccupied not only with the current problems in his life but
also with the meaning of life itself and the existence of God.
The way in which a novel can approach these problems has
been admirably dealt with by Erich Auerbach in *Mimesis* and
Lionel Trilling in *The Liberal Imagination*. *Romeo and Juliet* is
not just a love story; it's a reflection of the society of its time.
Stendahl's *The Red and the Black* would have no meaning

outside the social context that Julien Sorel moves in. It also needs the ideas of Rousseau which you find beneath Stendahl's narrative. You wouldn't have Dante without Thomist philosophy. The passions can be unleashed, or at least deformed, by the dominant ideas of the times. It would be madness to try to separate the passions from ideas, though some writers, having concluded that ideas are part of the territory of philosophy and science, have banned them from their works, becoming 'objectivists', though what they create is in fact a strange unreality.

For better or worse, man never ceases thinking, and there is no reason to make him do so when he becomes a character in a work of fiction. Just imagine what would remain of the work of Cervantes, Proust, Tolstoy, Joyce or Thomas Mann if we removed the ideas. On the other hand, ideas never appear in fiction in the abstract way that they do in philosophy. They always appear through the passions of the protagonists. The problem of good and evil, for example, is examined in *Crime and Punishment* through the killing of an old woman by a resentful young student.

The human being can't be limited, as some 'objectivists' would have it, to the movement of a piece of metal at the end of an arm, as if this movement were unaccompanied by sensations and emotions, not to mention thoughts. These thoughts don't even have to be primal, as in a criminal imbecile; you might find someone led to commit a crime by a system of ideas, as in the work of Dostoyevsky. His works seem to 'illustrate' some ghastly theory of ethics or metaphysics. Many great novels have profound discussions of ideas.

That doesn't mean that ideas should appear in an explicit way in all the great works of fiction. It's not even necessary that authors should be consciously aware of the ideas, as their immersion in their culture will provide a picture of dominant or rebellious ideas, of modern or very ancient ideologies. Neither Faulkner nor Melville make sense without certain kinds of Protestantism, even though neither of them was a believer. That is why they are great writers, more than mere storytellers.

The questions of good and evil, of freedom and determinism, all the things that you see even in the ancient religions, come alive through the misfortunes of their characters. Through these writers' genius these issues become grand and tragic; the devil helps give flesh and blood to the abstract ideas of theology and philosophy. It was with good reason that Camus said that the great novelists are novelist-philosophers. What is more, though the philosopher gives us an outline of reality, the poet gives a total image, an image that combines logic and magic. The artist speaks about both heaven and hell, telling us about the truth he suffers so intensely. A metaphysical poem to wake the reader from the everyday and from the commonplace is more inspired by demons than by the sacrament.

In re-establishing the fundamental value of the unconscious, of myths and of the passions, the modern novel in its greatest moments is much more than a description of the world in which we live or a confrontation of the great spiritual crises; it contributes to the salvation of alienated man.

Manuel Puig

Manuel Puig is one of the great innovators of Latin American writing, replacing narrative with a collage of voices and viewpoints. He is never evident as a voice but rather as an ear for idiom. Scavenging the non-literary language of letters, diaries, movies and psychological or police reports, he builds up stories in a fragmentary way that explores not so much events as the webs of self-deception, the lies and the hidden drives that lie behind them.

Puig once remarked that he began to experiment as a way to avoid the intimidatingly Castilian Spanish of the novels he'd read as a young man. His first novel, *Betrayed by Rita Hayworth* (1968), finds a very Argentinian voice, evoking the meanness of provincial life. At the same time it is a highly sophisticated piece of work that reflects the influence of William Faulkner, at least on the level of technique, as it weaves together the accounts of different characters. Puig studied philosophy at university and his technique reflects a concern with the themes raised by Ernesto Sábato: in philosophical terms the modern novel has to be formed from a sort of narrative diversity because modern thought offers the writer no authoritative line. In a sense, the authoritative voice of the omniscient narrator is an anachronism.

An awareness of what Ernesto Sábato termed 'inter-subjectivity' has a basic importance for Latin American writing. Vargas Llosa's novels, for example, are also narrated by an array of voices, though he differs from Manuel Puig in that he can be defined as a realist, whereas the emphasis in Puig's work is on the use of language as a clue to attitudes rather than events or situations. Sometimes Puig is almost clinical in this respect. Chapters may read like a case study or the record of a session in psychoanalysis.

The French psychoanalyst Jacques Lacan has been important here; his suggestion that the unconscious has the structure of a language may have contributed to Puig's focus on language rather than narrative action: what people say reveals more than what they do. However, this hasn't stopped Puig using that most narrative of genres, the detective story. *The Buenos Aires Affair* (1973) is about criminally abnormal sexuality, though the aim of the novel seems to be to draw uneasy parallels between the pathological and the normal.

Puig broke off his studies in philosophy to study film. His first novel grew out of a film script and in his subsequent works, with their peremptory cuts from scene to scene, the influence of film is still clear: the narrator switches viewpoints rather as a camera does. Screen mythology is also a rich source of material for Puig, who has a large personal film library.

Perhaps an oblique method of presentation is appropriate for a rather unassertive man with a sympathy for feminism. In *The Kiss of the Spider Woman* (1976) Puig comments that if men were like women, there would be no torturers, and in fact many of his views on sexuality have clearly political implications. At the time that I spoke to him, Puig was living in Rio de Janeiro. He subsequently moved to Mexico, where he died in July 1990.

GP What motivated you to choose philosophy when you went to university?

MP I really wanted to make films – to write them and direct them – but in Argentina there was no school for that in those days. Philosophy excited me as a discipline, I think mainly because it was so opposed to the popular character of films.

The territory of films was so vast and wild in the 1950s when I started college. The neo-realist school of criticism was just being born and Cahiers du Cinéma was just being founded – or perhaps that was a few years later. I needed some kind of mental order, so I studied philosophy and also languages, because, for me, English, French and Italian were the languages of film. I studied those three languages, and their literature, with a passion – I have a degree in Italian literature from the Dante Alighieri Society and a degree in French literature from the Alliance Française. I was trying to discover the world through reading. You, being from Australia, will understand this very easily. It is something to do with living in a country that is a long way from a cultural metropolis, from Paris or New York. Just after the war Paris was the centre of the cultural world, by 1950 New York was just starting to become more important.

While I was studying philosophy and languages the Italian institute awarded me a scholarship to go to a film school in Rome. However, I didn't complete the film course because I immediately sensed that directing wasn't the thing for me. I objected to the conditions of work. When you direct you must know exactly what you want and you must convince everyone else that you know. You have to like giving orders and doing many other things that I thoroughly dislike, such as getting up very early. I dislike pressure. Also, I want to have the space to re-do things.

Everything was pointing me in another direction, but I thought, 'Well, I can't really write for films either.' When I tried to do something serious in the form of a script it became my first novel – *Betrayed by Rita Hayworth*. The material itself asked for a different approach; the story I had to tell couldn't be made into the sort of synthesis that you need for a film. It is mostly a study of characters. The action isn't important at all.

GP You have said that when you started writing you lacked the confidence to write in classical Spanish.

MP Yes, on the surface it was that. I had a dislike for Castilian Spanish. I didn't feel it was my language. I was more interested in Argentinian Spanish, which is not really very different but it does have a different rhythm. A Spaniard will understand Argentinian Spanish but will notice a different flavour. I was interested in this flavour but didn't know how to capture it because the flavour is in the speech.

Another very important factor that determined my narrative technique was that I didn't have a point of view. What pushed me to write my first book was the need to understand better what had happened during my childhood and adolescence. I wanted to listen to my characters, to the people who had been close to me, and to myself as a child. I wanted to listen to those voices and then draw my conclusions. So it was impossible to use a third-person narrative. A third person would have demanded a point of view and I wanted to avoid that. I wanted to avoid pre-judging those characters; first I wanted to see what the story was about.

One thing was very clear from the beginning: I wasn't just interested in reproducing language. I wanted to create music and colour with the language, but the silly critics thought I was just working as a tape-recorder. My work has been published in twenty-four languages, but it is a miracle that literature manages to survive the nonsense of the critics. With very, very few exceptions the newspaper and magazine critics didn't understand anything. The academic critics were a little slow to understand my work, but that's a different story. The newspaper critics are the influential ones and they do a lot of harm.

GP But you've had great success – every time a book of yours comes out people rush to buy it. They can't have done much harm in the long run.

MP No, but it took a long time to get recognition.

GP Is your use of many different narrators inspired to some extent by your reading of modern philosophy – by the lack of an omniscient viewpoint and consequent lack of any single, right way of seeing things? Or did it perhaps come from reading Lacan?

MP It came mostly from reading psychology. I believe modern literature doesn't simply start with James Joyce. The discovery of the unconscious brought about a great change. In the nineteenth century writers could honestly believe that they understood a character, that they could embrace a character totally. Motivation lay in a character's consciousness, with a little dark margin for what in those days were called the instincts. Then with Freud we realized that consciousness was the tip of the iceberg, and writers could no longer pretend that they understood a character. Now you can have a kind of intuition about a character's dark motives but any attempt to describe or understand them has to be tentative.

For me, the big interest lies in gaining access to the realm of the collective unconscious. If I reveal some of it in a novel, if I succeed in showing some of a character's more intimate and hidden motives, that excites me. How do you approach that dark territory; how do you reveal that hidden material? It's a problem that drives writers to try new techniques. A third-person narrative won't get you very far. I may write part of a novel in that way, but I feel the need for other tools as well.

GP You like to explore that territory using unemotional material like official documents. It's as if you are doing scientific research and are careful not to venture any comment that you don't feel confident about. You just hint.

MP That's because such documents often reveal the collective unconscious. They have somehow accumulated a lot of hidden meaning in the language they use.

GP You've recently been writing plays. In the theatre you do have a single point of view, that of the spectator sitting in their seat. In *Under a Mantle of Stars* (1983) you solve this problem by having a number of different identities for each actor, but in some way the theatre limits your ability to use different kinds of language and different points of view.

MP There is unity of place, unity of time, but no unity of identity in that play, which has scared directors a lot more than I thought it would. Perhaps it is still waiting for the right production. It was done very well here, but who sees a play in Rio?

GP In the play you explore one of the themes that occurs in your novels: the idea that people tend to fantasize about each others identities rather than perceive them. You say that writing a novel is a process of discovery. Is writing a play also a process of discovery?

MP It's a different kind of operation. You must know more about what you want when you start writing a play, you must have clearer ideas.

GP There are many dreams in your novels. They are not like the dreams in Freud's case studies; in many ways they are like a cross between a dream and a Hollywood film script. There is also an element of the daydream. You don't seem to try and capture the apparent chaos or confusion or linguistic game-playing of dreams that Freud talked about.

MP Well, I can't reproduce a dream. It's impossible. So, since artifice comes into it, I might as well invite a whole cultural code to come in as well, to join the party. I always try to use some code that reveals something of the collective unconscious. That's where Hollywood is so useful. Hollywood movies were full of clues. The producers wanted to appeal to people, they didn't want to raise their consciousness. They wanted to cater to their needs, to give them their dreams, so they tried to guess what the desires of the audience were. When they found an actor who was exactly what women wanted, or who men wanted to resemble, such as Clarke Gable, they were on to a gold mine. It's not just chance that made James Dean or Marilyn Monroe such myths: they embodied the wishes of the masses. Hollywood movies are full of meaning. Look at *Rebecca*, for example. People never get tired of the story and there must be some reason for that. I've used elements from such films and will probably continue to do so. It's not that Hollywood created a dream. The dream existed and the producers reflected it. They created a product that people wanted.

GP Obviously there is an enormous ideological difference between the way Hollywood approached those dreams and the way you do.

MP Of course, but I want to have one point in common with them. They gave pleasure and I want the reading of my novels to give pleasure.

GP Why is it you write a lot about the 1930s?

MP For me it is the territory of myths, because it is the period of my early childhood – the mysteries are all there. The 1920s are too far away, out of reach, but I'm in contact with the 1930s. I lived the things I write about, albeit in a very childish way. I was just opening my eyes to the world.

GP You've said it's important for you to give pleasure to the reader and you seem to be interested in playing on dreams and desires, yet there is often a very clinical aspect to your writing. I was very struck by the end of *Heartbreak Tango*, where all the passionate letters, reflecting the great problems and the emotions that have been so important in the novel, are thrown into the fire. They just go up in smoke. Everything is suddenly seen from a great distance and all the issues appear tiny.

MP I think that in this life we have to cope with the fact that everything is very ephemeral.

GP Can we talk about some of the notions of sexuality in your work? One of your most striking images is that of the cobra in *Blood of Requited Love*. It suggests that male sexuality is particularly poisonous. It is linked to the desire to hurt people. The protagonist, even when he can't hurt someone, fantasizes about doing so. In *The Buenos Aires Affair* male sexuality seems to be linked to sadism. Do you think that is a general tendency?

MP I see sexual roles as quite artificial and think that they have produced a sickness. Male sexuality is linked to power and we know how dangerous power can be. I feel that the way sexuality has been seen until now is totally childish and wrong. There have been some improvements recently but we still need to see things more clearly.

For me, sexuality is an activity that belongs to our vegetative life. It is as important as eating or sleeping, which are the other activities of the vegetative life, but like them it is totally devoid of moral or transcendent meaning. It is simply fun and games. It's innocent though our culture doesn't see it that way. What I see as transcendent and charged with moral significance is the life of the affections. Sexuality, at some point in history, began to be seen as morally meaningful. One theory is that a patriarch invented the concept of sexual sin, so that he could differentiate the saintly woman at home from the whore in the street. He created a distinction between them in order to be able to control them.

GP Or to control himself, perhaps.

MP No, power doesn't want to be controlled. Power just wants more power. So, he succeeded in controlling women because they had to carry this strange moral weight that he'd invented. A man who had an insatiable sexual appetite was considered a stallion, a model of health. A woman who had a strong sexual appetite was considered a nymphomaniac. I use the word deliberately. 'Nymphomaniac' first began to appear in journalism at the beginning of the 1950s. Before that it was too strong a word for anyone to use. I remember it first being used in the American press linked to Tennessee Williams' heroines such as Blanche Dubois. A woman who needed sex was considered to be not in control of her glands; she was dominated by them. Also, being a nymphomaniac implied a dash of madness. A woman who needed sex was no model of health. She was a bit crazy. For me, this horrible word 'nymphomaniac' marked the peak of perfidy against women.

The moment you invent this moral significance for sex you take away its natural essence; as soon as sex becomes artificially meaningful on a moral level, identities are created on that basis. Sexual roles are created artificially. Women, for example, are then seen as sexually passive. Everything is constructed on an unreal basis. Everything that comes after that is sickness. There is frustration for the woman, while these ideas, invented by men for the convenience of men, substantiate male power. Since that distinction was first made, there has been an accumulation of power in the hands of the male. The male attributes suffer from a sort of elephantiasis.

As far as homosexuality and heterosexuality are concerned, when I'm asked for my opinions on the subject I say something shocking, such as, 'Homosexuality doesn't exist.' That is partly just to make people nervous, but it's also true in a way. The distinction between heterosexuality and homosexuality is really a creation of the reactionary mind; it's just a legacy of an old, old mistake. I think we should be very radical and accept the only healthy view, namely that a non-meaningful and non-transcendent act shouldn't be used to define identity. We should not allow ourselves to be manipulated by this archaic way of thinking.

I don't think we can really imagine what a world free of this old mistake would be like. Sex would be considered just what it is. I don't think that exclusive homosexuality or exclusive heterosexuality would exist because, technically, it's perfectly possible to get pleasure both ways. Things would happen in a totally different way. Another human being, of either sex, would present you with the possibility of pleasure and that is all.

GP You seem to make that point indirectly in *The Kiss of the Spider Woman*, with all your footnotes on homosexuality.

MP Well, I hadn't arrived at this point of view when I wrote the novel, though I was on the way. People often ask me, 'How can you say that sex has no transcendence when it is the basis of reproduction and of life itself? Life is given by the sexual act.' I have an answer for this. We are different from beasts, especially in terms of sex. What should count in human reproduction is the wish to bring a new being into the world. It shouldn't just be an accident, because someone forgot to take their pill. The sexual act is merely the means of fulfilling the wish. When a couple decide to bring a new being into the world, I think that is a sublime moment, a kind of affirmation of life. It's an act of love, of communion with God, and that is the thing that matters, not the physiological process that causes you to have a child. That's why I believe in abortion, because if there's no wish for a child, there shouldn't be a child.

GP You are talking about having wishes and making choices, but one of the things that comes through strongly in your books is that people are determined by their situation. They very rarely transcend their sexuality, their drives or their desires. They seem to be driven rather than choosing their fate.

MP Yes, because people believed, especially before the

sexual revolution, that the rules of our sick society were the rules of nature, that nature wanted things to be the way they were. During my adolescence, in the late 1940s, people believed that nature wanted women to be weak and men to be very strong. I remember women saying horrible things with total conviction, such as, 'I can only really love a man who makes me tremble when he embraces me. If I don't feel a little afraid of him I can't respect him. Sexual ecstasy isn't possible unless I feel dominated.'

GP You could still probably hear that today.

MP Yes, but you'd have your tongue in your cheek or you'd be letting go a little on the perverse side of things; it's no longer a law of nature. Women used to think: 'Nature has been unfair to us. We are the second sex. We don't make any decisions, but nature wants it that way, otherwise we'll be frustrated wives and mothers because men can't love a woman who doesn't know how to yield.'

GP Some modern feminists would say that the sexual act itself is an act of a man dominating a woman. There is a built-in, natural injustice.

MP I believe, on the contrary, that the man is sometimes a slave, doing his best to give the goddess a good time; but it's all part of this same sickness that has developed over the centuries.

GP Would you link male sexual dominance directly to political dictatorship?

MP Certainly; it's a logical development. It is all part of the old fallacy that in order to feel pleasure you must dominate or be dominated.

Luisa Valenzuela

President Juan Perón's populist economic policies during the late 1940s and early 1950s won great support, despite riding Argentina's post-war boom into national bankruptcy. Both he and his wife Eva built up a cult following; after her early death Eva was commemorated with almost religious intensity. Perón was, of course, criticized for his authoritarianism. The media, the universities and other sources of dissent were either controlled or intimidated. Jorge Luis Borges, Argentina's greatest writer, was dismissed as director of the national library and offered a job as inspector in the municipal fish markets.

Perón was re-elected in the early 1970s, though he died soon after taking office. In the ensuing uncertainty an army officer called Lopez Rega gained a great deal of influence and began to form death squads, operating initially against dissident members of his own Peronist party. In the military dictatorship that followed these squads operated on a larger scale and many thousands died or disappeared in a repression that is known as the dirty war.

How Argentina could fall prey to figures of such dangerous charisma is a question Luisa Valenzuela seems to ask herself in her novel *The Lizard's Tail* (1983). Lopez Rega is a model for the protagonist, whose menace emanates from a swamp kingdom where the vilest features of the unconscious seem to rule. Though based on real events, the novel makes no effort to be plausible, as Valenzuela tries to confront the irrational on its own territory. The narrator enters the novel as a combatant when the act of writing appears to reawaken the Lopez Rega figure, who had been inactive for some time. Boundaries between the political and the literary are dissolved to give access to some kind of collective unconscious. Symbol and historical fact mingle in a work full of conundrums and black humour. Interestingly, Valenzuela's treatment of her ghastly protagonist is often flippant, perhaps in order to puncture a reputation based on horror. The great torturer is revealed to be a pathetic creature, despite his acknowledged power.

Luisa Valenzuela has travelled widely, has lived in Paris and, for ten years, in New York. The influences on her work are very varied, ranging from the indigenous mythology so evident in *Up Among the Eagles* (title and date of original unknown; published by North Point Press, Berkeley, California, 1988) to the theories of Lacan, whose linking of language and the unconscious provides the cue for her often dream-like prose. Her wonderful short stories are puzzling in the same way that a dream is: a beguiling play of words and symbols teases at meaning.

Luisa Valenzuela's fiction shifts from social allegory to whimsy, making her stories as resistant to interpretation as the work of her great precursor, Borges. There is also a strong feminist aspect to her writing, though it is not a doctrinaire feminism; it inspires the reader to adopt the curious, questioning stance of the author.

GP As a child you saw quite a lot of the literary life in Buenos Aires during the 1950s, didn't you?

LV During the 1950s many writers, including people such as Ernesto Sábato and Jorge Luis Borges would come to visit my mother, the writer Luisa Mercedes Levinson. A lot of intellectuals were out of work because of the Peronist persecution and so they used to give seminars or lectures at our house in order to get a bit of money. The meetings were very intense, partly because they weren't quite legal. They had a surreptitious quality, even though they were usually quite innocent politically. Peronism did create a kind of solidarity amongst writers. When Perón fell everyone went around to Sábato's house and celebrated.

GP The figure of the messiah appears in many of your stories; Perón was looked upon almost as a messiah, wasn't he?

LV As a father figure, really. Argentina wanted a charismatic figure that would save it. I don't understand this need at all and that is why he appears in my novels. I'd like to understand how a supposedly sophisticated nation could feel this need for a father and mother like Juan and Eva Perón.

GP Is there something very Argentinian in this almost religious devotion to political figures? It doesn't seem to happen so much in Brazil or Peru or Chile.

LV It happened in Brazil with Gertúlio Vargas – there is a devotion to populist leaders which is the result of a need to find a national identity. They say the United States is a melting pot, but it is less so than Argentina, where racial and class differences have often been almost completely erased. Everything has been amalgamated – you are nothing in particular in the midst of a mixture of everything, an alphabet soup. This feeling is probably behind another worrying Argentine phenomenon, the devotion to almost mythical figures like Juan Moreira, who was really no more than a murderous gaucho. He lacked any ethical dimension and yet they venerate him. And though Borges was right in defending *Martín Fierro* as an important epic poem, Martín Fierro himself was a racist, a reprobate gaucho with a chip on his shoulder. We always venerate these outlaw figures, people who are culpable not only in the eyes of the legal system but also in terms of the essential ethical standards.

Perhaps it is a lack of a sense of identity that makes us cling to these figures, or then again maybe it has something to do with our identity. There is the story of the founding of Buenos Aires by Juan Díaz de Solís. Solís was sick with syphilis and couldn't leave his ship. He landed a handful of men and returned to Spain, leaving them in this place, which they called Santa María de Buen Aire, even though it had terrible air. These men stayed in a tiny stockade, unable to go out because the Indians surrounded them. They had no access to food and hardly any water, so they began to die. When they died they were tossed

outside the wall to avoid contamination, but after a few days
the living came out and took their legs or other parts of their
bodies to eat because they were dying of hunger. While this
Argentine cannibalism was taking place Solís was on his way
back from Spain. On his ship there was a poet, Martín del
Barco Centenera, who wrote an ode called La Argentina, that
portrayed Argentina as a place full of the figures of European
mythology, sirens and tritons and so on. It seems we are
descended from both cannibals and poets; sometimes one side
wins and sometimes the other.

GP You wrote in *The Lizard's Tail* that things don't live if
we don't give them names. Doesn't this run contrary to the
thought of Freud and Jung?

LV It doesn't run contrary to Lacan. Maybe not to Freud
either. Freud stopped elaborating his theories because he died,
but I think if he had lived, he would have reached post-Freudian
conclusions. In Freud's work the unconscious is implicitly structured like a language. When Freud expounded his theory of
dreams it was in terms of words. In fact, there's no possibility
of anything without the word for Freud.

GP But the emotions and the drives come first, the word
comes second.

LV I don't know whether it's a matter of coming first or
second. These are really false categories. Think of the small
child, without language and so without any perception of the
world. The word comes first. Any religion will tell you that.

GP I don't think it does. According to Piaget perception
comes before the word. Perception and the structure of reality
come without words. The child learns to think logically and
to order its perceptions to a very great extent before it even
speaks and it continues to develop mentally to a great extent
on a non-verbal level.

LV Well, these are both valid theories and I'm not going to
advocate either view; it's one thing to talk about the newborn
or young child, but which comes first, the chicken or the egg?
Remember we're not talking about the perception of the
newborn but of the *imago mundi*, which is the global perception

of the world that the adult has. When the developed person perceives the world the first thing is the word. If you can't name, you can't have a notion of anything. Things that don't have names almost don't exist. They are not categorized. You can't manipulate or play with them in any way.

GP Lacan said that the unconscious has the structure of a language. Does it also have the structure of a narrative?

LV Yes. Anyone who has gone to sleep with a question and woken up with the answer knows this. The unconscious is constantly at work. Say you are writing a scene and don't know how it is going to end; it all seems too complex and you don't know why you started it. Yet twenty pages later you know where you are going and exactly what value it has in the novel. The important thing is to break the barrier of censorship and let this happen. The word says itself through you if you don't spend all your time closing off the pathways. You have access to your dark side: desire, eroticism and things that frighten you and seem to have nothing to do with you.

Writing is now in many ways a process of listening. When I wrote my first novel, *Clara*, or the short stories in *The Heretics* it was a matter of seeing everything in images, rather like going to the cinema. Later, when I was writing *Scare Cat*, everything began to accelerate and I had no time to deal with images. I literally began to hear voices; this is a way of delving much deeper into language and that's what I love about the act of writing: the moment when words become transparent and allow you to discover the hidden meaning and reveal the logic of what is coming next.

This is one reason why I don't use much autobiographical material. I already know all about it and it would bore me. With invented characters, I am following a thread in the dark. You enter into metaphor and it is not what's said that is important but rather how much of the unsaid flowers despite what you say. If you say everything, you exhaust the pleasure of reading, even for yourself, because that pleasure is a dark one. It is the pleasure of putting yourself in a cavern and finding treasures.

GP This way of working is rather reminiscent of Plato – it sounds as though the world is knowable through introspection.

LV No, facts are important but they need to be digested or what you write will be merely literal. If I were to choose a philosophical line, it would be a matter not only of Plato and his cave but of someone like Heraclitus, where opposites are always meeting and things are constantly transforming into their opposites.

GP How does inspiration come to you? Is it a matter of dreams or accidents or things you read?

LV Inspiration is very much a matter of chance. It usually comes from some combination of words, a phrase I hear or read or that just comes to mind. It can be a question. *The Lizard's Tail* came about because I wanted to understand this story of power and how a nation as cultivated as the Argentinians could have fallen into the hands of a sorcerer – though cultivation and the occult are different sides of the same coin. Then there are themes that seen so fascinating or are already so literary in themselves that I have to use them. For example, the piece of theatre I have been working on has this theme of painted faces, inspired by the way rebellious Argentinian officers have painted their faces before going into combat. So there are stories or phrases that I hear or overhear. I almost never have the whole plot; it would be quite intolerable and boring to write something with a plot that I already knew. I need to surprise myself. I need to be surprised in order to surprise the readers. When I write, my sensation is of walking a tightrope without a net or diving without knowing if there is any water below. From time to time you suffer some pretty brutal surprises but it is interesting to throw yourself in and see what happens.

GP The narrator in *The Lizard's Tail* implies at one point that if she doesn't write about the witch doctor, he won't create problems. Are the psychological drives he represents really harmless and tranquil until stumbled across in the process of writing?

LV No, these things can't be dealt with by ignoring them,

any more than the crimes of the dictatorship will cease to be crimes if we remain silent. On the contrary, the only way of exorcizing our personal demons is to name them, and if you close your mouth, they simply grow or reappear in another guise.

GP So the narrator's fear that she ought to stop writing isn't something that you share?

LV Fear always exists. There is no life without fear, but you can face it in an active or a passive way. For example, when I was very young I was very much afraid of a grandfather clock which stood in our house, at the end of a corridor that at the time seemed enormously long. The clock was made more frightening by the many closed doors you had to go through as you walked along the corridor. I only heard the clock chime at night, especially in the middle of the night, and this sent me into a state of panic. I thought that there was some sort of creature touching the clock to make it chime and the only way I could get to sleep was to get up and make sure nothing was there. If I put my head under the blankets and tried to ignore it, I would just lie awake. The only way to beat the fear was not to let it paralyse me. If fear makes you do things and carries you forward, it can be creative. Writing can be a process of going to face up to that monster.

GP Because when the monster is seen in the light it isn't a monster?

LV It is a monster, but at least one you know and have some possibility of dealing with, not one that is going to grow in neglect until it becomes immeasurably large, a real devourer. Every human being is a prey to monsters and phantoms and to want to see them is a way of accepting their reality and a way of carrying on, knowing that at least this particular monster won't frighten you again.

Of course, there are some that continue to be frightening, such as the military dictatorship. That is a monster whose face I've seen and it always frightens me, so I prefer to mention it and keep it in mind as a way of coping.

GP I suppose it would be impossible for you to write a

novel in the way generally favoured by the English, where common sense has, with some exceptions, precluded the introduction of the fantastic into serious literature.

LV The common sense of the English leaves a lot to be desired. It is curious considering that the Gothic novel and the ghost story originated in England. We are really talking about metaphors: metaphors for very deep feelings, prominent among which is the Judaeo-Christian sense of guilt, the vestiges of Puritanism, and the sense of sexual shame, which is alive and well in England. I think that common sense is a mask that serves to hide a whole range of powerful interior forces, which you may or may not want to call monsters.

GP In an important sense *The Lizard's Tail* is about masks and reality ...

LV I don't have much confidence in this word reality. What we are used to calling reality is a tiny percentage of what reality may be when you think of what we could have access to through the unconscious. In medical terms the separation of what happens inside and outside the mind is now breaking down. It seems that imagining events can be as effective a cure in cases of trauma as if those events really happened. If you dream a love story it seems that the cerebral chemistry behaves in the same way as if you were really in love. So where is reality and what are its limits? Of course, there is a great deal that passes completely outside the limits of our perception and in that sense reality is irremediably limited, but the task for the Latin American writer ought to be to open up the fan of our perceptions, to look a little into the world of shadows and those regions we aren't used to paying attention to, and to write about that.

GP The English novel seems to focus more readily on the small scale, on issues that are important at a private, personal level. Do such matters lack importance in the more turbulent Latin American context?

LV No. Nothing lacks importance because everything is part of a chain. As the Lacandon Indians say, when a tree falls a star falls. A tiny, intimate wound can have its repercussions and it can also be a metaphor for something that happens on a much larger scale. In a small, intimate story there can be the seed of a story of a whole people or of a war. Why does one have to separate things in this way? Why must we deal with the great themes and not the minor ones? In *Other Weapons* I tried to show how the small, everyday tortures are linked to the great national tortures or the multinational ones.

GP Yes, but the structures of a nation are not the structures of a personality.

LV I don't know whether they are so different. I don't know whether individuals letting themselves be victimized by someone else are so different from a people letting itself be victimized by its leaders or a nation letting itself be victimized by a great power. I don't know if a husband or wife's desire to dominate in the household is so different from a head of state's will to dominate a nation. There is a question of scale, but otherwise is the difference so great?

An important Argentinian anthropologist was telling me recently that it isn't right to talk so much about the *desaparecidos* because it isn't true that 30,000 have disappeared. Some estimates put it as low as 9,000 and what are 9,000 compared to the millions that die or disappear in a world war? I began to wonder whether I was speaking to an anthropologist or some kind of national accountant. What was this idea of keeping books on the dead? What a monstrosity! Two deaths or even one is a monstrosity. If the small evils don't move you in any way, how will the great evils?

GP When I spoke to José Donoso he seemed to imply that the unconscious was equivalent to the poor part of his nation. The poor had drifted to the city, lost their culture, become quite primitive and even lost some of their capacity for reason.

LV I'd like to read what he said because I have the feeling you are oversimplifying. The poor might correspond to the unconscious but only in the sense that they are abandoned and rejected and silenced. We don't want to hear about the condition of these people. At the same time it is important to remember that the unconscious has the structure of an intelligence and works with a logical and mathematical precision that I find quite astounding. I feel that the unconscious is infinitely wiser than I am, able to speak on a level that touches all of us. It has a capacity for elaboration and precision that we don't have at the conscious level because of the barriers we put up and the way we limit our perceptions.

I think that the writer acts as a mirror for others. It is not only that the monsters of one person are often the monsters of many, but that the memory of certain horrors ought to be a collective one. Writing can also dislodge people from the paths they are used to following. Changing paths means thinking laterally and so writers need to surprise themselves and then hope that this will surprise the readers, or at least the good readers, the active ones.

GP Argentinians as a group seem remarkably gracious and charming. When you see them in the street, for example, they relate with such a mixture of propriety and good humour. Argentina is the last place where you'd expect the barbarities of the 1970s to occur. What happened?

LV However charming people may be in the street, a background of great repression, or perhaps a lack of repression, can be seen in the history of fascist nationalism in Argentina. This is something you notice from time to time when, for example, you are talking to taxi drivers in Argentina. They are always asking for a hard line to be taken with the country. This is a kind of immaturity. They are incapable of imposing any internal order so they need some external order to be imposed on them, the discipline of the military who arrive as some sort of messiah.

GP In *The Lizard's Tail* the occult is a factor in politics. I suppose this isn't a completely Argentinian phenomenon, if you remember rumours of Nancy Reagan planning her husband's engagements through astrology.

LV The Nazis were very interested in astrology, which is where Perón picked it up. I don't have anything against astrologers. On the contrary, I think they have some interesting things to say. What I'm against is the messianic idea of using such means to avoid taking responsibility for your actions, to say that the stars took your decisions for you, so you torture not on your own account but for your country and in obedience to some sort of greater command.

GP So on a national level myths enter politics?

LV Myths are always a part of politics. Politics need a mythic dimension to exist – otherwise how can you explain that the facts of the Irangate scandal didn't completely undermine the government of Ronald Reagan? The myth, which is something completely real, was stronger.

GP There is a feminist dimension in *The Lizard's Tail*, in that inside the female writer a man appears to be fighting to control her. Up to what point is the unconscious a masculine entity in the woman?

LV You mean Jung's notion of the anima inside the man and the animus inside the woman?

GP Something a bit different. As the book deals with political issues and with barbarities that have generally been carried out by men, I wondered if you felt that male qualities were responsible for brutality in both men and women.

LV It is a matter of trying to denounce the barbarities, political or otherwise, carried out by men – by men because they've had the opportunity. If women had had power in recent centuries, or rather millenia, we would now be in the position of having to denounce women, because the key factor is power.

I do agree that in every human being the opposite sex is alive in some region, some part of their soul, their body or sex or heart or ear, or wherever you want to locate it. None of us are pure or absolute as a gender. That would be monstrous.

GP I must say that, as a man, I'm rather irritated by the apparent line of some feminists that everything evil in the world comes from the masculine side.

LV And, being a woman, it bothers me that all the blemishes, weaknesses and defects in the world should come from the female side. I do believe that all the evil in the world comes from the male side, but not because men individually are to blame. Rather, the individual man is just as much a victim as the woman. The evil comes from the system of machismo that makes victims out of both men and women. On the men's side, of course, there is the question of territoriality. Men have territory and they are fighting to keep it, not as individuals, perhaps, but collectively. It is the system that is to blame, a system where a woman has very little space or respect and what respect she does receive is really designed to minimize her actions and keep her out of circulation and to make her behave in a way that has more to do with men's image of a woman than what a woman might really be.

Robert Graves has the interesting notion that if women were able to behave differently, you might not have this phenomenon of male competitiveness. The defect of the male is portrayed as one of his greatest virtues, as expressed in the cult of the hero. I think that the cult of the hero is something that kills us. It is at the root of the dictatorships, because they incarnate the figure of the mythic hero. We women don't have this notion of the mythic hero. To us this heroism is grotesque and ridiculous.

It is true that women are driven by ideology to kill as much or more than men. In Latin American the number of women who have fought is enormous and the number of women in the struggle for liberation, whether as individuals or as part of a group, is almost preponderant. Yet there is no cult of the hero or heroine. There is no personalization. I feel the world would be run better in this way, though this is an idealization, because we haven't had the opportunity to demonstrate that this is so. It is something that is easy to say from the position of the vanquished.

GP Is competition not more deeply rooted? It seems to be not just a social characteristic or even a human one, because it is a factor in most mammals, where competition amongst the males is often a way to decide who has the opportunity to pass on their genes.

LV Perhaps, but in the case of human beings there are more women than men and there is no reason why any man should be anxious about missing his opportunity. It is also one thing to pass on your genes and quite another to dominate the world, in which case your genes would be the only ones in the universe. It is fine that a man has many more opportunities to reproduce than a woman, but that doesn't mean he should treat all women as receptacles, which is what the man appears to want because power is erotic and eroticizing. It is as if a dictator is fornicating with everyone under his power, which is to enter into another dimension of madness.

PARAGUAY

.

Augusto Roa Bastos

In the War of the Triple Alliance (1865–70) Argentina, Brazil and Uruguay, with the support of the British, joined forces against Paraguay, which was under the rule of the dictator Francisco Solano López. Allied propaganda portrayed the war as a fight to unseat a tyrant, but the Paraguayans defended this alleged tyranny with such ferocity that they fought to the last able-bodied man, losing half the population. The Paraguayan nation was destroyed.

Acknowledged as one of the greatest modern Latin American novels, Augusto Roa Bastos' *I the Supreme* (1974) focuses on the years of growth that led up to the war. The novel is about José Gaspar Rodríguez de Francia, the dictator who between 1814 and 1840 set Paraguay on the course that made it the most economically independent and, in some respects, the most technologically advanced nation in the region. Though it doesn't deal with the eventual decimation of Paraguay, this is always implicit. However, *I the Supreme* plays some strange games with history: all the facts are rather dubious and the book reads like the diary of a maniac. Francia was one of the most highly educated men on the continent and Roa Bastos shows his astuteness as a statesman. At the same time he was capable of playing cruel and vengeful jokes on his enemies. He could be childish, even demented. He was certainly paranoid, though in the circumstances paranoia may have been a sane reaction.

Francia is something of a mythic figure in Paraguay; *I the Supreme* examines the myth, both contributing to it and undermining it, revealing the visionary and the madman.

Sometimes The Supreme spouts grandiosely about his achievements, intolerant of the slightest criticism, while at others he seems to see straight through himself. The appropriate shifts of style move from the realistic to the Kafkaesque.

I the Supreme is a remarkably detached view of dictatorship from a man who has spent a great part of his adult life in exile. Long before the publication of *I the Supreme* Roa Bastos was unpopular with General Alfredo Stroessner, one of South America's most infamous dictators, who ruled Paraguay from 1954. Perhaps because his earlier masterful short stories and the novel *Son of Man* (1961) were written in Paraguay, these works lack the distancing effect of humour. They represent the nation as a kind of expressionist mask that it utterly convincing, given the authority and commitment of the writing.

Augusto Roa Bastos now lives in France and works at the University of Toulouse. Following the fall of General Stroessner in 1989 he visited Paraguay and was given a hero's reception, though, with typical modesty, he turned down posts offered by the new government.

GP You have said that a book is not a placard. To what extent do you think literature is socially important?

ARB Literature does have an important social role, but it's not true that 'literature will save Latin America' as some of our best writers seem to feel, perhaps having been carried away by their own writing. One shouldn't create myths about an activity that, despite its importance, has definite limitations and its own specific functions.

GP You are a very prominent person in Paraguay, despite the fact that there is a high rate of illiteracy, so the majority of the population can't read your work.

ARB That is mainly due to the myths that have sprung up during twenty-two years of exile. Time and distance are flattering. It is true that in Paraguay there are few readers, especially for works of fiction. Narrative literature doesn't really exist in Paraguay. There are a few novels, among them my own, but no literary corpus. The tradition of the novel in

Paraguay begins only in the 1940s, a century later than in the rest of Latin America. That is an interesting phenomenon, which social historians haven't paid much attention to. They haven't analysed the causes of this backwardness, though there are very evident social, political and economic factors.

Paraguay was completely destroyed by the war of 1865–70, which left the country almost without men. There were only women, children, the elderly and invalids left. So for the last century the country has been trying to reconstruct itself, which has proved impossible because of its position of dependence. It has been a beaten nation, dominated not just by the great powers but by its Latin American neighbours, such as Argentina and Brazil. Paraguay's cultural evolution has been held back, in particular in terms of a culture that produces literature.

GP The words 'civilization' and 'barbarism' have had a special meaning for Paraguay, because the war that destroyed Paraguay was seen by some as a struggle of civilization against barbarism.

ARB The pretext for the war was the destruction of the tyrant, Francisco Solano López, who ruled Paraguay. In fact, it had more to do with the introduction of free trade, which Paraguay had opposed. In the years following independence from Spain in 1811 Paraguay had achieved a degree of self-sufficiency and self-determination that made it perhaps the most advanced nation in Latin America, not only in material but in cultural terms. Foreign technicians were brought in and quite quickly it developed an industrial base. It could process its own primary materials, so it wasn't dependent on imports. When British free-trade interests were victorious in the Río de la Plata region, both through economic and military means, they saw Paraguay as a stronghold of opposition. If the aim of the war had been the destruction of a tyrant, that would have been fine – I'm against tyranny – but what they destroyed was the country.

It is the task of the writer to investigate the interests that lie concealed behind theories of cultural superiority. This investigation is the reason for everything I have written. My writing rests very much on the opposition of civilization and barbarism, because it is true that in many ways Latin America is still struggling to emerge from barbarism, to find a just system which can act as a bulwark against barbarism, against the bloodbaths and the exterminations of enormous numbers of people that are still going on.

At the same time you can't apply Sarmiento's opposition as an exact model. As a writer you have to try to see more profoundly than that and to create your own myths, by turning a critical eye on our history, which has been, after all, written by the victors.

GP *I the Supreme* could be seen as a revision of history. You show that the dictator Francia did many good things, despite his reputation.

ARB Yes, Francia had the great misfortune of being constantly misunderstood, both by his supporters and his detractors, but the important thing is that, despite all the concessions I make, I remain opposed to dictatorship and to absolute power. On the positive side, he stood for Paraguay's independence. Moreover I think he saw the possibility of defending the sovereignty of a nation that was even older than modern Paraguay. There was already a people here before the arrival of the Spanish – the Guaraní – just as there were the Incas in Peru and the Aztecs in Mexico. These were strong and advanced civilizations, ones that already had the shape of nations, perhaps not in the political sense suggested by Rousseau or Montesquieu, but at least in their social structure. Francia managed to create the basis for a nation state which, after he disappeared, could become the most advanced in Latin America.

GP Did you have personal experience of the Chaco War between Paraguay and Bolivia in the 1930s?

ARB Yes, I ran away from school with some friends at about fourteen. We went off to the war as a great adventure. Because of our age they wouldn't let us join the troops at the front, so we became auxiliaries, transporting food or ammunition and helping out behind the lines. At that time the reasons for the war were very unclear. We Paraguayans had the firm conviction that we were fighting to defend our national territory. No doubt the Bolivians felt the same way. Really, an economic conflict lay behind the war. It was a matter of petroleum reserves. Paraguay lost 60,000 or 70,000 men over the three years of the war and there were 100,000 deaths on the Bolivian side. There was also the corresponding destruction of each country's economy. Things like this, when you look closely, always turn out to be products of larger economic and political factors.

GP In *I the Supreme* you quote Pascal's saying that truth never belongs to just one person. It begins with two or more, which is relevant to both Latin American history and to the novel. There are always multiple perspectives: the Indians, the Europeans, the mestizos and so on.

ARB Ethnically and culturally Latin America is mestizo and our literature has come about through a kind of fermentation. Of course the literary norms originally came from outside. The indigenous peoples had no novels, though they had myths, sacred songs, hymns, rituals and ceremonies. The novel is above all a bourgeois form which, over the last two centuries, has gradually been assimilated and adapted to our fundamentally mestizo nature.

GP Is that why you include Guaraní words?

ARB I do that less and less. I don't want Guaraní to appear just on the surface but to be an internal radiation. I've been trying to achieve this through restructuring the semantics of Spanish, which is not a language with fixed norms. In Paraguay quite a lot of standard Spanish has been lost, as has a lot of Guaraní. We speak a mestizo Guaraní, very Hispanified.

Spanish is an artificial language for most Paraguayans. This is something that has impeded the development of the novel. In what language does one write? I can't write in Guaraní because it is not my first language and also because I don't want to reproduce in my writing yet another symbolic enclosure for the country. I want to project the Paraguayan being towards universality. I'm not interested in the picturesque or in writing folkloric or regionalist fiction. My deepest aspiration is that my stories about Paraguay could be read in Japan, where the readers know nothing of the language or the history. If a novel doesn't move foreign readers, it is false and ought to be thrown out.

I feel that the opposition of the Hispanic and indigenous cultures is very important in Paraguay. I've read quite a lot of anthropology, and I've studied the way the indigenous families live in Paraguay, although as an observer rather than as a scientist. The two cultures are enemies: the Indian still suffers the oppression and persecution of the white culture. The mixing of the races doesn't seem to have moderated this. From early times the indigenous woman would give her language to her mestizo son but the son would inherit the vices of his Spanish father and in fact become an even crueller master. Of course there were great men amongst the mestizos, the liberators like San Martín or Artigas, but the majority were cruel oppressors of the indigenous people. Even today in Paraguay many of the Indians live marginalized and unprotected lives.

The dialectic between Indian and mestizo culture has been crucial in my work; it is the sort of social dialectic that is central to all literature. Even the most apparently socially evasive writing is grounded in a web of relations in which it finds its deepest meaning. Take the case of Borges. As far as I'm concerned, Borges is the greatest writer the continent has seen. I say that without embarrassment and in the confidence that it is true. In his writing you find all the currents of Latin American culture, including cosmopolitanism, which is very important. He also had a deep appreciation of popular life. In much of his writing Borges is an admirer of gaucho literature, such as *Martín Fierro*. There is the influence of *lunfardo*, the slang of the Buenos Aires underworld, and of the marginal dialects. Then came the definitive, classical period when he rejected all these shadows of the past and dedicated himself to writing his own quintessential, pure and crystalline literature. Even then, the larger Latin American universe is integrated into the Borgesian one.

Some of my leftist colleagues have said that I commit an injustice in praising Borges. That is not true. I don't praise

Borges; I praise his writing, which is the most revolutionary of Latin American reality. Of course I am aware of the dark side of his world. As a person Borges was just as fallible and fragile as any other writer. You can't suggest that such perfect writing could come from a perfect man. The two things would have destroyed each other. Borges' writing was perfect because he was imperfect. He was a man full of fissures and traps, of enormous desperation in the face of the infinite, time and death. He had a sinister, black humour and made jokes about everything sacred in Latin America, which is fine by me, because I believe Latin Americans could do with a little more courageous humour instead of this eternal game of factions.

GP You use humour quite a lot in your work. There is black humour in *I the Supreme*. I like the mention of a *de fatuo* government, which is appropriate in a book where there are a lot of fatuous moments.

ARB I haven't thought much about that. *I the Supreme* is my best work because I gave myself over to it and the book used me as a mediator. I'm not the author of *I the Supreme*. Partly for that reason I introduced the figure of the compiler. He is a metaphor for the writer who wants to enter the world that he's elaborating. The compiler can set the novel up but he can't enter it. I wanted a figure who could give new life to this dark and mysterious drama.

I am waging a war against literature because I am a little against everything. I don't feel a blind devotion to literature, nor to history – I am also fighting against history. *I the Supreme* isn't a historical novel; it is anti-historical, counter-history, because I was looking for collisions that would produce fissures in the narrative material, so that you could see or guess what was behind the thick web of lies that make up the surface. History, after all, is a kind of fiction, like the novel. What do historians mean by the statement that history is infallible because it employs documents? I can use the same documents and come up with a completely different history. The novel called history is more fictional than the novel. I have less confidence in history than in novels created with a writer's whole being, with all the cosmic sense that you can find in even the smallest cultural fact. At the same time, I'm also against the novel.

GP In *I the Supreme* you mention memory a number of times but you don't talk about history. Is it that memory is more personal, popular and therefore more important than history?

ARB The two are complementary. There is a kind of writing that records facts in documents and then there is history as lived by certain people. It is this lived history that generates a collective memory, the old and beautiful memory of the tribe. The collective memory has moments of confusion and obscurity, when it is important to look for a different angle. You can find that not only in the written history but in popular culture, whether written or oral.

I have a lot of confidence in the collective memory. Collective memory is something you can see very clearly in closed societies, where a culture is cut off and hasn't lost its internal structure, and the web that links past and future is still intact, as in Paraguay. Collective memory is also prominent in cultures such as the Mexican, where the oral tradition is still strong. It is less evident in Argentina, which has had a lot of immigration and where the web of the past has been remade and edged with new patterns.

GP In *Son of Man* there is a conflict between this collective memory and the forces represented by Miguel Vera, the bourgeois who always betrays his community.

ARB In *Son of Man* I wanted to show the opposition between the bourgeois anti-hero, in this case Miguel Vera, a man full of weaknesses and cowardice, lacking in integrity, crushed by events, and the popular heroes, who are nameless and who pass the baton to each other from chapter to chapter.

GP You spoke of Borges as being a revolutionary writer. I think he was revolutionary in that he could distil a continent into a symbol, the labyrinth, which captures the bewildering complexity and the conundrums one constantly encounters there. Then there is the aspect of cruelty and the macabre. Octavio Paz insisted that the labyrinth is a symbol for all men, but don't you think it has a special meaning for Latin Americans?

ARB The labyrinth as the Cretans conceived it has no particular relevance to Latin America. However, there is the labyrinth of nature – the jungle, the desert, the mountains, the vast rivers that form their labyrinths of water – and above all there is the cultural labyrinth, the historical labyrinth where opposing currents constantly mix. Everything is thrown together with violence and without a destiny. As for Borges the revolutionary, leaving aside his unsound ideology, you find that the labyrinth is a potent symbol because of what he introduced into it. His labyrinth contains the great universal myths, presented by his erudition but transformed into something else.

The whole Borgesian universe breathes anxiety, the anguish of the labyrinth. During a whole epoch of his life, up to the point when he began to go blind, the intellect completely ruled his literature. It was all a mental construction. The body didn't speak. When his blindness provoked this uncertainty and his sense of mortality he began to feel existential anguish and to remember his body. He had a body, which was the only place he could write stories and, specifically, his own story. He didn't remember his body until his oncoming blindness converted it into a physical metaphor, the labyrinth.

Nothing is gratuitous in Borges. Everything that happened to him happened as a kind of premonition or as the carrying out of a secret law. And so I make the distinction between the reactionary and the visionary Borges, able to see infinitesimal details. It is not for nothing that he invented the metaphor of the aleph, which also didn't surface until blindness took him by the back of the neck, as the true monsters do. Uncertainty, mortality and anguish were expressed through his body because that was where he was wounded. All the late poetry is a song about death – his death. He wrote not only about the strange and the fantastic but about his own tragedy. There is little Latin American writing that includes as much violence as the stories of Borges, where there are always at least one or two deaths.

This too relates to his uncertainty, unknown to the clear-minded or Platonic Greeks.

GP The grotesque is another element of the labyrinth. Latin America can be divided into the north, where you find the literature of magic realism, and the south, where the grotesque is more evident. In this respect you could oppose people such as José Donoso and Ernesto Sábato to writers such as Alejo Carpentier and García Márquez.

ARB Yes, but this is an issue we won't resolve now. It is something that may become clear in a few centuries time, when the culture of Latin America has become coherent and this labyrinth has shown its exits. The grotesque has certainly inspired a whole current of Argentinian literature, especially that centred on Buenos Aires. I'm not a literary critic but I have the impression that the grotesque, at least in the case of Borges, came from his own personal feelings. Borges reacted with some violence against the phenomenon of massive immigration into Argentina. With the great influx of Italian migrants the heroic universe, the world of both the gaucho and the patrician – patriarchal Buenos Aires, with its old established families – began to crumble, producing a current of theatrical literature, very influenced by the grotesque, by the lack of adaption of the Italians to the local surroundings.

There are elements of the grotesque in my work. I couldn't have avoided it. I used it a lot in *I the Supreme* because it offers an avenue into one of the means of dismantling history, parody. You can't repeat written history. You can only parody it. You make a pastiche and that comes out as a grotesque parody of history. As part of this process you also find strong, expressionist elements.

GP In your writing, and in that of Sábato, Donoso, Vargas Llosa and Borges, there is European romanticism as well as expressionism.

ARB Yes, indeed, above all French romanticism, which is what we have read most of and which has been powerful since the time of Latin American independence. It has given us arms with which to fight the persistence of the dominant literature of Spain. Before I read the European romantics I had read only Spanish classics. When I began to read the romantics I felt a kind of liberation – I began to see that romanticism was a strong ally in combating the relics of colonialism and cultural domination.

Afterwards I discovered the great English-speaking writers, such as Faulkner, Hemingway and Dos Passos. As for James Joyce, I couldn't read him well in the original, whereas I could read Beckett and he impressed me much more. Joyce reflects one aspect of the universal destruction, the pre-apocalypse, but Beckett is already inside the apocalypse.

GP You have combined some aspects of Beckett and Faulkner by investigating the fragmentation of character. In Beckett there is often one interior voice that narrates; in Faulkner there are various interior narrative voices belonging to different characters. In *I the Supreme* you have many voices inside one character, which is a new twist.

ARB Whether or not there is anything new there, it is the point of view that gives sense to the narrative. The presence of internal narrators has great importance; it gives the novel its internal geometry.

GP You seem to stand apart from the literary groups and factions in Latin America.

ARB In my opinion the greatest Latin American poet was César Vallejo, who died in complete misery in 1938. Now writing has become an industry and some writers are multi-millionaires, which is a great weight for a writer. Austerity is scarcely possible any more. Isolation is a way of maintaining a kind of liberty and the right to see the world in your own way.

I don't want to be part of any faction or party, nor to march under any banner that I haven't invented myself. Recently the main Paraguayan opposition party offered me a seat in the senate but I said that I wasn't suited to be a senator. Now they have offered me an ambassadorship to UNESCO. I won't accept that either, because I know that in three months they will throw me out for saying things they won't like. Why take a post where you can't do anything? The only thing they are interested in is my name, which, after all, is not much. It's not that well known, although our literature is becoming more widely read, which is good; the English-speaking nations have given a great and influential literature to the world and now it is time for us to give a little back.

GP Why did you stop writing for so long between *Son of Man* and *I the Supreme*?

ARB It's the way I work. I have two or three novels maturing inside me. I don't take notes or make résumés, I live with these novels and sometimes I forget that it is necessary to write them. I recently finished writing a novel called *El fiscal*, some 1,500 pages representing three years' work. Partly because of the current situation in Paraguay and partly because the work was flawed I decided it was wrong to publish it, so I burnt it, just as I did with *Son of Man*. *Son of Man* also took me three years. It was written while I was holding down three badly paid jobs in exile in Buenos Aires. I burnt the manuscript and then, three months later, the novel came out quickly, by itself. So I don't abandon the novel, just the flawed form.

I don't publish a great deal because while I don't feel the need to write I don't write. You could write a novel a year at the rate of three pages a day. The cultural industry permits you to work this way because now they don't sell books for their value but for their signature. They'd publish anything of mine now, no matter how poor the quality. That doesn't seem very moral. I don't see why writers like Vargas Llosa or García Márquez feel the need to publish a book every once in a while, as if the world depended on three or four books more or less.

As I said at the beginning, this idea that literature can save Latin America is false. Writing makes an important contribution to culture, but it doesn't save a nation or a people. The great Jewish literature didn't save the Jews from the holocaust. Equally, no totalitarian regime, no government led by a Hitler, a Mussolini or a Stroessner, has ever produced great literature.

BRAZIL

·

Márcio Souza

The years of the Brazilian 'economic miracle', 1967 to 1973, were a period of rapid modernization driven by a nationalistic military dictatorship. Brazil emerged not as yet another source of raw materials for the economies of the developed world but as a competitor, first in the field of heavy industry and later in that of advanced technology. Brazil now has one of the world's largest car industries, is one of the largest arms manufacturers and has begun to produce computers. In the process of development, however, Brazil has become a rich nation full of poor people. Those not part of the growing economy have become invisible to the nation's book-keepers, though they remain very evident in the slums that intersperse even the wealthy areas of Brazilian cities.

The Brazilian dictators were more moderate than the Chileans or the Argentinians but nevertheless the media were censored and critics faced possible imprisonment or torture. Writers who published critical material ran a risk; Márcio Souza's *The Order of the Day* (1983) would probably not have appeared had the military not been moving towards re-democratization.

The Order of the Day is deceptively whimsical. It could be read as a breezy, entertaining piece of science fiction. On another level it is a political satire whose critical thrust is concealed by a lightness that distinguishes it from the more sombre writing of Spanish-speaking America. The serious message behind this lightness is a call for sleepers to wake. The novel describes apathy in the face of a takeover by malevolent aliens, a comment on the political quietism that many observers saw in the Brazil of the 1960s and 1970s.

In *Mad Maria* (1980) Souza casts a satirical eye on the notion of progress. This is a much harsher book, written with black humour. It deals with the building of a railway line through tracts of rainforest at a terrible cost in lives. The irony is that the project leads from nowhere to nowhere – it is merely a scheme cooked up by some politicians in a financial swindle. This is particularly pertinent to Brazil, where there are doubts about how money for development has been spent.

Though a critic, Souza is in many respects a nationalist, as is testified by his humorous work *The Flying Brazilian* (1986), a historical account of the adventures of a Brazilian aviator in Europe. The book grew out of Souza's work as a screenwriter and film director. He has also been very much involved in the theatre in Rio de Janeiro, where he now lives. He co-directs a publishing house, having suffered one of the cruellest blows for a satirist, an improvement in the government. However, though the dictators stepped down in 1985, there is still much uncertainty about Brazil's future. Charges of corruption and cronyism surface from time to time and the conditions of life for most Brazilians have failed to improve.

Márcio Souza's thought-provoking fiction, with its wonderful flights of the imagination, tackles concerns relevant not only to Brazil or the Third World but also to the countries of the developed world.

GP Is being a Brazilian writer very different from being a Spanish-speaking Latin American writer?

MS There is a lot of difference. We are a huge Quebec, as different from Spanish-speaking writers as French Canadian writers are from the rest of Canada. That is because of our Portuguese background and because Brazil is the only modern country in Latin America.

There are only two countries on the continent that have a continuous, unbroken literary history: Brazil and the United States. Our literature goes back 300 years. Brazil is much older than the United States. The Spanish-speaking literature consists of a lot of different moments from different countries – you have to join up important contributions from Argentina, Mexico, and Peru to make a literary history. When Jorge Icaza died in Ecuador, for example, it finished Ecuadorean literature. In Brazil we have an independent literary tradition going back to the seventeenth century.

GP Did Brazil have more independence under the Portuguese than the rest of Latin America had under Spain? Was it less repressed?

MS I don't think so. We don't have a history of liberalism. Our history is the same as Spanish-speaking America in that sense. It is true that there was a difference in the methods of colonization. The Portuguese had much more experience than the Spanish. They had been forming colonies since the fourteenth century. In the sixteenth century they were establishing themselves in China and Japan, and they were the first Europeans to go to the Far East. Portugal itself was a mixture of Arabs, Africans and people from different parts of Europe. The Portuguese, with their greater experience, had a more objective, direct approach to the colonization. For example, you never find any Portuguese looking for a fountain of youth, like some of the crazy Spaniards; colonization was just a military and administrative operation. In the eighteenth century Brazil had a very powerful bourgeoisie and there was already an independence movement, though it wasn't successful.

GP Do you see Brazil's literary history as different from the rest of Latin America?

MS Yes; when we think of a Latin American novel we think of one in Spanish. We don't feel that the term 'Latin American' applies to Brazilians. Of course we are Latin American in the sense that we are Latins in America, as the Italians are in the United States – Mario Puzo is Latin American. The mafia is Latin American.

A novel like *One Hundred Years of Solitude* is about things that no longer exist in Brazil but which are contemporary in Colombia. García Márquez writes about his present but for us the book could be set in the 1930s or even in the nineteenth century. There was a Brazilian novel very like *One Hundred Years of Solitude* written during the nineteenth century.

GP A fantastic yet realistic novel?

MS No, it wasn't that kind of book, because we Portuguese (or 'new' Portuguese) are much more realistic, more objective. Even so, there was a strong tradition of fantasy in Portuguese-speaking literature.

GP In *Mad Maria* you set out to write a strictly realistic novel but what is real in Brazil is fantastic anywhere else, so in that sense you have similarities with literature from the Caribbean. Yet your novel *The Order of the Day* is not magic realism. It's full of flying saucers. Both you and Ignácio de Loyola Brandão seem to owe more to science fiction or science fantasy than to García Márquez.

MS Yes. The book is a mock-fantasy, of course, because it was written as a satirical novel about the military.

GP On the cover of *The Flying Brazilian* you describe the story as 'lighter than air' and you say at the beginning that it is just an entertainment, but I am suspicious of a writer who declares his work to be merely entertainment. With Graham Greene I find the 'entertainments' are as profound as his more serious novels. *Our Man in Havana*, for example, reveals an enormous amount about Latin American reality, but in a very light way.

MS It's a fantastic book, one of the few to show Cuba before the revolution.

GP Are you working in a similar vein, writing to entertain but also to bring controversial ideas before the general public? Your books are political and controversial.

MS It is not difficult for me to write in that way. The path has already been beaten by other Brazilian writers, for example Lima Barreto a black writer from the turn of the century. He wrote light novels, yet he was highly critical of the slave society and feudalistic morality of Brazil at the time. Our greatest writer, Machado de Assis, wrote his best novel about the ruling class, which is portrayed as just a few idle, very rich guys. It's a kind of romance, written with a great sense of humour, a humour that Henry James, for example, doesn't have. De Assis wrote as Henry James wrote about society, about good and evil and human nature, but he is much better than Henry James. I like Henry James a lot but I prefer the corrosive humour of Machado de Assis.

There is a lot to read in Brazilian literature. In the 1920s, when Joyce and other avant-garde writers were working in Paris, there was an experimental, modernist movement in Brazil. There was nothing else like it on the continent, not even in the United States. There, modernism meant someone like Katherine Anne Porter writing very realistic fiction. In the 1930s we had 'critical realism', which was similar, but for us modernism means the avant-garde novel of writers like Oswaldo de Andrade and Mário de Andrade.

GP There was a 'boom' in Spanish Latin American literature during the 1960s, but we are much less aware of Brazilian literature. Is that just a matter of lack of publicity?

MS No. First of all we have a huge market here for any kind of fiction. Writers can make a living working just for the Brazilian market. Also, we don't have the habit of giving our writers posts in the diplomatic corps. Octavio Paz, Carlos Fuentes, even Julio Cortázar, worked for the government at one time or another and lived in Europe. They managed to keep quite a high profile in France. They could make contacts, promote their own work and the work of others, whereas no one from Brazil was working to try to sell books outside Brazil.

When we were finally 'discovered' in the early 1970s a literary agency in Barcelona signed contracts with a lot of Brazilian writers, but then they just forgot about Brazilian writing. In the case of Darcy Ribeiro, who had a best-selling novel in Brazil, when European publishers went to the agency they were told the price was something like 50,000 dollars, so high that no one wanted to buy. We publish a lot of Spanish-speaking literature in Brazil, but they never publish us in Spanish.

GP You mean that since the beginning of the 1970s the best

Brazilian writers have been kept out of circulation because they are under contract?

MS Not any more – eventually people began to wake up. But there is something rather curious at work here. In Brazil you often hear the argument that we must integrate with Latin America. In a commercial and cultural sense I think it is important, just as it is important that we have contacts with other cultures. Yet we present a certain challenge to the other Latin American countries – we are a threat; we are too big. Once when I was giving a talk at the University of San Marcos in Lima I asked the students why they didn't learn Portuguese. Portuguese-speakers can understand some Spanish but Portuguese is pretty incomprehensible for Spanish-speakers. Still, we read Spanish; why don't they make the effort to read Portuguese? They answered me quite angrily, saying that Brazil is an imperialist country, that there was already enough Brazilian music on Peruvian radio stations and now we wanted to flood their market with our literature. There is a fear of us in the Spanish-speaking countries.

GP *The Order of the Day* is a mixture of satire and allegory; is your choice of form a result of not wanting to be too direct in your criticism of the military?

MS It was almost the only novel mocking the military to appear during the dictatorship and it was published by my own publishing house. My partners decided to take out insurance policies in case there was trouble. I invited a general, a member of the opposition who was a military outcast at that time, to write a preface. When I asked his opinion he said it would be dangerous to publish; it would be better to wait. However, I wanted to publish it then, in 1983; politically it was the right time.

When there were no reprisals it was a sign to many people that there was a decline in the power of the military; they were no longer able to be as repressive as they wanted to be. There was a very strong, organized public opposition and that year there was a move towards a so-called democratic opening.

GP When the villagers in *The Order of the Day* see flying

saucers they forget about it and carry on as if nothing had happened. Is the book meant to be a satire on political passivity?

MS Yes, but it is also about the 'power' of the repressive system. It is a satirical look at the system of information created by the military – readers not living in Brazil would miss some of the references but they would get the general sense of a crazy political system. At the same time it is an adventure story, it's funny.

GP You seem to be deliberately vague about who the aliens in the novel are. They don't represent the military, nor the CIA, nor any political party. They are not even a metaphor for the Chilean subversives who are supposed to be behind a lot of what is going on. Did you not want to put your finger on any one cause of the problems?

MS I didn't want to take a partisan viewpoint, whether of the right or left. The aliens are a product of poetic licence. I didn't want to follow any specific ideological line. That wouldn't be right for a Brazilian novel. You see, we are one of the big countries: we belong to the same family as Australia, Canada, the Soviet Union, the United States, India and China.

GP I'd say that Australia really belongs to the little countries, at least in terms of population.

MS Yes, but it is big in resources. In Brazil we have both resources and population density. Also, unlike India, we have one culture throughout the country. I'm from the north, I write novels about the north, but a southern reader can understand them perfectly. Even a reader from Portugal or Portuguese-speaking Africa can make sense of them. That doesn't happen in India, where there are so many different languages and cultures. We have a country with cultural variety – it is a melting pot – but there is one mainstream culture, the Portuguese, Latin, Iberian culture that holds everything else together.

Another point is that all our national territory is usable land, which makes us different from Canada and Australia, where some land is frozen or a desert. All of Brazil can be used to produce agricultural goods, so we are big enough to be

independent. Our future isn't linked with the United States or
the Soviet Union. We are very dangerous because we can be
the Third Way and not just the Third World.

GP Perón thought that Argentina could be the Third Way.

MS They also have a lot of resources in Argentina. I think
the connections that are starting to appear between Brazil and
Argentina are very important.

GP If Latin America were unified, it would be a very
powerful force.

MS The problem is the difference between the cultures.
Brazil has the tenth largest economy in the world and a very
advanced industrial sector, so it is difficult for us to deal with
Paraguay, Bolivia or Nicaragua, for instance. We have very
strong ties with Nicaragua – even during the military dictatorship the government supported the Sandinistas – and Nicaragua's main economic aid comes from Brazil, not from the
Soviet Union.* But what can Nicaragua exchange with Brazil?
We produce our own coffee and sugar, all the agricultural
products we need. If there were a common market here, the
others would buy from us but what would they sell?

We don't have an imperial tradition in Brazil. That has never
been part of our mentality, perhaps because our Portuguese
culture is a dialectic: change is gradual. Everybody talks; you
give a little, I give a little. It is slow but sure and steady. *One
Hundred Years of Solitude* could never be written here, but one
day someone might write *One Hundred Years of Solidity*. Also,
the Latin culture is deeply entrenched in the Brazilian mind
and no Latin country in the world wants to be imperialistic
again. We have tried imperialism many times and we know it
is not the best way. The Latin culture was imperialistic in
Roman times, in the Renaissance, in the nineteenth century;
the experience is shared because there are many connections
between Italy, Portugal, France and Spain.

If Brazil had wanted to, in the nineteenth century it could
have stretched its borders to the Pacific Ocean. At the end of

* This interview was recorded while the Sandinistas were still in power.

the nineteenth century we had the best army and navy in the region, even more modern than that of the United States. We could have invaded all the neighbouring territories, but we didn't because we were more preoccupied with what was happening internally. We were busy making ourselves one nation, spreading this Latin culture and the Portuguese language all over the country.

By the mid nineteenth century Portuguese was supposed to be the official language spoken in schools and government departments in the Amazon region, where I come from. When the emperor, Pedro II, commissioned a poet to go to the north and prepare a report on how the national education programme was going, he found that classes were being given in Portuguese but that as soon as the classes were dismissed the teachers and the students would start talking in Indian languages. The emperor then took more measures to establish a uniform culture. Some people say that this was a terrible thing to do, but there is no turning back. I can't go back to speaking an Indian language, nor would the writers from other Portuguese colonies want to revert to theirs. In Portugal's African colonies tribal languages are no longer spoken; they can't go back to writing in their old languages any more than we can.

GP Were the Portuguese better at assimilating the Indians? Were the conditions for Indians and slaves as bad here as they were in, say, Peru?

MS Yes, they were. Brazil was the last country to liberate its slaves and that was only because of English pressure – they blockaded the ports and intercepted the slave ships. Yet despite the brutality of Portuguese colonialism, the Portuguese mixed much more with the local cultures than did the Spanish, the English or the French. Significantly, when Mozambique became independent the Africans pulled down all the monuments to the heroes of the colonization but left the statues to the writers standing.

I remember attending a meeting of African writers in Germany. The French-speaking writers, who had wonderful Parisian accents, were attacking the imperialist, colonialist lan-

guage of France and proposing to go back to their tribal
languages. The English-speakers didn't quite understand what
was going on, while one of the Portuguese-speaking writers
objected that his language was Portuguese. 'We have taken this
language from the colonialists,' he said 'and now it belongs to
us. They exploited our country and took away a lot of wealth,
but we took the riches of this language from them.' The French-
speakers thought this was an absurd position and even the
English-speakers had misgivings, but I understood perfectly
what he meant.

GP In *Mad Maria* you seem to be attacking the way foreign
capital moved into Brazil in the nineteenth century.

MS Well, we have a colonial past and we have to deal with
this. Just as in Australia, a lot of hooligans came to Brazil in
the early days, but they were the people who organized and
created the country. They didn't know that they were creating
a country but they were. Do you think those hooligans who
went to Australia knew what they were starting? They couldn't
have imagined that a few centuries later there would be an
opera house on Sydney harbour.

GP Feminist themes appear quite often in your work. In
The Order of the Day the central character is a woman and she
finally kills the alien. In one scene she is trying to talk some
sense into one of the male characters and you describe him
looking at her with arrogance bordering on sadism. Is the
position of women holding back progress in Brazil?

MS There is a strong womens' movement here now. Latin
culture has always been very male-oriented, ever since Roman
times. Also we are marked by having been a slave society,
which affected the relationship between male and female.
However, since the modernization of the country began in the
1930s, there have been changes, especially in the big cities.
Women can do all kinds of jobs now. The situation here is
similar to that in Italy, where there is a strong feminist movement but women also have a very strong traditional role in the
family.

GP In *Mad Maria* men are compared to scorpions. Life

becomes so cheap because of the oppressive conditions. Class divisions and poor working conditions are still very much a reality in Brazil and there doesn't seem to be much improvement.

MS There is a strong fight for improvement here. The main concern of the current return to democracy is to establish the concept of citizenship. You cannot construct a democracy without citizens. Even before the military dictatorship the population was divided into first- and second-class citizens. That was another legacy of the slave society, the attitude that you don't need to work because you have some 'nigger' to do it for you. Now, with industrialization, you can no longer get cheap Indian or Negro servants, because they get better money working in the factories. Wages are going up.

There is also a movement to ensure that everyone has the same rights as a citizen. If you go to any political meeting the rhetoric will not be the anti-American-imperialism kind that you'll find in many parts of Latin America. We are concerned about foreign influence but the main issue is civil rights. This is the preoccupation of the people who are writing the new constitution.

A few years ago you couldn't imagine a black girl denouncing soldiers who murdered her brother, but that happened recently. The military were very surprised by the trial, but the law has to be for everybody, not just for those who can pay. That's the way it has to be if you want a democracy and I think many people amongst the ruling class and the industrialists do want a democracy because they are afraid of the current levels of discontent.

Ignácio de Loyola Brandão

São Paolo is South America's largest city. It is also Brazil's industrial heart. Set on a cool plateau, it is a grimy, matter-of-fact place of grey, wintry stone and grit in the air. Wastelands are given over to squatters, starving in makeshift houses beside high-rise luxury apartments where children only go out to play inside security fences and where residents deal with the constant fear of attack by removing all jewellery and valuables before stepping on to the street, or opening the garage door by remote control. With its skyscrapers, motorways, flyovers and concrete towers, the city suggests Fritz Lang's *Metropolis*, and it is perhaps an Orwellian sobriety that you see in the eyes of the pedestrians. In São Paolo you don't need to be told that Brazil is a giant. Here the novels of Ignácio de Loyola Brandão become credible.

Zero (1975) and *And Still the Earth* (1982) have an edge of anger and desperation not present in the work of Brandão's friend, Márcio Souza, even though they share the theme of apathy. *Zero* traces the path of a small, inoffensive loser, who is victimized and turned out of his home by a police raid. Through a series of bizarre and brutal adventures he becomes a political radical and outgrows his initial identity as a nobody, the zero of the title. Written during the dictatorship, the effect of an authoritarian state on personal identity is the central concern of this novel, which has no really developed characters – all the figures seem bleached by the corrosive atmosphere.

The bizarre is a strong element not only in *Zero* but also in *And Still the Earth*, where Brandão has projected current trends into a truly ghastly future. Brazil has become a vast desert; the Amazon river has been concreted over and the climate so disturbed that small pockets of air are hot enough to grill a human being in a few moments. The upsetting thing about this future is that it is not sufficiently unlikely. Nor does the complete rewriting of history by an impenetrable bureaucracy seem sufficiently strange in modern Brazil, where the control of information is highly centralized. Such themes have also been explored by writers of the developed world, though rarely with Brandão's inventiveness or sense of urgency.

And Still the Earth is similar to *Zero* in that it is a journey of discovery. It follows the path of a weak man who wanders deeper and deeper into forbidden parts of a nightmarish metropolis. Discovery of the true state of affairs and an impulse to rebel correspond to personal growth, a humanization that represents a small victory for the protagonist over the state. It is a very small victory, however, as the ending is deeply pessimistic.

Brandão's fiction is a call for concern and action. His passionate involvement with matters social, ecological and political fuels writing of great emotional force. As an inventor of ghastly futures he is similar to Orwell, except that in Brandão's case too much of that future has been visible by merely looking out of the window of his São Paolo apartment.

GP Do you come from São Paolo?

IB I'm from the interior of the state of São Paolo, not from the capital. I was born into a fairly poor family. My father worked on the railways. I started work as a journalist at sixteen, writing cinema criticism. Afterwards I worked on two local papers between 1952 and 1957. I founded a cinema club and in the late 1950s we made a sixteen-millimetre film about our city. I was also part of a theatre group and a photography club.

In 1957 I started working for the paper *Ultima Hora* in São Paolo. It was a paper of the centre-left and was a very formative influence. I started writing on social and political matters, though I also wrote about cinema, theatre and television. It was there that I began to develop a literary style. Themes and plots kept turning up – I was constantly faced with situations that I've later been able to use in my writing. *Zero* was the product of the views I formed there. Everything in *Zero* came from events that really occurred under the military dictatorship in the 1960s. I took the facts and transformed them, a little the way John Dos Passos did. Dos Passos was a great influence on me.

GP It's not so obvious that *Zero* was based on real events – it reads like a satire, or a possible future that you've invented.

IB It was actually an impossible past. That was the problem. I used the satirical form because I was writing at a very difficult time. There was severe censorship and I thought that the only way to get the book past the censors was to make it so absurd and fantastic that they wouldn't realize what I was saying. In fact they did realize and the book was banned.

Of course, irony is a characteristic of everything I've written. I find that irony is the only way to confront the harshness of life here – it is a way of softening very harsh facts, and of trapping your readers and not letting them escape. In a book like *Zero* where the situation is completely black, gloomy and violent, and there are continual shocks, irony is the only way to keep a hold on the reader.

GP Perhaps Brazilian readers have a certain resistance to realism because Brazilians may see shocking things every day; irony may be the only way of surprising people and making them think again.

IB Exactly. The public always has an escapist attitude. They run away from reality and the things they have to face here. They won't follow the path of a work of art that returns them to that reality.

GP Is irony typical of Brazil – as it is in England, where it is a part of everyday speech – is it a personal trait?

IB I feel that Brazilians do have a sense of irony. It is not the subtle irony of the British, which is a matter of hidden meanings. Brazilian irony is more direct and cruel, it's quicker and undisguised, and it is related to one of our great problems – the fact that Brazilians face everything with such good humour. Even in the worst situations Brazilians tend to lack the very important qualities of indignation and rebelliousness. If something terrible happens, people advise you not to worry – you'll get over it, you'll manage. I think it is time people stopped coping and started protesting and rebelling.

GP *Zero* and *And Still the Earth* both incite the readers to action, they are both a rejection of quietism.

IB Quietism, apathy, accommodation; Brazilians are always passive. That doesn't mean they are peaceful, just passive; they don't react.

GP Yet machismo is very important in Brazil. Isn't calling a Brazilian man passive an insult?

IB No, machismo means being active, but only in relation to women. Brazilian men are macho in relation to women but not to the system. Deep down they are not macho at all.

GP In your books the protagonists progress from being sexually rather inadequate to being more adequate as they become more rebellious. Political growth parallels sexual power.

IB I find that those who haven't discovered themselves, who aren't satisfied with what they are and who accept everything, lose a number of their qualities. They are less than full human beings. As you develop you discover yourself and learn to appreciate yourself. You begin to appreciate others. When you have an objective in life you start to be transformed and that transformation necessarily includes sex. I've seen this a lot. When someone is in this state of quietism and passivity there is really no sexual life. If they transform themselves, their sexual life changes because their conception of love changes.

GP Political repression implies repression of the personality?

IB It reaches the point of annihilating the personality, of turning it into a zero. That was very clear in Brazil in the 1970s.

Today there is a different kind of repression. There is no dictatorship but neither is there real democracy. We are living under a pseudo-democracy that has caused great economic problems and the economic situation is affecting people in exactly the same way as the dictatorship did. People today are sad, without hope, without a future and without faith. The government has no credibility. No one believes a word of what the government says, nor are they convinced by any action the government takes. People are empty.

All this is similar to the psychology that developed under the dictatorship, when there was no possibility of fighting. We still have no real possibility of fighting because the fight is against a whole economic system and the resolve of the people isn't firm enough. The solution might be the appearance of a great leader, or something like that, but the characteristics of Brazilians today are very similar to those of the difficult years of the 1970s.

GP In your books the state is rather like Big Brother. Last night I discovered that on all of the fifteen or twenty radio stations there were only two voices reading the news. You have no alternative but to listen to what they are saying. Is it true that the news comes from only two sources?

IB Between 7 and 8 p.m. all the radio stations in Brazil are obliged to transmit an hour of an official programme, *The Hour of Brazil*, written by a government company, The Brazilian News Agency. This was something I put in *Zero* – the moment when, whether you are in Amazonas or Rio Grande do Sul, you will hear the same news item read by the same voice.

GP To what extent has the obvious control of information by the dictatorship been replaced by more subtle means of control?

IB There is no subtle control of the means of communication; there's total control. The government gives concessions to private companies who want to own television stations. The companies fear losing their concessions so they never oppose the government. Those who control the media are generally politicians with links in the government. They are very rich people who have economic power, so political and economic power controls the media. The media are always in favour of the government. You occasionally hear discord, voices attacking the government, but the criticism is always attenuated, never violent.

GP In the newspapers the criticism is harsher.

IB Yes, because the newspapers don't operate on government concessions. Still, the papers are under the control of only two groups, and the most important medium is television. All Brazilian homes have television.

GP What does this mean for a writer who wants a wide audience?

IB It means that you don't reach people, though it is not really because of television. It is because we have a very high rate of illiteracy, practically 50 per cent, though the official figure is 30 per cent. The education system is in ruins because the dictatorship closed almost all the schools. There are only 600 bookshops in the whole country, serving 8 million square hectares and 140 million people. Of the 600 bookshops only 100 are any good. Cuba, with a tenth of our population, has 200 good bookshops. Argentina has 600 in the city of Buenos Aires alone. Public libraries are practically non-existent here and those that do exist are deficient. So, we write for nobody.

GP But Márcio Souza told me that Brazil had the second-largest book market on the continent.

IB If you are thinking of technical books there is a market. There is a market for school books and for best-sellers. General literature is another story. If you sell 10,000 copies, it is newsworthy. If you sell 50,000, you are a big success.

Curiously *Zero* was very popular. No one knows why. It was a difficult book but a popular one. *And Still the Earth* sold 180,000 copies in eight years, which was fantastic. Every couple of years there seems to be a very popular book. I'm not talking about foreign books; the best-sellers always sell well.

GP Yet the quality of Brazilian literature is very high.

IB But there are preconceptions in Brazil. There is a prejudice against Brazilian literature. The critics are all against it, as are big magazines like *Veja*. There are Brazilian academics who refuse to teach Brazilian literature. We suffer from a virtual boycott within our own country.

GP This is very different to the situation of Spanish-speaking writers such as Vargas Llosa, who are like heroes to many of their readers.

IB Yes. It is part of the Brazilian psychology, which is a psychology of destruction. We can't have idols. A kind of cultural cannibalism operates here. Mário de Andrade, the great Brazilian writer, was heavily criticized; we eat ourselves.

Brazil is completely open to foreign culture. We are being colonized culturally. In the universities there are important teachers who completely disregard our culture. Talk to any writer about this; it is almost a deliberate campaign.

GP What means did the government use to control culture during the dictatorship?

IB Censorship. Complete censorship. It operated over all the media – books, cinema and theatre, radio, television and music.

GP Critical works like yours were banned. What else did they find dangerous?

IB They destroyed the education system. The curricula were all modified and narrowed. Many teachers were harassed, taken prisoner or exiled. Many magazines which published fiction, philosophy or sociology were closed. Sociological research groups were harassed.

GP The protagonist of *And Still the Earth* was one of these people, wasn't he? He was a teacher who had been sacked because his students had asked too many questions.

IB Everything in the novel really happened at that time, though I set some of the facts in the past. In my book the present was the past. The future setting was a device I used to portray what was happening in Brazil at that time. It was quite common then, as in the book, to have pupils enrolled in schools who weren't really students – they were spies, government agents. This was especially common in the faculties of literature and philosophy, but in the end even the technical faculties had students who were keeping watch on the teachers. It's a sad fact that from 1964 to 1975 we had no academic conferences or debates because discussion was prohibited – another means of keeping a lid on things.

GP An intellectual in Chile was telling me that the police often gathered information on those participating in a demonstration, for example, but take no action. You have no indication of exactly how much they know about you and are never sure how much it takes to make them act, so you become excessively cautious. Fear kills everything.

IB Yes, it kills everything. The poem at the beginning of *Zero* says that fear turns everyone into rats. The telephones of all the intellectuals, teachers and scientists were tapped. You heard noises, so sometimes you knew they were tapping you. At other times you heard nothing but still couldn't be sure; you were still afraid.

GP In both *Zero* and *And Still the Earth* time passes very quickly. Time is not real time, it's telescoped. You go from a bad situation to a ghastly one with strange speed.

IB Time doesn't interest me. What interested me were the situations, the facts and the people involved. The events were the important thing.

GP Was *And Still the Earth* a way of warning people that if society stayed on a certain path they would end up with the situation in the novel, where the country was a vast desert?

IB Exactly. *And Still the Earth* was a continuation of *Zero*, which was something that few people noticed. It is also a novel of a possible future, and that future has already begun – in the way the Amazon forest is disappearing, and the rivers are polluted, without fish.

As in the book, nobody knows anything about the government. At this moment we can't say who is governing Brazil. Is it President Sarney? Is it the military? We have no idea if Sarney or the military are behind the orders that are given. They set up organizations in such a way that we don't know about them. We can't intervene. By the time we discover something it is too late, because everything has been finalized, which is another thing that gives you a feeling of impotence. Brazil's great problem at the moment is the feeling of impotence.

Take corruption, for example. If you denounce it, there is no response. There may be a news item, perhaps, and then another and another, until after five articles the original issues have been forgotten. There is a wall between the government and the people; nothing penetrates it. It is like a medieval fortress.

Lygia Fagundes Telles

Lygia Fagundes Telles' early novel *The Marble Dance* (1954) is told from the point of view of a well-born young girl who is afflicted by a deep and crippling sense of shame. Telles' language verges on the fantastic and the novel's sense of the dramatic and the uncanny is reminiscent of *Wuthering Heights*. It reflects facets of Brazilian society that echo nineteenth-century Europe, though themes of religious guilt, sexuality and romance are developed in a thoroughly modern way, with the heroine reaching a level of strength and independence that would have been unthinkable in earlier writing.

Telles is known not only for her novels such as *The Girl in the Photograph* (1973) but for her short stories. The tales in the anthology *Tigrela and Other Stories* (1977) nibble away at the tenets of realist fiction; in 'The Ants' the behaviour of ants is enough to drive two travellers from a hotel room. Her political concern is evident in an implicit pessimism, as if injustices are so entrenched that only supernatural vengeance can have any effect. In one tale the poor have eaten all the cats and a rat plague of frightening proportions ensues – rats literally take over the house of a government minister and destroy it with an almost apocalyptic force. Some of Telles' stories have a dream-like quality but there is also a very conscious, gleeful sense of anarchy, which surfaces, say, when a lunatic takes over the doctor's role at an asylum. At times Telles' work is close to the fairy-tale; like Márcio Souza and Ignácio de Loyola Brandão she is willing to use forms of fiction that, in the English-speaking world, might be thought peripheral.

The grotesque or the fantastic often enter through the motif of insects. Insects provide a forlorn emblem for the protagonist of *The Marble Dance*, Virginia, who feels she is no more than a bug. Tiny creatures appear in humanized form on the edges of Telles' stories, sometimes intruding in mysterious ways on human relations. The motif is, perhaps, emblematic of being a woman writer in a society where, until recently, even middle-class women had very little power. Small events loom large, with a sense of absoluteness and finality.

While Telles seems to be pushed in the same direction as Donoso and Sábato, she is deflected by her lively sense of humour and of the macabre. She takes pleasure in writing the story as a game and distancing expressions of anger or anxiety. She has the same glee as a prankster getting revenge. In this sense she has more in common with Luisa Valenzuela; flippancy can be the gentlest form of attack.

GP As a writer, do you feel threatened?

LT In my book *The Discipline of Love* I suggest that in Brazil there are three species in danger of extinction – the Indian, the tree and the writer. As regards the Indian, all we have to do is read the papers to see the struggle that is going on. The Indians are fighting for a dignified way of living and a legitimate place in society. They are being persecuted because they own land and that land has become very valuable. A fight to the death is going on. We used to think of the Indian in a romantic, literary way, cerebrally, from a distance; but the Indians are no longer figures in some sentimental poem. They make demands, they want their own space and a measure of dignity in their lives. They have become an inconvenience and so are on the way to extinction.

As for the trees, I don't know if you've realized that the tree is also an inconvenience, even though it is also extremely important. It is obviously important from an economic point of view. It has thousands of uses. In 1980, when I wrote *The Discipline of Love*, they were killing 2 million trees each day. I don't know how much longer our forests will last. Our land is being turned into a desert.

Then there is the writer. In a nation with a literacy problem as great as ours, what future can a writer have? What's more, this is a Third World country where even those who know how to read look down on Brazilian literature. They prefer North American literature. There are also those who know how to read but have no money to buy books. Books are considered luxury items, costly and superfluous. So, the writer is in danger of extinction. Who do we write for? Who is going to read us? Nevertheless, we keep writing. I still believe in and have hope for my profession; if this hope runs out, all that remains to do is to cover one's head with ashes and wait for death. This may sound bleak but we need to be realistic at the moment when our planet is sick, sicker than it has ever been.

GP Have you had difficulty in being recognized by the Brazilian critics?

LT It is very difficult. There is a terrible ill will towards Brazilian literature and this is in great measure due to our colonial mentality. We still feel that we are colonists, so the most important writers must belong to the colonizers: Brazilian writers can't be important. At the moment, I must confess, I don't give this very much thought – I go on writing and give no consideration to the critics and their possible reactions, but when I was younger I was very hurt by their discrimination, which was double in my case. I was not just a Brazilian writer but also a woman. Now criticism doesn't affect me so much.

At the moment I am working on a new novel and giving it the best form I can, writing with all my love and passion. When I write I fight with the word. I draw blood from it and it draws blood from me. At times when we are attacking each other it is almost like an act of love. I'm like a boxer who attacks the opponent just to stay on his feet. You see, you need a lot of courage to be a writer and courage, for me, is the greatest virtue. The second greatest is patience, which ought not to be confused with conformity. Conformity is something horrible and completely different.

GP What extra barriers did you have to overcome as a woman writer?

LT Brazil has its cultural origins in Portugal, which has always been a country with terrible prejudices. Portugal is a very conventional country. The women there have always known their place, which is to have children, to sew and at most to play the piano or sing.

GP I can see that that would make it harder for a woman to begin writing because it means stepping outside the circle of permissible activities. But suppose someone has the courage to write; suppose she has written a good book; what more is there to overcome?

LT That pre-supposes a lot, because a woman is meant to have little culture and never to find out if she'd like to write. But if she does overcome the difficulties and writes something good, she still has further to go than a man. Take a thirty-year-old man and a thirty-year-old woman of equal social and economic status and the same political background; if readers have to choose between the two, they will automatically prefer the book by the man. The woman's book is an object of mistrust.

GP You mean that women readers mistrust their own sex?

LT Yes, very much, because they have been accustomed to competing with other women. They compete amongst themselves but always in a state of servitude that creates a sense of insecurity and a lack of confidence in their own sex. The other sex is the one that protects them and makes them feel secure. They don't realize what they themselves can do and say. There is an aggressive mistrust. When someone opens a door for them they are like caged birds, afraid to fly out; they are afraid of liberty. Alternatively, they may accept liberty, but it's as if they are stunned by their sudden freedom, so they use it badly, like the many women at the moment who have become obsessed with the exploration of their own bodies. They end up playing miserable roles because they don't know how to use the liberty that has been given to them. Some of the birds scorn those who are really taking flight, while others admire and fear them. They fear those who have dared to do what they haven't been able to do and so there is a feeling of mistrust and irritation.

Men also mistrust us because they are used to women being inferior. They are frightened if a person who ought to be inferior comes out and says, 'I wrote this,' 'I painted this,' or 'I composed this.' When a woman tries to step out of her inferior role she is disturbing a state of affairs that men find very comfortable. This is the mistrust that affects the critics. I said once in an interview that in order to be intellectually respected a woman has to kill three lions, while a man only has to kill one, or even none.

GP So, other things being equal, will this be reflected in the sales in the bookshop?

LT Happily, this state of affairs is now being overcome, because readers are beginning to forget about the sex of the author. Sex is becoming less relevant as a means of determining identity. My books are selling very well. People forget that I'm a woman and see me simply as an author. It is also true that the prejudices I've been talking about are weaker amongst the readers than the critics and intellectuals. Readers now look for something interesting. If it's interesting, they will buy it and read it. This is a change that has come from below, not from an intellectual élite or from the critics. We are seeing a revolution in the attitudes towards women and women who write.

GP So once you've got into print there is hope?

LT That's right. One of my books, *The Marble Dance* has been published in English. It is something I wrote when I was very young, and I feel very satisfied that after all these years this book continues to sell. It's in its twentieth edition in the Third World. I am a writer of the Third World and it's something unusual and important that this book of my youth can reach its twentieth edition.

GP *The Marble Dance* reminded me of the Brontës.

LT I adored them when I was young. I used to cry when I read them. I was desperately looking for my own Heathcliffe but I never met one, or if I did, I failed to recognize him. Their books affected me a lot. Think of the way things are now, as we're entering the twenty-first century, and then try to imagine the fight those women must have had to write what they wrote in their time – the trials, the humiliations, the terrible things they must have gone through to keep themselves writing. As I said, for me the greatest virtue is courage, and they were courageous; patient, too, but never conformists.

GP One of the things your work has in common with theirs is that the passion of women is so evident – the women have such striking emotional energy.

LT That is something very important. It reminds me of Rimbaud, who said, 'The day women write freely, my God, what great works we'll have!' Rimbaud, as you know, was an extraordinary man. He was an ambiguous person, and a homosexual. He had a lot in common with women and he realized that women have an extraordinary vision. The great magicians and witches were all women. Rimbaud saw the magic that women have and knew how wonderfully women could write if only they did so with freedom.

GP It's clear that men have a feminine side and women have a masculine side, but I couldn't imagine a man writing a book like *The Marble Dance*. I don't think men ever have that sense of being so enclosed, so imprisoned, and with so few means of escape. They don't have a similar sense of shame, of feeling both bad and ugly at the same time, at least not in the way your heroine does.

LT But there have been great male writers who have managed to see the woman's point of view very well – Flaubert, for example. When asked who Madame Bovary was he replied, '*Madame Bovary c'est moi.*' The Brazilian writer Machado de Assis wrote a marvellous book, *Dom Casmurro*, whose principal character is a woman; he might have replied in the same way as Flaubert.

GP But how convinced are you, as a woman, by these portrayals of women written by men? Don't you sometimes think, 'A woman doesn't think like that. This is a man projecting himself on to a woman'?

LT Writers like these are so extraordinary, so above sex and good or evil, that they manage to overcome their own sexuality and become beings without sex – or perhaps they are a third or a fourth sex. They overcome sexual preconceptions; that is the mark of a genius.

When I write about men I try to forget I'm a woman. I may try to see women in the way that a man does; I don't know if I succeed, but as a writer you have an obligation to forget about your own condition. A writer has no sex. The writer is neither man nor woman, but androgynous. If the writer writes about a child, then the writer is a child, if about an insect, then an insect, if a fish, then a fish. Think of Hemingway's best novel, *The Old Man and the Sea*. At certain moments the fisherman is the fish that he is trying to catch. The feeling he has for this fish is remarkable, the struggle is beautiful because the man sees himself as the fish. The quality of the author is to disappear, to become a form. The writer is no more than an essence which has neither sex nor heart nor country nor people. The writer is a chemical!

GP Manuel Puig said that he thought sexual roles were merely a social convention and ought to be discarded. This is quite different to what you are saying, because you are talking about something metaphysical and mysterious. In your stories there is a feeling for insects, leaves, animals . . .

LT And cats. I have an obsession with cats. I enjoy reading Baudelaire very much; he knows cats well. Insects attract me a lot. They seem to have a right to almost nothing, not even life, yet they do have this right because they are living things, they are on our side. I always want to speak for them; we ought to give them their own space. I've tried this in a few stories. A few of my characters are insects.

GP Woman isn't a passive being in your stories, she's very competitive. Amongst themselves the women are ferocious, aggressive, in a different way to men, but they do get angry, enraged.

LT They have a will and at times they can be perverse, because they have been servile, submissive, living in the dark, in silence. The moment she is able to, woman will put out her claws and then ... she wreaks vengeance for the time she has been obliged to stay inside her shell. Woman has always been kept inside a shell. Now that shell has opened and she's on the high seas; it's dangerous but beautiful.

GP A number of people have told me how, in the early 1960s, there was a movement to create a new, integrated, fully Brazilian culture. Then the dictatorship rolled everything back.

LT There were attempts to create a horrible conformity here in Brazil but people who were working towards something continued working. Even though the fight is disguised or silenced, it continues. My novel *The Girls* was translated at the height of the dictatorship. It contains a description of torture, though I put the description in the mouth of one of the characters and not the narrator's, so that I would have a bit of distance if the censor objected. The description was an accurate one, based on a pamphlet written by one of the victims of torture in which he describes his experiences. So you see, even at the worst moments under the dictatorship it was possible to break the state of silence.

GP Did they ban the book?

LT No, because they didn't read many books, they didn't have the patience. My book passed without changes, fortunately. They picked on a few authors, Ignácio de Loyola Brandão, for example, but most of their attention was devoted to the theatre or the cinema. The writers worked on. The process continued because these things are stronger than the systems or institutions that want to impose something on a people.

I have a lot of hope for man. Man, as the Bible says, is going to survive. Despite all the horrendous things that happen, man will survive. I've told you about the horrible things they are doing in the Amazon, about the millions of trees they are killing, but I believe the tree will also survive somehow.

GP I hope so, but I don't have the same confidence. The

thing that impressed me most about the Amazon was its fragility.

LT 'Trans-Amazon, Trans-Bitterness', that's what they are calling the highway that is opening up the region. The earth bleeds through that road.

GP You are now very well known in Brazil, though not as well known overseas as you ought to be.

LT At the moment things are going very well for Brazilian writers, despite the difficulties posed by our language – our language is our splendour and our sepulchre, in the words of one of our poets. Still, we are making our own way now, we are managing to break down the barriers of speaking a minority language. It makes me happy to see my books spreading. They are spreading slowly, but paths are being opened up and that is important. The books are conquering. They are like the settlers who went into the forest and founded the first towns and cities – pioneers. It's good to be a pioneer but it's also sad, because the pioneers don't reap the benefits of their work. That is for those who come later. Still, I don't complain. I was happy to learn that a young woman at Harvard now teaches my work. In Paris one of my books was published recently to excellent reviews. Things like that make it easier; they make you realize that you've got to go on hoping and working. I keep working, albeit slowly.

GP There are very many paintings in your house. Is painting a source of inspiration?

LT Yes, but music is even more important. I love the cinema too; not so much the theatre, which has always seemed to me to be very limited – I'm always just sitting there in a seat, whereas the cinema transports me somewhere else entirely.

My husband, who died in 1977, was a man of the cinema. He founded many cinema schools in Brazil and he was a cinema critic. He felt that my way of using language was very cinematographic – he'd visualize what he read because the words were creating images. I was very happy to hear that because when I write I always try to see the characters. I see them as if they're projected on to a screen inside my head.

GP The language of the cinema tends to be opposed to one of the main currents in Latin American art, the baroque. Cinema is usually condensed, pared down and unadorned.

LT When you go to Salvador you'll see some wonderful baroque architecture. We do have baroque writers, principally poets, and there is also the great Brazilian film director, Rocha. Everything he did was baroque. His work was like a cascade, a torrent, a wild river. In my case, I prefer the depths of the river or the sea – still waters. I prefer to swim down and look for my pearls. I go with my knife between my teeth, searching. I couldn't say, like Picasso, 'I don't seek, I find.'

GP One of the notable things about Latin American fiction is the way it mixes so many different concerns – social, political, intellectual and philosophical. Perhaps the baroque style is the only way of fitting all that in. I suspect that a major reason for the richness of Latin American fiction is that it springs from so many concerns, it has so much material.

LT Exactly. Our sources are like the Amazon forest. There is a whole horizon open inside us, a horizon that is sometimes disturbing. It might have been better to be born in a tiny country with only a few things to write about because the magical variety of themes is intoxicating. You can spend your life a little dazed and groggy. The important thing is to choose what you want and to be sure about what doesn't interest you.

I see everything but I prefer to pay attention to a detail, something minute, as if I'm examining a tiny object and discovering splendours in it. In our beautiful Bahian churches there are marvellous baroque Christs, so rich in detail, but then your attention will be caught by one tiny drop of blood and you realize that this drop of blood is more important than everything else you've seen. It's things like this that impassion me. I see through a magnifying glass.

GP Hemingway said that when he wrote he'd visualize a scene and try to identify exactly what the detail was that had caused him to feel an emotion, then he'd forget the rest.

LT Exactly. You find the thing that moves you and forget the rest, otherwise it would be impossible. There is so much around us. Man is the richest of creatures. If you look at a man through a magnifying glass, you'll see so much – there's so much even in one hair. You have to find all the important things that make up a map of what you're looking at.

GP Is this where the expressionist aspect of your work comes from? When you look through a magnifying glass you find things no longer have a human perspective; they look almost grotesque.

LT At times they are grotesque, as man is in his battles and his sufferings and his despair. Dostoyevsky is an author I like very much; he studies and manipulates the human condition with such despair that it sometimes seems grotesque, like a caricature of his own pain and despair. Faulkner is a little like this too.

I remember when Faulkner came to Brazil he couldn't even say 'Good-day' in Portuguese. At a party attended by Brazilian literary figures he sat next to me. He'd never read any Brazilian literature and as my English was terrible, I was as silent as a fish. I think he was happy to be sitting next to this young woman who didn't say anything because he didn't have to say anything either. Eventually he turned to me and asked, 'Is this Chicago?' 'No,' I said, 'It's São Paolo.' 'Ah,' he said. A little later he suddenly remarked, 'You've got nice eyes.' I simply said, 'Thank you,' but a friend of mine overheard and burst out laughing. 'You can put that in your next book,' he told me. 'That's the only opinion William Faulkner has on Brazilian writers.'

I believe we have very important writers here, who are capturing the Brazilian reality, each in their own way. A writer for whom I have the greatest admiration, Juan Rulfo, one of the founders of the modern Latin American novel, has said that Brazilian literature is the richest, the most profound and the most diverse in the Americas.

João Ubaldo Ribeiro

Brazil is diverse not only geographically but culturally. While São Paolo was strongly influenced by the technological know-how brought by Italian and Japanese migrants, the northern states were dominated by the plantation culture initially built on black slavery. Many of the social issues in the north go back to long before Brazil's push for modernization from 1967 to 1973. Land has been the major source of wealth and, as Jorge Amado's novels testify, has been fiercely fought over. The north was, and still is in some parts, a frontier region where power is seized by the strongest.

João Ubaldo Ribeiro's novel *Vila Real* (1979) is based on one of these battles between the weak and the strong as a rural community fights the influence of big landowners. Political though the book may be, it is most remarkable for the intensity of its language. Ribeiro's prose is as emotionally dense as poetry: rough and ready poetry that expresses the often brutal conditions of the north-east.

Sergeant Getúlio (1971) is essentially the story of a thug in uniform. It is a long monologue by a man who is gradually slipping towards megalomania. The narrative bristles with logical twists and turns, hawk-eyed perceptions and bursts of sound and fury as the drift into madness shifts the gritty realism of the earlier passages into the realm of myth. In one sense the novel is an exploration of Brazilian machismo; Getúlio perceives the political opposition as weak, unmanly and meriting the treatment he hands out, and he knifes his pregnant wife without a second thought when he suspects her of adultery. Remarkably, the novel also elicits a certain respect, even a degree of sympathy, for this repulsive character, as we follow his attempts to stick by a barbarous code of honour in the face of orders from duplicitous and amoral superiors. Sergeant Getúlio is one of fiction's great anti-heroes.

An Invincible Memory (1984) is a work on a much broader canvas which traces the history of the Bahia region through anecdotes that wickedly send up a whole series of historical preconceptions. Literary preconceptions are also fair game for Ribeiro, who works to capture a specifically Brazilian tone; he is opposed to any notion of *belles-lettres* or literary élitism; he writes with a rare gusto that is reminiscent of Rabelais.

Ribeiro lives on the island of Itaparica, across the bay from the state capital, Salvador. The main town on the island is a small cluster of brightly painted buildings and there are almost no cars. The interview turned out to be very convivial as we sat at an outdoor table in the shade of one of the palm trees in the main square, facing the translucent blue of the sea and drinking a few bottles of Brazilian beer, with the locals passing the time of day. Ribeiro has the exuberance of some of his characters and he spoke with the irreverence and irony that make his novels some of the finest to be written in Latin America in recent years.

GP I understand you translated *Sergeant Getúlio* into English yourself and now you are working on *An Invincible Memory*. Beckett was one writer who translated his own works, but I can't think of many other instances.

JR There was Nabokov – he was a bilingual writer, and Conrad learned English very late in life.

GP Have you read *Nostromo*?

JR No. I don't read much any more. I read the same books over and over again. Classics generally, the craziest mixture you can imagine. Some Brazilian classics, some Portuguese classics and people like Rabelais and the Latin classics; a lot of Homer.

GP The beginning of *Vila Real* is a parody of *The Iliad* in the way you treat the characters as heroes, isn't it?

JR That's right – you could make a very pretentious comparison between *The Iliad* and *Vila Real*, and between *Sergeant Getúlio* and *The Odyssey*. *Sergeant Getúlio* is a journey; *Vila Real* is more of an epic. It encompasses the fight of a people, or rather of a whole community. But to get back to translating, I did that by coincidence. *Sergeant Getúlio* was coming out in the United States and the publisher's translator wasn't sufficiently familiar with the way they speak in the backlands of Sergipe, a state north of here. This led to a disastrous first thirty pages – they were unpublishable. I then volunteered to translate it because it was important for me. This was my first book to be published outside Brazil. *Sergeant Getúlio* was much easier to translate than *An Invincible Memory* which I hope is the last one I ever do under any pretext. My agent persuaded me to do it because he thought I was the only qualified person. In a way he was right because you'd have to have an almost encyclopaedic knowledge of Brazil to be able to make sense of that whole area.

GP *An Invincible Memory* is a bit like a historical encyclopaedia of Brazil.

JR That wasn't the intention. It's just a novel, but it encompasses three and a bit centuries, although most of the action takes place from the 1830s onwards. All the references to the history of Brazil, to local customs and cultural differences make it difficult for the translator. I used no footnotes, but if it had been an academic work, it would have ended up longer than the Los Angeles telephone directory. Celebrated translators in the United States who have translated some very difficult Brazilian classics have footnoted them heavily because they were translating for a largely academic audience. I turned to their translations for help with words like *mucama* – a Portuguese word that referred to black girls who were household slaves – but I found that it was impossible to translate. Then there were other problems. For instance if we use the word 'nigger' in a translation it sounds like Faulkner. The word 'Negro' has unwelcome connotations in the US, but in Portuguese *negro* simply means black. It is not derogatory at all and in fact the black movement here prefers *negro* to *preto*, which is the more usual word for black.

GP So you're very conscious of the words you use?

JR Oh very. I hate to tell you this, but I've literally spent a whole day looking for one word. I am a big fan of Simenon's, although I haven't read much by him; I'm not really interested in mystery novels but what I like is the craftsmanship. You read pages of his work and you think, 'This is really good copy.' In interviews I've read he says he hates adjectives and adverbs. I'm addicted to adjectives and I suffer for them. I think I can use them well. Adverbs are practically adjectives naturalized and I suffer a lot trying to choose them too.

GP Did you do research for *An Invincible Memory* or was it written from experience you'd accumulated over a lifetime?

JR Mainly from experience. I'm not a very organized person, so I would do rather frantic research when I needed to know something.

GP You write a lot of parody. You take myths or literary stereotypes and reverse them. *Sergeant Getúlio*, for example, is like a Western. The sergeant is the marshall but he's also the bad guy. And in *An Invincible Memory* you turn cannibalism into a joke – the hero, Capiroba, eats Dutchmen.

JR I think cannibalism *is* a joke. I think it's all made up. I try to caricature it in the book because there is anthropological data to confirm that cannibalism, as a natural practice among primitive peoples, is mostly mythical – at least in Brazil. And besides, even if it wasn't a myth, Capiroba's cannibalism perfectly balances the metaphorical cannibalism of the Europeans here. In my book the natives learn about cannibalism from the Europeans. The Jesuits tell the Indians horrible stories about how bad they've been, about how they've eaten missionaries and settlers. The Indians are astonished that they have been capable of doing such wicked things yet they can't remember anything about them. Everyone starts suspecting everybody else: you know, 'He must have done it because the priests wouldn't lie.' Capiroba, who can't master the whole cosmogony that has been imposed on them, and who can't handle

the whole thing, goes a bit crazy. He runs away and kills his
first Portuguese, a priest. Capiroba was hungry and then he
thought, 'These guys said you could eat people, so why not?'
He ends up being a connoisseur and having a preference for
Nordic meat.

GP Going back to Sergeant Getúlio, it's curious that in some
ways he is an attractive person.

JR Yes, this is a question that people always bring up. I
think I have an answer, at least a partial one. In Portuguese the
book is preceded by what may be a cryptic comment which
says, 'This is a story of "Arete".' *Arete* is a Greek word which
means 'virtue' – the virtue of the Greek hero, not the Christian
idea of virtue. When I did the English translation I decided to
use the word 'virtue', so it is 'a tale of virtue'. Even people who
don't know much about the north-east of Brazil perceive that
Sergeant Getúlio was a man of integrity: he was faithful to his
values. If you do know north-eastern Brazil, you realize that
he was a person with a social function: he was part of the social
fabric and he was an honest man, although he was a thug, a
bloodthirsty criminal. He was only doing things that according
to his society and his culture were right. He was faithful to his
principles and he was a victim, after all. The system that
produced him, that raised him for this type of occupation and
function in society, then destroyed him after society started to
change and have different needs. He was cruel to his prisoners
because he was supposed to be. He was a kind of Pavlovian
dog, conditioned to see his political prisoners as evil. They had
committed crimes. When his universe was destroyed all of a
sudden he refused to yield. He stuck with it to the end. That's
why I think people feel for him. His tragedy is a palpable one
that people anywhere can feel.

GP As the book goes on he gets either more poetic or more
Faulknerian, I'm not sure which.

JR He identifies very closely with his own country. To him
there is little difference between the land, the trees, the animals
and people.

GP He says things like, 'I was born from a hole in the ground,' and 'I'm going to pick my teeth with calf ribs.'

JR That is part of the epic tradition of north-eastern Brazilian tales with their superhuman heroes.

GP Are you drawing on Greek mythology or local mythology?

JR It is all second-hand, in a way. It came through our medieval Portuguese heritage, which was both preserved and modified here.

GP The north-east is a frontier culture and frontiers seem to be the places people make myths about. The novel seems to contrast the north-east and the south; is there a cultural division between the two?

JR This is an extremely complicated question. It is very difficult to explain to a public that barely knows where Brazil is what the issues are in such a diversified, complex society. This is a huge country with a huge population, a rich history and a great variety of social patterns. It's impossible to give a simple picture. If you were a Brazilian I would refuse to discuss the issue of the north-east because we would go on for ever. But, in the final analysis the backwardness of the region makes it easy for the voters to be manipulated in very indecent ways to provide a power base for the conservatives: the basic thing is to keep the ruling class in power, no matter how.

GP I've heard people talk about cultural and economic imperialism coming from the south to the north, and it is evident in *Sergeant Getúlio* that the south is where the orders come from; the south is corrupt, inconsistent and, in a sense, morally inferior to even the barbarous Sergeant Getúlio. On the other hand, the morality seems to be the rule of the strongest. It's like the law of the jungle: anything goes.

JR Yes, but there are principles that should be respected. The sergeant is suddenly confronted by two different sets of values, which happens in Brazil all the time. Across the bay here you have an old and in many senses decrepit town, Salvador, yet it is still one of the biggest cities in the country – one of the biggest cities in the world, in fact: bigger that San

Francisco, for instance. On this side of the bay – you could swim across if you wanted to – you are in a different world. This is a big island, over thirty kilometres long with so many settlements that are anachronisms: very backward places where there is no electricity, no running water, people who have never seen a television in their whole life. And people don't talk the way people talk just a few miles away; there are different vocabularies, as well as different accents.

This coexistence of contradictory realities is still evident in Brazil. If you go to São Paolo, you can feel you are in New York or Chicago. You can live there without ever seeing anything but a megalopolis, yet in the same city there are patterns of living that are practically stone-age. It's crazy. Brazil produces good wine; an American wouldn't believe that, because how can you make good wine in the Amazon? Brazil has a computer industry, yet it is one of the most backward countries in the world. You have all these islands inside the country. That is why I could never write an essay – it would be too troublesome to combine all these different things into a homogeneous perspective. It's probably why I write fiction.

GP But you do write some non-fiction. I was reading your book *Política*.

JR Yes. Well, I wanted to contribute something. I wanted to make it as simple as possible for literate people to understand a few basic things. I don't know if it worked, but it has been adopted by university courses and has been widely read, I think.

GP It tackles the really basic social questions.

JR Yes, things that a fourteen-year-old would know in other countries.

GP I'm not sure about that. I think that Latin Americans are often more politically aware than educated Westerners – not so much in Brazil but in Argentina, or even Chile. In Brazil the problem seems to be not so much apathy as simply a lack of education.

JR Yes; that's why I wrote the book.

GP Why did you come to this island to write?

JR I was born here. I'm not a rich writer, and it was difficult to live anywhere else. Also, there is the question of age. I'm forty-seven now and have decided that I have the right to be radical. I want to do nothing but write. I want to abide by as few rules as possible. I do not want to explain anything to people. I do not want to be doing literary odd jobs all the time, as I had to in Rio. The house I have here is the one where I was born. It still belongs to my family; I don't pay any rent. I don't spend any money on clothes. Here I'm like a rich person. I eat better food than I would eat in Rio.

GP Did you work as a journalist in Rio?

JR I used to write a weekly article for the newspaper *O Globo*. I quit less that a year ago, after seven years. I was very well treated but I just couldn't stand it any more. I knew my little jokes by heart; I knew all the tricks. Now I don't want to do anything that will give me unnecessary stress. I think it is stressful enough to do what I think I have to do.

GP How did you manage to write enormous books like *An Invisible Memory* when you were working on other projects?

JR I've been writing for newspapers ever since I was seventeen. I'm used to it. It's all a lot of tricks. Of course you have to have a certain penchant for it, a certain knack, but if you have that after a while you develop a way of producing things that people think are clever but which are really just done by rote. There are major tricks and minor tricks. Writers get together from time to time and maybe they get drunk; they exchange tricks and laugh at the readers for falling for them. You begin to feel this contradiction: if you are going to be a pure writer, you have to write what needs to be written; if you live as a writer you have to write things that are not really needed, except by your family – you've got to buy the bread. There is something uncomfortable about that.

GP What drew you to journalism?

JR It probably had something to do with my childhood. My father was, in fact still is, a very strict man as well as being a high-powered intellectual. I had a classic relationship with him – one with all the trimmings, as they say about hamburgers.

When I was a kid I played soccer and did everything that normal Brazilian kids are supposed to do but I also had to write book reviews for my father. An examination result of less than 70 per cent, even in subjects like fine arts where I was really all thumbs, was enough to get me ostracized for a month; it was an absolute catastrophe.

GP Did you go to school here on Itaparica?

JR For a very short time. My mother's family is a traditional one here; or used to be. Most of the legitimate line had daughters and they took their husbands' names, so the official family disappeared. Of course, genetically it's the same thing, but onomastically it's not. I don't know a lot of my relatives any more. We've spread out. But my mother's family was one of the ruling families.

This place used to be very different. We had a certain 'home rule' because there were no big supermarkets, no mass distribution system, so there were shoe shops and metal-working shops which provided everything the community needed. Then Brazil started developing in a way that destroyed that world. This is now a resort town. It became impossible for a dentist to live here because people couldn't pay him any more.

Take the example of transportation. The bay here is almost as large as Guanabara Bay, in Rio. The transportation of goods in this area was by *saveiro*, a kind of wooden boat that has no exact equivalent anywhere else. They are elegant boats, beautiful boats. The *saveiros* would transport merchandise, papayas and other kinds of food, from all over the bay to Salvador, back and forth. So there were a lot of *saveiro* builders – people specialized in building and designing them, in making masts, sails, ropes, or people were sailors. Now the ferries have made the boats obsolete so these people don't have anything to do any more. I can remember when this bay was crawling with *saveiros* going back and forth. They were like the blood of the economy. Then things were centralized in such a brutal way that it destroyed all that. Now we are supposed to eat whatever someone in Rio de Janeiro eats because we are industrialized and there is an efficient distribution system. Everything local just withers away.

There were so many important activities here that have been destroyed by the implacable accumulation of wealth. It's like a biblical curse: 'They will take everything from you.' There is a passage in the Portuguese version of the Bible which says (to make a terrible translation) that those who have will have more, and those who have not will have less. The saying is applicable to what happened here: we were destroyed by prosperity.

The independent sugar and tobacco production in this area was destroyed by this invasion of progress, as was our local infrastructure. The end result is that many people now survive only by going down to the beach and catching fish. We've undergone a kind of economic castration. This is a country where you even have to have a licence to go to one of our city dumps and pick up garbage for survival. Yet the country is so rich that if you spit out a seed it grows. The official name for the garbage-picking profession that exists everywhere in Brazil is *parameiro*. You have to go through a bureaucratic maze to obtain a licence; if you don't have a three by four picture of yourself and if you don't present your certificate of this or that and proof that you voted in the last elections, you don't get the licence. The bureaucracy is an unbeatable machine, a juggernaut.

GP In Argentina they have big economic problems but there the unions and all the major interest groups have power so they are fighting it out amongst themselves. In Brazil it looks as though only one group really has power.

JR Again, this is a complex issue. The unions in Brazil have been reduced to worrying about medical care and providing a little party for the children at Easter and a gold watch on retirement. This is the end result of Getúlio Vargas' actions as a leader of the labour faction and the workers of Brazil. 'Workers of Brazil,' that's how he used to begin his speeches. For me, he was one of the most noxious influences in Brazilian history. We now have union leaders who are state employees and are mainly concerned with improving their own lot. They see to it that things run smoothly.

Brazil has a reputation for being a passive country with very nice, mild-mannered, easy-going people, but it's not so. If you look at the history of this country, you will see it's a history of violence. You can be sure that people are being killed here in the state right now, and not only Indians, which is the thing that fascinates Europeans and foreigners in general. We've just massacred thirty or so Indians, according to the papers. Of course it is immoral when an Indian is killed but the fact that he is an Indian is not the point. He is simply an obstacle in someone's rush to get land and get rich. One of the most absurd forms of violence is leaving kids of five or six in the street to scratch out a living. No bullets are involved there, but we have one of the highest infant mortality rates in the world. It's not just the violence we read about in the papers; we massacre people's minds, too, by preventing them from assuming their own identity.

The violence here is not a simple thing. It's not just a matter of the poor striking back, because if poverty were enough to generate violence, Bombay would be a much more violent city than São Paolo. It is not only poverty. It is a civil war. People are not satisfied with just robbing you. They want to rape your wife, rape your children in front of you; they want to kill you even if you give them all your money. They strip you naked in the street in Rio de Janeiro and then they look at you and they shoot you. It reminds me of a story one of my many lying friends told me (Márcio Souza, perhaps – a good liar; I lie back to him of course). There was an Indian in the United States who cut off his wife's head because she was unfaithful to him. Then he said, 'I wonder if this woman has been sufficiently punished.' That's the same syndrome.

We are used to civil wars like the American one where you have Grants and Lees facing each other in battle. It's not like that here. Middle-class people in the big cities are incarcerated. They live in penitentiaries, big blocks with wire around them, while the bums, or whatever you want to call them, are free to roam about. People are so afraid that they lock themselves up; children are raised looking out from behind bars. Yet if you go to states like Paraná, you might think you're in Germany — the good parts of Germany; everything is prosperous. Brazil isn't a simple country to understand.

GP As a writer the social turmoil must cause you problems.

JR No, if you are obsessed with what you are doing, I don't think that happens — if you are able to abstract yourself. Now I have to do only one thing and that way I can be efficient. I've decided that I have to keep away from things for a while because otherwise I'd be too involved. I'd be a bad writer and a bad journalist. I wouldn't be anything.

There comes a time to say, 'I want to do this and I do not want to consider other alternatives because I cannot examine them with all due care. If I do, I'll end up like the great philosopher who has doubts every time he has to decide between having a coke or a beer.'

GP Have you been writing something new as well as working on your translation of *An Invincible Memory* since you've been here?

JR I'm writing a new novel. I'm supposed to finish it two or three months from now but there is no chance of that. Writing it has been one of the most difficult things I've done in my whole life. About 150 pages are done and I think it's starting to take off now, but sometimes it took me four days to write five lines. It was terrible. My wife thought I was going crazy — she knows I'm crazy but she thought I was getting worse. I'd sit in my house and go, 'O God, I can't write any more.' But now it's coming out. It's called *The Smile of the Lizard.*

GP Was writing easier and faster for you before, when you were living in Rio — not such an anguished process?

JR Well, I'm only human. I'm faced with the prospect of writing and this time it just has to work.

GP Because your writing is supporting you?

JR Yes, but at the same time I don't give a damn about what people say about the book. I just want to write the book

I want to write. I'm trying to be honest, but I go home and I look at my children and say to myself, 'Shouldn't I just make a little concession here and there?' Writers are basically liars. A friend of mine, a movie director, used to say, 'Artists are incorruptible,' and that is true, although a real artist can be the biggest bastard imaginable. When you are writing you can play all kinds of dirty tricks on everyone – you might fool your friends, two-time your wife – you can do anything, but you do have to be honest. I don't want to make writing sound nobler than any other human endeavour. I think it is the same in other fields, though I don't know about other people except in the sense that I am every one of my characters.

You see, I think I am capable of writing cheap literature. The only thing I couldn't do is write a good pornographic novel. That requires a tremendous amount of talent. Still, sometimes I feel that I could write something designed to woo ten thousand dollars from someone; as Vargas Llosa once said, when you sit down at your typewriter you decide whether you want to be a good writer or a bad writer. That is very true, though it is an oversimplification; at the precise moment you put your sheet in the typewriter you decide. It's a crucial decision. If you don't stick to it you are dead.

For instance, I think Mickey Spillane is a serious writer. He made a serious decision – he said, 'I have no readers, I have clients,' or something like that – and he was faithful to it, which is abundantly corroborated by his career. He is precisely what he set out to be. I made a decision as to the kind of writer I wanted to be even though I may not have been aware of it at the time. So I can't write a bad novel – at least from my viewpoint!

GP In Brazil this choice must be particularly difficult because, although you have an enormous book market here, there is only a very small market for so-called serious writing.

JR In Brazil we have a saying, '*Faz parte*' which is a very succinct way of saying, 'It's all part of the job.' Like very serious people who snort coke for the first time and offer their wife to someone, or whatever. The next day they say, 'What did I do?

I made these homosexual overtures to someone and then I said my wife could screw anyone in the house. I'm so embarrassed.' To which someone will reply, '*Faz parte*': it's part of it. If you snort, you fart. So, if you write you fight. Life can't be all fluffy clouds.

There's an old saying here in the north-east which has a Chinese equivalent. Here they say, 'Heaven is not near,' and in China they say, 'Heaven is not near and the Emperor lives far away,' or, as the Americans would say, 'There is no such thing as a free lunch,' though the idea of having to pay a price is a very vulgar way of looking at things; it's more that you have to realize that things are reachable through dedication and effort and obsession. The only way to achieve anything, I believe, is to be obsessive.

GP Machismo is another aspect of your books, isn't it?

JR Yes, because you have to suffer. My theory is that it is much harder being a *macho* than a *fêmea* because you're not supposed to cry, you're not supposed to cringe, you're not supposed to flinch, you're not supposed to break any of the thousand mysterious rules of a very tough code. That takes its toll. I know because when I was a kid in Sergipe at school they used to twist my arm and make me kiss their hand and ask their blessing like you do to your godfather or father; and I would rather have them tear my arm off than do that, which is silly. We were brought up not to cry, not to complain – like the probably apocryphal story about a Spartan kid (told by Plutarch, I think), who stole a fox and kept it under his toga during class. Then the fox started nibbling away at his stomach. He never said a thing and he died. That's a bit like the ethos of Sergeant Getúlio.

The human race keeps repeating itself, which makes me think of the book I'm working on, *The Smile of the Lizard*. A crazy Canadian has put forward the hypothesis that, if conditions on another planet were the same as on earth, evolution would tend to privilege lizards and other reptiles with intelligence. According to this man, what happened on earth in the mesozoic period – people say that a comet or the impact of a

meteorite caused a cooling in the climate and killed the dino-
saurs – was just an accident and that we are just freaks. This
Canadian is a professor at the University in Toronto. I started
thinking about this theory and somehow *The Smile of the Lizard*
developed. I was thinking about the way we betray intelligence
and evolution whenever we deny the consistency of morality
with our specific importance as a species. (I'm being pleonastic.)
I think that it is part of our specificity to be moral and ethical.
People think of evolution as being only physical; I think our
moral and ethical sense is also part of it. When we are not
ethical we betray our destiny as a species. This is what I've been
writing about. Of course the whole thing may end up being
just one great big turkey.

The turkey! I'll leave you with a final comment. The turkey
is an animal with an identity problem: in English the bird is
called a 'turkey' because people thought that it came from
Turkey. In Brazil a turkey is called '*Peru*' because people
thought it came from Peru. In French a turkey is a '*coq d'Inde*'
because they thought it came from India. In Peru itself, the
turkey is known as '*pavo*', which means 'peacock'. So, the
turkey is born with a built-in identity problem. In fact it
originally came from the United States, from New England.
It was a wild bird. But everywhere you go it's, 'Hey, look,
there's a Pakistani Sparrow!'

Jorge Amado

Jorge Amado is Brazil's most prominent writer. He is much loved and respected by Brazilian readers, especially in the Bahia area, where nearly all his novels have been set. Amado has a great talent for creating a social panorama of vividly drawn, memorable characters who bustle through long, entertaining books that have often been compared with the novels of Dickens. They do have rather Dickensian moments of pathos, but there is also a very Brazilian sense of warmth and a very un-Dickensian emphasis on sexuality.

Amado is often read as light entertainment, yet he is a serious writer who is easily misunderstood. Each of his novels raises important issues. *Gabriela, Clove and Cinnamon* (1958) deals with adultery by women. In Brazil it was long accepted that a man could reasonably kill his wife if she were unfaithful, and even today, Brazilian courts find it notoriously difficult to get convictions against jealous husbands. In *Gabriela* Amado presents female desire in a positive way and, judging from the response of women readers, with a rare understanding. The inequities of the double standard are exposed not through preaching but by making the reader empathize with the characters. Female sexuality is again the subject in *Dona Flor and Her Two Husbands* (1966), a great comic novel in which the eager, prospective adulterer is the ghost of Dona Flor's first husband.

Many of Amado's early novels have a much grimmer tone. *Suor* (1934), for example, had an unflinchingly political aspect, dealing with the bleak and desperate lives of a group of people who live in a tenement. His later works are equally committed but written more optimistically. *Jubiabá* (1935) is one of the novels that established Amado as a portrait painter of his region. The hero grows up living on his wits, leaving a slum to become a rich man's ward, then becoming a street kid, a plantation worker, a boxer and eventually earning a little money as a writer of local songs. *Jubiabá* offers a glimpse of all levels of society and shows Amado to be not only a consummate storyteller but also a persuader, a man whose sympathy and concern elicits the same response from the reader.

Jorge Amado's beliefs have been sufficiently controversial to earn him imprisonment on a number of occasions. Nor has the sometimes innocuous surface of his novels saved them from censorship. His work has been banned for considerable periods of time and he was unconstitutionally turned out of office after his election to the Brazilian senate in 1946.

Not surprisingly, Amado has lived a good part of his life abroad. Now in his late seventies he spends most of the year in Paris, where I found him still at work, with the warmth and good humour that is so clear in his books.

GP Could you tell me a little about your family?

JA My father came from Sergipe, a small, very poor state in the north of Bahia. The people there had no chance at all of improving their life so many of them left. My father started work when he was ten, cleaning floors. At the age of nineteen he had risen to become what was known as the 'chief employee' in one of the wealthier households. This was as far as he could go. About that time they were starting to grow cacao for the first time in the south of Bahia. The Jesuits had brought the plant from the Amazon and had recognized that the soil was perfect for cultivation. When the plantations opened up many people migrated from Sergipe; also from the Middle East, Syria and Lebanon. The area was considered a kind of El Dorado and so my father was attracted to move there.

Those were violent times. I had an uncle who had only two fingers on one hand because of a bullet and had lost an eye to another. By the time I was born my father had spent ten years in the area and had a small piece of land, though that didn't mean things were secure. When I was fourteen months old there was a great flood which destroyed my father's plantation.

GP Was that the basis for the flood in your novel *Showdown*?

JA Yes, to an extent. At about the same time, my father was wounded in an ambush while he was cutting some sugar-cane. After that the family made its way to Ilheus. We lived in one of the poorest parts of town and my parents survived by making and selling wooden sandals until my father was able to get back to the land. He was quite well off by the time the crash of 1929 occurred and that ruined him again. He ran into debt and lost most of his land, but he managed to keep a small plot on which he supported himself until the end of his life.

I had three brothers, one who died at the age of three, when I was still very young. I can only remember the night of his death and my grandmother going past in the corridor, saying, 'He's dead. He's dead.' We didn't know what the illness was. He really died for lack of a good doctor. Later, another brother was born and he is now a doctor in São Paolo. My third brother is a journalist and has written some criticism and fiction.

I couldn't tell you where my father's family came from. There are Amados in Spain and Portugal, even in Holland I think. I once met a Syrian called Jorge Amado. We didn't talk much about my mother's family when I was young because my grandmother had been abandoned by her husband. She was an Indian who had been taken from her tribe during one of the raids they used to make. They captured her as if she were an animal and she bore my grandfather's first child when she was eleven years old. When he abandoned her at the age of nineteen she had had nine children, including three sets of twins. One of the twins was my godfather. Another died of tuberculosis at the age of three. My grandmother never spoke of my grandfather. She was a remarkable woman. She sup-ported her large family by starting a small street stall selling fruit and vegetables. She raised her children well and two of them became owners of big cacao plantations.

On my father's side there are all the possible mixtures of blood, certainly some Portuguese and some Negro. On my mother's side there is Indian blood, so you could say I'm a true Brazilian.

GP What were the forces that politicized you?

JA Well, as you may know, the 1930s were a time of great political upheaval in Brazil. Before the 'revolution' of 1930 the presidency was shared between the richer groups of society, the owners of the mines, the cacao and coffee planters, and the graziers. You'd have four years of rule by one faction followed by four years by another. In 1929 there was a disagreement between the ruling parties and that meant a real opposition candidate had a chance to emerge. There was some popular unrest and then a military rebellion. Before a battle actually took place there was, as so often happens in Brazil, a reconciliation of the parties.

Brazil has a long tradition of flexibility, thanks mostly to the Portuguese, who were much less brutal than the Spaniards and better negotiators. That is perhaps why Brazil is one nation today while Spanish-speaking America fragmented after independence. You can see Brazil's unity and cohesion and its political astuteness in the way the recent military dictators stepped down. Unlike the Uruguayan or Argentinian dictators, there was no controversy when they left. There is also a real, popular tradition of co-existence in Brazil and a strong, national culture.

GP I've heard that at one time Brazil had the largest communist movement in the continent. Did the communists work for co-existence?

JA Brazil did have the largest communist movement, but you have to ask yourself what kind of communism it was. You could also say we had a very strong fascist movement, though it was very different to the Italian or German models. I think that both the right and left wing fostered fundamentally nationalist movements. A large number of so-called right-wing thinkers ended up in the so-called socialist camp. Really, both were nationalist movements, reacting against the imperialism, firstly of Britain and later of the United States.

GP Your writing is always political to some extent, isn't it?

JA Yes, though I've written only two books with strictly political themes, *Pen, Sword and Camisole* and *Os Subterráneos da Libertade*, which are both about the fight against the new state of the Vargas regime during the 1930s. Otherwise the main concern of my work has been social, which leads to a political element in books such as *Jubiabá* or *Captains of the Sand*. Social concerns have remained a constant in my work for over fifty years. What has changed is the language of the novels, which has become more finely honed, and the structure has become more complex. My early novels are much simpler than my recent one, *Showdown*. The characters have become more complex with time. In the beginning everything was black and white.

GP In *Showdown* you seem to bring together many of your earlier themes in one novel.

JA That's true. *Showdown* brings together the various strands that have run through my work, especially the rural ones. The novel I am working on now brings together all the urban themes. In one respect it's a testament to Bahia. I've said everything there that I want to say.

GP It's important to you that your books should be entertaining, isn't it?

JA The great writers are not the ones that people find heavy, tedious or hard-going. Writing has to give pleasure and not just to a small circle of intellectuals.

GP Your novels seem to be rhetorical and designed to galvanize the reader into action. *Jubiabá*, for example, follows the course of a man who learns to fight not just in the boxing ring but in the political arena. The novel seems to be trying to persuade people to protest more and demand more.

JA Perhaps, but when I write I basically want to tell a story. I don't want to prove anything, although in *Jubiabá* I wanted to explore certain themes such as racism and to show the gradual evolution of the consciousness of the protagonist, Antônio Balduíno. He began by fighting against racism in an almost unconscious way but in the end he realized that there was not one but many forms of racism. He saw that the solution was not for whites and blacks to fight each other; the problem was not a matter of race but of class.

GP There is the comment that all the poor have become black.

JA Yes, in Brazil a rich Negro was effectively white and a poor white was black. However, when I started writing the book I didn't realize it would end that way. The action and the characters took me there.

GP I'm surprised to hear that, because the plots of your novels are often very intricate.

JA I don't know why, but I am unable to write a novel that I've worked out beforehand. I never know what's going to happen from one page to the next. Never. The narrative is something that evolves from day to day. The characters make the narrative.

When I wrote *Showdown* I was trying to write a different story – about religious syncretism. I started writing: the beginnings are always very difficult for me. I established some characters, a few relations between them and a sense of mood. At one point a priest arrived in Bahia and this started me thinking about the relationship of the Church and the poor, which then moved the book off in a different direction entirely; in the finished novel the priests arrive only towards the end.

At other times you want a character to do something but it's not possible because he doesn't have it in him. The character, once established, does what he wants to do, not what the author wants him to. For example, when I was writing *Jubiabá* I wanted to use a phrase that I'd heard from a *campesino* – 'The poor are so unlucky that if shit is ever worth money their arseholes will tighten up.' I initially wanted Antônio Balduíno, the hero of the novel, to say this, but it didn't seem to fit. He was a young man and a fighter. He wouldn't say anything so pessimistic. Then I thought Jubiabá might say it. But despite being old and having suffered a lot, he wasn't really a beaten man. I had to create a new character, an old *campesino* who had lost his land and his wife and whose daughter had become a prostitute. The sentence could finally be said by him.

GP It almost seems that all your novels are part of one great novel. They even cross over into each other at times. There's the tale of the boat race across the harbour, which is won by the sailor whose woman sings. That story appears, from different perspectives, in *Jubiabá* and *Sea of Death*.

JA The race with Manuel and Maria Clara appears in five or six novels, including my most recent one. Themes and characters often repeat themselves because my concerns have remained the same. My writing is very repetitive. *Jubiabá* and *Tent of Miracles* are the same novel. The same strike appears in both novels. Their theme is the same – the formation of Brazil as a nation and a culture. Of course, twenty-five years lie between the writing of one novel and the other. The author has changed and evolved a lot in that time. *Tent of Miracles* is richer and more complex. You say that my novels are all one novel. I think that's correct.

GP Perhaps it is one great portrait of the life of Bahia in its many different aspects.

JA Above all the popular life. People in Bahia will sometimes say, 'There goes Antônio Balduíno', which is a recognition that the work has been a kind of portrait.

GP I've heard that a number of people have sued you for defamation, believing that you've described them in your novels. Didn't one woman think she was Dona Flor?

JA When I wrote *Gabriela* there was quite a scandal. A number of people were pointed out as being Gabriela and there were angry denials. Now that the novels have been made into films and television programmes people have stopped making denials and have started claiming that they're such and such a character.

GP To what extent are real-life people the basis for your characters?

JA One person is never enough to make a character. Generally a character is made up of many people; also, someone like Gabriela grew through a number of novels – *The Violent Land*, for instance. She'd been in my mind for a long time because of people I'd known. The matter is complicated by the

fact that I like to give my characters the names of my friends.
It's a sort of homage I make towards a friend. But even if you
have taken a real person as the basis of a character, the moment
this character becomes a part of the text he or she starts respond-
ing to new problems, to other characters and to different
moods. The novel is an entirely different world and makes its
own changes.

GP In an early novel of yours, *Suor*, the characters are
beaten, weak and miserable. In more recent novels they tend
to be more heroic, stronger. The novels are epic, to an extent.
Why the change?

JA Not a change, an evolution. I wrote *Suor* in 1934, when
I was twenty-two. My experience of life and literature was
very slight. As time passed my experience naturally grew and
my books became more complex. When you're young it's a
fine thing to be a pessimist. It suits you to be doubtful. As you
grow older you begin to see that life can be lived fully.

Despite this evolution, my writing has remained constant in
another sense. From the first book to the last I defend certain
values such as liberty, justice and human rights, those who fight
against prejudice, above all racial prejudice, and those who
fight against misery, oppression and militarism.

GP You also fight against sexism, don't you?

JA Brazil is a country where there are many vestiges of the
Middle Ages. There are semi-feudal attitudes, one of them
being that the man is superior to the woman. Women in
Brazil are doubly exploited. While men suffer class exploitation,
women are exploited both in terms of class and sex. In my
novels I try to show women fighting against this state of affairs.
Even in *Suor* there is a woman who is stronger than the
men. There is Rosa Palmeirão in *Showdown*. There are always
women who fight. *Tereza Batista: Home from the Wars* has
become, in certain places, a feminist emblem. In Milan a group
of very combative feminists has adopted her name.

GP The humorous aspect of your novels has become more
notable with time. Is that for tactical and rhetorical reasons?

JA No. Humour is something else that comes with maturity.

In my early books there was always a commentary that ran alongside the action. 'Listen,' the reader would be told, 'this is wrong and has to be changed.' The commentary has been replaced by humour, which is a much stronger weapon. Laughter is much more powerful than an angry shout.

GP Would you agree with Ignácio de Loyola Brandão that one of the Brazilians' main problems is apathy? When something terrible happens to the Brazilians, he said, they don't feel indignation. When something bad happens to them their friends say, 'Don't worry. You'll get over it.' Do you agree?

JA I don't know. I wouldn't want the Brazilian character to be different. The Brazilian is a genial person, happy, someone who lives fully. I think the Brazilian's amicable, easy-going nature is very important. Indignation is an important quality because you need to know when to fight, but it's also necessary to maintain a certain serenity. That gives you the ability to push ahead. If you shout and make a lot of noise you stay where you are. What you need is to move ahead. So, in answer to your question, any suggestion of changing the Brazilian character makes me uneasy.

GP In *Suor* there is a scene where the characters tell each other stories that are exaggerated, like the one about the strong man who was hit by a car but walked away, while the car had to go to the garage. Would you say your writing is a little exaggerated, so as to give comfort to people in the way that these stories did?

JA Writing is a re-creation of life but it's also an exaggeration of life. My literature is very influenced by popular literature. If you listen to the storytellers you'll find that there is always exaggeration, which allows you to get the true measure of reality. If you don't exaggerate, the reader sees the world of the text as being less than life size.

GP Would you say that the emotional life of the Brazilian is on a larger scale than in some other countries?

JA The Brazilian is very emotional. We have the easy tears of the Portuguese and the easy laughter of the Africans.

GP Why is it that you've never been interested in the experiments of the Brazilian modernists?

JA The modernists were active in the 1920s; they were concerned with form, while the revolution of 1930 made writers more concerned with content and social problems. This coincided to some extent with the great literary generation of the United States – writers like Hemingway and Steinbeck, who were also very concerned with social issues. Brazilian modernism had no influence on the writers of the 1930s. None of us followed that path.

GP Haven't you ever felt the desire to experiment in the way that many of the Spanish-speaking novelists have done?

JA I'd say that no Spanish-speaking novelist has experimented as much with the novel as João Guimarães Rosa.

GP I was thinking that your novels are quite traditional, close to the novels of Dickens, for example.

JA Perhaps. I've always been totally uninterested in fashion. There are many people who experiment and who do it very well, but that is no reason for me to follow them. I'm a writer, not a member of the literati. I try to re-create life in my writing and formal questions are always secondary.

If you take the case of Guimarães Rosa, you'll find that, when translated into Spanish, his work loses something. It loses more when translated into French and still more in English. By the time you've gone into Russian or Chinese, there is nothing of his form left. What's left is the life he created, his men and women. That lives on. The form disappears.

I feel that life is more important than literature and that life in literature is more important than the literary elements. There is literature written in blood and there is literature written in ink. The literature written in ink can have great beauty but that written in blood is more permanent.

GP It's also a matter of making literature well understood, isn't it? *Gabriela* makes a satirical point when a pretentious poet sends the heroine to sleep. Dona Flor is also sent to sleep by her husband's high-flown speech. Is your style simple so that it's accessible to more people?

JA You write to be read. If you didn't write to be read, you wouldn't publish. The classics have generally been very popular, Cervantes, Dickens or Mark Twain, for example.

GP The 1940s must have been a very difficult time for a Brazilian writer. How did you cope with censorship?

JA My books were banned in Brazil for many years. From 1937 to 1943 none of my books could be sold. I was in exile in 1941 and 1942. I returned to Brazil and was put in prison. I've been to jail eleven times in all. In 1937 I was a prisoner in Manaus, in the Amazon. Then they sent me to Rio by ship. In 1942 I was a prisoner in the south, in Porto Alegre, until they sent me off elsewhere by train. So I've toured the whole country as a prisoner. The last time was in 1945.

GP How is it that you became a deputy in the parliament?

JA When the dictatorship ended there were elections and I was a candidate. I was elected deputy for São Paolo in 1946. Two years later I was expelled from the parliament and left the country for Europe, where I spent the next five years.

GP Your novels are often historical, or at least set a good thirty years ago. Would you consider that you are rewriting history?

JA The official history is always a false one. It's always written from the point of view of the powerful. Novelists re-create history and though the details of their stories may not be accurate, they get closer to the truth than historians. The novelist can write from the point of view of those who are not powerful. *Showdown* is exactly this, the negation of the official story. I tell what really happened.

GP Namely that Brazil doesn't owe progress and development to the rich and powerful?

JA That's right. Life isn't a function of wealth.

GP Your novels could be seen as stories that tell the Christian myth in reverse. Dona Flor, for example, is saved by her rather devilish husband.

JA Possibly. That's an interpretation for the critics to make. When I write I don't think about either Christianity or materialism. I'm just telling my story.

Ana Miranda

Ana Miranda's historical novel *The Mouth of Hell* (1989) does not seem to share the experimentalism of Latin American writing, but the society it depicts so vividly cannot but appear extraordinary to the modern reader. Its characters move on a grand scale and with a gusto that most readers would be familiar with only in tragic drama or in a book on Renaissance history.

While basically a realist novel, it is adventurous in its structure. It borrows a great deal from drama, and the characters are given to philosophizing from time to time, in dialogue if not in dramatic soliloquies. Miranda carries this off brilliantly, reminding us that realism is merely another means of making us suspend disbelief.

The Mouth of Hell tackles one of the questions implicit in Machiavelli's work: what is the meaning of morality in a corrupt society? The novel is set in colonial Brazil at the end of the seventeenth century, when government was an intricate game of intrigue involving corrupt royal appointees and an equally opportunistic local upper class. The novel portrays a web of duplicity that is as baroque in its ramifications as the speech of the time.

The book is also a romance. The protagonist is a Don Juan figure, Gregorio de Matos, who wrote ribald and profane poetry. His unlikely love is the innocent Maria Berco, and as they are both swept up in the dramatic events of the plot, the novel addresses profound issues relating to the sexual mores of the age and the nature of sexuality itself.

The Mouth of Hell is a remarkable achievement. Its complex world view is communicated with a degree of subtlety, balance and literary judgement that makes Ana Miranda one of the most important writers to appear in Latin America in recent years.

GP *The Mouth of Hell* does not have the elements of fantasy that many English-speaking readers have come to associate with Latin American writing. Did you make a conscious decision not to incorporate the fantastic?

AM Each story has its own specific characteristics and problems. I wanted to write about our colonial life, the language of our baroque period, the formation of our literature and other things that are quite real. There was no reason to choose the fantastic style.

GP The novel draws on both prose and drama. In particular, the way narrative action alternates with philosophical observations by the characters reminds me of Shakespeare.

AM I found that alternating action, dialogue, description, reflection and commentary was the best way to tell the story and to gain greater harmony and movement. Technically this presented many problems; the proportions of each of these narrative forms depend on an awareness of the ebb and flow of the different elements in the narrative. In fact, this was the fundamental question to be solved in the construction of the novel, which is an exercise in rhythm and should be an almost musical experience for the reader. Shakespeare has always interested me and I am very struck by your reference to him, because I read a great deal of his work while I was writing. I felt I could learn from him, especially with regard to the techniques of writing dialogue and the incorporation of brutality in dialogue in a graceful way; there were also his characters, so human and so classical at the same time. Another important influence was Dostoyevsky, the first writer I ever read of my own accord, at the age of thirteen, and who continues to fascinate me.

GP By having an omniscient and sometimes intrusive narrator the novel moves away from some techniques favoured by modern writers. Were you trying to match the novel's style to the historical period?

AM Yes, even though at that time there was no such thing as a historical novel. I used the omniscient and intrusive narrator to gain greater mobility and opportunities for scene setting. This was important in portraying a period so little known to the readers. At first I tried writing in the first person, in the character of Maria Berco. This would have allowed me to write from the woman's point of view, but the language and style became very restricted and limited, the view of the world so naïve and inexperienced, that the historical forces represented by de Matos and Vieira were lost. Then I tried having Gregorio de Matos himself but it made the book excessively reflective and meant the whole narrative would have had to be in the baroque manner, which, in the end, appeared only in the dialogues. After that I tried a limited third-person narrative, giving the point of view of only one character, but this too was restrictive. Finally, I chose an omniscient narrator who used an atemporal language and could appear everywhere. This was ideal for the portrayal of colonial life and the first manifestations of our literature. There was the added advantage that the classical language of the omniscient narrator contrasts with the baroque language of the dialogues, giving more vigour and liberty to the narrative.

GP How did you research the novel?

AM I tried to do the research not as a scientist but as a traveller. I wanted to absorb the spirit of the age, to become an observer of colonial Brazil. At times I felt I was really there, that the characters were of flesh and blood, had their own scent, movements, presence and will. I felt them by my side not as phantoms but as living beings. I was the phantom. I read hundreds of books, documents, returned to the archives again and again, in an attempt to imbue myself with the iconography of the age. Each investigation led to another in an unending chain of discoveries. My greatest problem was to know what to use and what not to use, to decide what had a function and what did not.

At the same time, I was often troubled by a lack of information. The period is very incompletely documented and the archive material is badly organized and sometimes inaccessible. The most important book on the life of Gregorio de Matos, by Professor Fernando da Rocha Peres, is a mere 120 pages. There are critics who conclude that Gregorio de Matos did not even exist. His poems are for the most part apocryphal and authorship is impossible to ascribe with certainty. However, even if the poems didn't come from his pen, they were unmistakably an expression of the age and valuable documents in themselves. When I couldn't find the information I was seeking I worked by deduction and checked the situation in Portugal. At other times it was simply a matter of using the imagination. Unfortunately, I had no institutional support for research and no chance to travel to Salvador or even to dedicate myself fully to the work, so finishing the book took a lot of determination.

GP What sparked off your interest in this period of history?

AM In the first version of my book, which was set in 1720, Gregorio de Matos was merely mentioned by a character, an old blind woman with long white hair who said she had been his lover. In order to write this scene I had to research his life and became so enthusiastic that I returned to 1683, when he was still alive. I had studied the baroque period at school but knew almost nothing of Gregorio de Matos, having read only an expurgated edition of his poems, without the satires. I had heard that he was an unlucky and much abused poet, though I didn't know why he was so abused. When I read the manuscripts of his poems, and stumbled across the episode of the killing of the mayor, with the involvement of de Matos and Vieira, I was fascinated. It was an intensely dramatic story, Shakespearian, and very rich in characters. It also revealed a great deal about Brazil. Here was an unexplored period of our history, one that no one had yet written about.

GP For the reader, the novel seems to move towards a grand denouement but then the documentary elements reassert themselves and there is no dramatic climax. The resolution is more like real life than fiction. Did you have to fight against the storytelling impulse in order to stick to the patterns of contingency common in history?

AM There was an intense struggle to fit the history and the fiction together. I decided to limit myself to two areas: the crime and the dismissal of the governor, Braço de Prata. I could have worked within a larger context, as from 1683 Gregorio de Matos had an increasingly dramatic life, culminating in his being banished to Africa on a caravel with some of the king's horses. That might have provided one climax to the book. Alternatively, the love between Gregorio de Matos and María Berco could have had some sort of consummation. I was free to write this in, as it was a fictional history. However, I preferred not to write a dramatic climax because the story does not finish on the last page of the narrative. It continues through the last section 'Destinies' and up to the present day. A climax would have given a false impression that there was an end to the story. History never finishes. I wanted to write a story resembling real life.

There were also personal factors; I am not given to paroxysms of passion. The structure of the book is also the structure of my mind. The curve of the story is the curve of my emotions and in this respect I don't know if I could have written it differently.

The battle to make the history fit the fiction was hardest in the purely fictional scenes and in the dialogues. Events had to appear not just possible but probable. That demanded caution as well as imagination. As in any work of literature, language was the most important element, but at the same time language is not everything.

GP The hell of the title seems to refer not only to the city but also to the relations between men and women in that society. Was the novel an attempt to trace the ramifications of sexual politics in the larger political sphere?

AM No. *The Mouth of Hell* was the nickname given to Gregorio de Matos – they called him that because of his cruel satires and obscene verses. But the true hell was between men and men, the political enemies. Between men and women there was a mixture of inferno and paradise. The term inferno also has a sexual connotation; one of the most common and condemned sins at that time was libertinism. The devil and hell were always being used by the priests as a kind of threat. Inferno also refers to the lower part of the world, this southern colony. Antonil, a writer of the time, wrote that Brazil was a hell for blacks, a purgatory for whites and a paradise for mulattos. Hell was the colonization, the Inquisition, the monarchy, slavery; hell was misery and hunger.

GP At one point Braço de Prata says that hate will always be victorious over coolness or love. The failed attempt to kill him seems to support this view. Is the novel arguing that virtues are for losers?

AM The loser is not always virtuous, nor are the virtuous always losers. The book is not meant to establish any Manichaean struggle between good and evil. The characters have the same mixture of strengths and failings as real people.

GP Gregorio de Matos seems to be at the mercy of drives that result in suffering for women. Do the needs of men and women inevitably conflict?

AM No. Needs vary from person to person, though it is also clear that the sexual nature and demands of men and women are different. At the moment I feel that there is a greater understanding between the sexes; in the seventeenth century there was an enormous conflict. Women were sharply divided into the fallen and the virtuous. Iberian culture had absorbed a great deal of Moorish influence in its treatment of women. They were kept in jealous seclusion. The only way to escape was to enter a convent, where there was intellectual freedom, because there were no men. The female writers of the time were mostly nuns. It is interesting that in many convents during the sixteenth and seventeenth centuries the nuns still had the freedom to receive visits from lovers. I wrote an essay about this which was published in a Brazilian magazine.

GP Should the literature of Brazil be profane and popular, like the poetry of Gregorio de Matos?

AM No, literature should never follow precepts. There is great variety in Brazilian writing. Clarice Lispector, one of our most expressive writers, wrote intimate, psychological works.

Guimarães Rosa, the leader of an experimental regionalist school, wrote works of great sophistication and beauty. In the nineteenth century, Machado de Assis wrote of our customs with a fine irony. Amongst contemporaries there is Rubem Fonseca, who is highly sophisticated even when he is dealing with brutality.

GP Portugal, being far away and the apparent source of justice in the novel, plays heaven to the hell of Salvador. What are the chief positive and negative aspects of European culture, from a Brazilian writer's point of view?

AM European culture was of course the most important factor in the formation of Brazilian culture. The positive things included the Portuguese love of adventure, their capacity for adaption and social flexibility and their love of personal independence. They brought beautiful architecture, music, theatre, clothing and literary tradition. On the other hand, they also brought an obstinate bureaucracy, a tendency to obscurantism, religious and racial persecution, an abhorrence of manual labour, the concept of slavery, religious indoctrination, the impunity of the rich, nepotism, the catholic philosophy against worldly wealth, obedience as a basis for discipline, the irrationality of privileges and hierarchies, to name but a few things.

It is also true that the Portuguese saw Brazil as a sort of kitchen garden where the colonizers could throw their problems and their criminals. They monopolized the economy and they implanted a tendency towards monoculture that has had destructive economic effects to this day. They failed to construct, to plan, to lay foundations, preferring to capture easy riches. Some of the areas that were richest at the beginning of the colonization are the poorest today. The old Iberian culture was based on the impossibility of solid social organization and on social injustice. It is also worrying that culture was simply imported. At times I feel that our culture is inappropriate for our part of the world – for our climate, our landscape and our people.

GP How universal is the political hell of Salvador?

AM The fight for power is universal. I don't know of any

civilization that does not have this characteristic.

GP How does the historical portrait in the novel relate to the social issues of modern Brazil? Is there an equivalent of the Inquisition or the persecution of the Jews, for example?

AM The recent military governors were inquisitorial. There have been other periods when restrictions were imposed on civil rights, such as during the rule of Getúlio Vargas. At the moment we have a constitution that is modern in its attitude towards society and justice. Everyone seems disposed to respect it. As far as religious and racial persecutions are concerned, there has not been anything very severe in recent times, though there is a detestable racial prejudice against Negroes, disguised as class prejudice. The great majority of Negroes in Brazil are poor. There is a very subtle anti-Semitism, which manifests itself through drollery and mockery, but I don't think it is a result of nationalist sentiments; it is rather a tendency, common among human beings to reject what is different.

GP In what ways did the political and social concerns of modern Brazil prompt you to write the novel?

AM I knew when I started the book that all our vices and virtues had deep roots in our colonial past. The first document written in Brazil, a letter from Pero Vaz de Caminha, ends with an appeal for employment on behalf of his son-in-law. Nepotism is very common in Brazil and is only now being fought. It has been the right of the élite to traffic in posts and privileges. I kept coming across things like that. At the same time, research was an adventure for me and I was fascinated by what I encountered; it helped me not only to understand but to love my country more.

EL SALVADOR

.

Manlio Argueta

In the small Central American nations land has been a key issue. Land ownership has been centralized in the hands of a very small minority, in an economy built on the plantation system. In the absence of slave labour, indigenous people have been employed on starvation wages. Left to themselves, the indigenous people would have preferred to continue as subsistence farmers, but their land has often been taken and allowed to lie unused to force them to depend on the cash economy. Attempts to reoccupy land, even with government approval, have often been met with more violence. In El Salvador demands for basic civil rights in the 1930s led to the massacre of some 40,000 people. It is perhaps not surprising that guerilla groups eventually formed, leading to the present civil war that has taken 70,000 lives.

Manlio Argueta's fiction is based on true accounts; moral necessity has driven him to explore the borders of fiction and non-fiction. He writes in the concrete, immediate and matter-of-fact manner of a survivor recounting a story to a friend, an approach that allows him to narrate the truly disturbing without falling into the trap of sounding shrill or exaggerated. There is a healing sense of acceptance that allows the reader to take the same point of view as the survivor. This distance and understanding help make the writing much more than documentary.

The novels also work on a number of levels: flashbacks and changes in viewpoint imply a sense of history even when the attention is very focused, as in *One Day of Life* (1980), and in *Cuzcatlan* (1986), which weaves together the accounts of three generations to provide an overview of the Salvadorean situation. Surprisingly, the novel ends without rancour, more in pity than bitterness.

Argueta is also a poet and his prose style is often lyrical rather than documentary. The poetry is evident not in rhythm or rhyme but in moments of perception or epiphany that subtly blend with the matter-of-fact narration.

Argueta's characters are remarkable for their strength. Much of this strength comes from a culture that has survived in the face of great difficulty. Argueta captures a voice that is rarely heard, as the indigenous culture has always been predisposed to stoicism and silence. Elements of magic and myth enter the writing, as do the simple rituals of a life that has been pared right down.

Manlio Argueta lives in San José, Costa Rica, where he runs a cultural centre from a small office that is bare except for a couple of chairs and a desk.

GP I was surprised to find that you are running a theatre here.

MA This is the Costa Rican and Salvadorean Cultural Institute, which I founded in 1981 with the help of some Costa Rican friends. The idea was to help Salvadorean refugees – there were about 12,000 in Costa Rica at that time. We also wanted to present the Salvadorean point of view to Costa Rica. Everyone in the institute is Salvadorean. All the work we do is voluntary, supported by donations from private companies and some friends who are involved in the theatre.

GP Do you put on a lot of plays?

MA Yes, though most of the time Costa Rican groups use the auditorium. Four or five years ago we had a number of Salvadorean theatre companies but recently fewer people have been arriving, while many of those living here have left. It's not easy for them to find work here so they go to Canada, for example, or to Australia. A few have even returned to El Salvador. Still, this institute remains as a kind of meeting place for the Salvadorean community.

GP When did you come to Costa Rica?

MA About twelve years ago, after the army stormed the University of El Salvador. I worked in the University of Costa Rica for eight years, teaching Central American literature. I wanted to concentrate on that because it receives so little attention.

GP Do you live from your writing at the moment?

MA Yes, I get by on the royalties of *One Day of Life*. *Cuzcatlan* has also been translated into English recently.

GP So your time is split between writing and helping the Salvadorean refugees who arrive in Costa Rica?

MA Yes. We have a lot of cultural exchange projects: we have sent some Costa Rican artists to El Salvador, mostly musicians, and Salvadorean painters, writers and musicians have come here.

GP Do these people have difficulties leaving and re-entering El Salvador?

MA The point is that Salvadorean artists are hemmed in by the conditions there. They can't get themselves or their work known. It's difficult enough for any Central American but it is much worse for a Salvadorean. One of the aims of this institute is to get our artists known abroad, as well as introducing Salvadoreans to the culture of other parts of Central America. It's a way of making people more aware and in a way it is a contribution towards peace in Central America.

GP One of the preoccupations of your novels is the way people are alienated from their own history and culture. Culture is frowned on because the military see it as a form of opposition.

MA That is especially true in El Salvador, where any expression of one's own values is very difficult. Military regimes feel threatened by freedom of expression. They are happier if our feelings are kept in prison. That is true for the individual and for the nation; our frontiers are like the bars of a cell. Even though Central American countries have the same historical characteristics, the same language and the same religion, it is extremely difficult to move from one country to another, because culture is conceived of in terms of repression and domination. Everyone has to lock themselves in their piece of feudal territory. We feel that it is time to communicate more and know each other better.

GP Did you start writing very young?

MA Yes, I began to write poetry when I was in primary school. I began to read quite early and that awoke my interest in literature. When I started writing seriously it was as a poet. Then, when I matured, I began to write novels. Can you imagine what it would be like to be a poet in El Salvador? The illiteracy rate is very high and most people are struggling to avoid death by starvation. It is very difficult to find the money to buy books. Also, the military regimes which have been in power for over fifty years have no interest in seeing books published. Writers have had to concentrate on poetry because it can at least be recited. The publishing houses used to be in the hands of the government, though in the last fifteen years that has changed a little, thanks to the universities. The University of El Salvador published quite a lot before it was closed and the Catholic University is doing great work in this field; it even manages to publish texts directly related to the conflict in our country.

Universities in Central America (with the exception of Costa Rica) are centres for social and cultural movements. They fill a gap in our societies, which don't have a tradition of political involvement. The only political party has been the army, with gun in hand. So in the last twenty years political thought has been channelled through the universities and expressed by the intellectuals. From that point of view the university has played an important role in raising the level of awareness in El Salvador, especially since 1960.

El Salvador was without political parties for fifty-five years. The first political party with permission to operate openly was the Christian Democratic Party, which was formed in 1961 at the instigation of John F. Kennedy, who was worried that El Salvador was turning into the detonator for a great explosion in Central America. The party was founded by José Napoléon Duarte, who later betrayed it and allied himself with the very officers who organized a coup against him. More recently other political parties have been formed but as there is still no genuine freedom of expression, they haven't been able to do a great deal.

I was the director of a publishing house that operated from the University of El Salvador. We were trying to publish books that were otherwise unavailable, whether for economic reasons or because the censors didn't allow them to be imported. Our best-known poet, Roque Dalton, was published for the first time – he'd been given an important Latin American literary award but he hadn't appeared in print.

The country's main cultural and literary expressions came out of the university and this was what provoked the military to intervene in the late 1970s. The university was completely destroyed by the army. Everything went, from the window panes to the libraries and the laboratories. All the typewriters disappeared. It was turned into a barracks for two years. All the books were destroyed. Then there was the earthquake in 1986, which finished off the buildings that had been left standing. Still, the university is operating at the moment – there is a great spirit despite the problems of accommodation and infrastructure. Even when it had been taken over by the army the university managed to rent places to give classes. The students took the initiative and organized classes, even though it was at the risk of their lives.

GP Is it difficult to enter university in El Salvador if you are not middle class?

MA It is a little easier than you might think in Central America because there are generally no fees. I suppose I was middle class, but it is difficult to know how to classify yourself in a developing country like El Salvador.

GP In *One Day of Life* and *Cuzcatlan* you put yourself inside the heads of the *campesinos*. How did you manage to write so convincingly from this point of view?

MA My novels are written through a poetic method, using memory, and my early childhood had a lot to do with the life of the *campesino*, which enables me to interpret things from that point of view. I've also done research, but I think that

without working poetically, through remembrance, I couldn't
authentically interpret some aspects of the *campesino*'s spiritual
life.

I am from San Miguel, in one of the provinces, and I lived
on the outskirts of the city. I had more to do with the country
than the city, although my parents worked in the city, doing
simple jobs. We were never well off.

Even though I became interested in reading and writing at
an early age, I didn't have any encouragement. I had no help
from my parents or my teachers, who had no idea of what I
needed or what writing meant to me. I didn't respect my
teachers; I'd read quite a lot and used to argue with them.
There was only my mother, who liked poetry, despite being
poorly educated. She'd read when she was young and she
recited poems to me from memory because there were no
books in the house. Until I was twelve I had only the books
that were set for school, so I read only one book a year. Then
I gained access to some books through a lucky accident, which
I'm writing about in the novel I'm working on at the moment.
I found a public library where I managed to borrow books and
read.

I concentrated on poetry. At least that appeared in the newspapers, though it was poetry fifty years behind the times. So,
before I started university I'd read some Latin American
poetry – people like Neruda or Spanish poets such as García
Lorca. Again, it was through my own initiative that I managed
to get hold of these books. My teachers were of no help.

GP Do you have any idea what first interested you in
literature?

MA No – unless it was my sensitivity to the landscape, or
the fact that I was often alone and so liked to write. When I
was twenty I won a national prize for poetry, without having
any reputation in El Salvador. I began to meet some of the
important poets who lived in San Salvador when I arrived to
study at the university. I met other writers of my generation.
We didn't have many forebears because, although there had
been excellent writers in El Salvador, their works had been

suppressed. We managed to become known by uniting, by shouting and demanding our rights; we were the first generation to become a literary force. We published our own magazines; we made the debate on the problem of Salvadorean art and culture a public one. We talked openly about the injustice and repression in the country.

GP Was that because, with the formation of the Christian Democratic Party, there was a little more freedom of expression?

MA No. They were never any help. The Christian Democrats were really only interested in gaining positions of political power. Even though they initially made some attempts to change things, they later lost interest. The main assistance came from the university, which gave us a certain discipline in our studies and also an infrastructure.

Almost all the writers were gathered in the university and as we were really the only significant opposition to the government, we were harassed. Some of us were imprisoned; others were expelled from the country. There is no poet of that era who hasn't experienced prison or expulsion. We have all been imprisoned six or seven times, exiled or handed over to the military in Guatemala or Nicaragua.

You may wonder what poets were doing so mixed up in politics. It's as I said, there were no other means of political expression. It wasn't until 1961 when the Alliance for Progress got under way that laws were passed to permit political parties or any form of social security was introduced. The United States began investing in El Salvador to make it a lynchpin in the establishment of a Central American market and to develop some sort of modern industry. The idea was also to create an internal market in the country. However, these plans were effectively derailed by the Salvadorean oligarchy, who saw them as a threat to their power. They wanted to keep exploiting the workers as they'd always done, and they were competing with the more recently formed Honduran oligarchy. Both groups wanted dominance for their exports in Costa Rica and Guatemala.

This struggle culminated in the so-called Football War of 1968, which ended any hopes for a Central American market. The frontiers were closed and things returned to how they had been. Also in 1968, there was an agrarian reform in El Salvador. The universities helped plan this and there had even been some support among the military. Then the oligarchy stepped in and rolled things back.

GP Was poetry primarily concerned with expressing political concern?

MA Our poems were always ones of protest. They were almost always concerned with injustice. We also participated in demonstrations against the dictatorship, which had been in power since 1932. There had been fifty years without any sort of change. When I write about my early childhood I find myself wondering whether life is different for children today. I don't think it is, except that conditions are even worse now than when I was young. The struggle that you see in El Salvador is the result of more than a hundred years of injustice. It is not possible for the oligarchy to calm things down with small changes or reforms because this has been building up for so long.

GP In *La valle de las hamacas* there is a dialogue about Ionesco, which made me wonder how much your reading of twentieth-century literature had influenced you.

MA The university offered an alternative culture. We staged Ionesco plays; I even acted in one of them. We were also very interested in what was happening in the rest of the world, especially in other parts of Latin America. We got to know world literature through our magazines. Roque Dalton, for example, knew a great deal about European literature. He'd trained in El Salvador as a Jesuit and then travelled in Europe. He passed on a lot of what he knew.

GP Yet in your novels, you seem to return to an oral tradition that is uniquely Salvadorean – in one sense you made no use of what you'd read.

MA My reading helped create a basis for what I wrote. If you read Roque Dalton, you can see how much he has absorbed other literatures, even though all his poetry is about El Salvador. The same thing happened to me. I needed to find ways of letting the poor speak. They have their own forms of spiritual and aesthetic expression but no way of making them known. Realizing that the poor had great sensitivity and a special sense of beauty was very important for me. At the same time, I had to absorb the techniques of the European and American novel, especially the American novel of the 1930s and 1940s – great writers like Hemingway, Steinbeck and Dos Passos.

GP Simplicity and clarity are very important in your work, aren't they? You began by listening to literature, by hearing your mother recite poems. Reading your novels, I feel as if I am listening to someone speak. It's like being there with the characters and listening to them.

MA Yes, I wanted to recapture some of the richness and beauty of oral literature, and even of everyday speech – the way people can speak to you with great sensitivity and emotion. It is just a matter of organizing what they say and putting it into some sort of literary code. In order to do that you need to master the techniques of fiction.

One Day of Life is a real story. Almost all of it consists of real statements. I met a *campesina* who told me her story. It began as an interview I was doing for a paper. I was very moved by what she told me. They had put out her husband's eyes – which is the main strand of the plot – and brought him into town. Everyone was afraid to recognize him. Even she had to deny him because they were going to kill anyone who knew him. I had a recording of this interview and it inspired me to write the novel.

The husband's story is on file in the Human Rights section of the Organization of American States. He was the director of the Rural Federation of Christian Workers. His name was Justo Mejía. The town where the novel was set, San Antonio de los Ranchos, has been so badly bombarded that it has almost been wiped off the map. They have created a new San Antonio de los Ranchos because almost nothing is left of the original.

GP Did the army come and disperse the community?

MA Yes, the *campesinos* and the Federation of Christian Workers were very active in this region, Chalatenango, which is in the north; it is the poorest and most miserable part of El Salvador. Almost everyone left for Honduras, though they've now returned, with the help of the United Nations. There is a movement called Repopulation. Duarte didn't want anyone to return to certain areas. He wanted them to return to San Salvador. No one was willing to do that because it would have meant living as beggars. People wanted to return to where they had their houses, and they are living there now, even though they risk being killed and conditions are very difficult. Sometimes the army refuses to let food or medicine from international aid agencies into the area.

It is hard for the *campesinos* but even in Honduras they had many problems. They were kept in camps. The Honduran army made life difficult and even killed some of them – that's well documented. Children were becoming young adults, having spent years in these camps, and so despite the war and the repression in El Salvador, people wanted to return. They are very organized. Some even learnt trades while they were in Honduras. Though they were harassed by the army and were virtual prisoners in the camps, there was a lot of international aid. They had their own schools and were able to set up small workshops to teach carpentry, for example. You'd see seven-year-old children working. They had little else to do as there was no chance of working on the land.

GP In *Cuzcatlan*, which tells the story of three generations, you changed your style a little. It is more complex and ambitious than *One Day in Life*. Does this book also have documentary foundations?

MA Yes, it is almost all based on real events. Some of the material comes from interviews. There is also some autobiography, especially in the poetic aspects of the writing. I tried to bring my style as a poet into the writing of the novel.

GP When you talk of your novels being poetic, it is a poetry without metaphors or symbols or imagery. The poetry seems to come from the flow of the prose, the way you portray the landscape and your perception of the spiritual aspects of your characters.

MA I am very influenced by the landscape and I draw my images from that. I'm also influenced by other poets: Saint-John Perse, for example, Cavafy or Maxim Gimet, also classic Latin American poets like Pablo Neruda or César Vallejo. But I give priority to the poetic idea, rather than to the word, to language or rhetoric. Poetry is emotion and El Salvador is a country with a lot of emotions and upheavals. You can't go 100 kilometres without feeling shaken. There is a cataclysm in your body when you are confronted with the way things are. This is a great source for poetry.

Of course, I'm also absorbed in our landscape, in our colours. It's a matter of expressing the feeling of wonder you have at the landscape, or the stars.

GP You've turned the *campesino*'s sense of magic and mythology into a kind of poetry.

MA Yes. In *Cuzcatlan* some of the stories come from our sacred book the *Popol Vuh*. For example, there is the story of how men were created first from wood, then from earth and then from maize. On the first attempt, when they were made from wood, men couldn't think. When they were made from earth they had problems when it rained. The successful attempt was with maize.

GP And there's the story you tell of the woman in the river, who is a kind of devil.

MA This is the story of the *Siguanaba*, which the *campesinos* always accept as true.

GP In your novels there is no hint of the magic realism of Alejo Carpentier. Nor have you followed the tradition of the great Guatemalan writer Miguel Angel Asturias. In your works the magic is in people's minds, whereas in magic realism it is part of the world. Magic is always a mental thing for you.

MA Yes, because I am interested in the emotions and the interior world, perhaps more than in the external world. The external world is expressed through the landscapes, but the main thing is what lies inside. That comes from the fact that we are oppressed so harshly that we create interior worlds. I want to express this. We feel close to the Peruvian poet César Vallejo, for example, because he shows the interiority of the indigenous people. He reveals the Peruvian culture.

The indigenous people hide in their interior world as a way of escaping repression. It is a very rich world, a great culture that is kept hidden as a means of preservation. They have no forms of expression; I feel that the tendency of Central American literature to testify to this reality is a step towards making our own culture known.

I remember that when we started writing poetry we said that the poetry was in the idea. That was partly to distinguish ourselves from the dominant school of poetry of the time, that centred on Neruda, who was writing a more external kind of poetry. The same is true of García Márquez and *One Hundred Years of Solitude*, which is a great, extraordinary novel, showing the tempestuous, external world of Latin America. What we wanted was to express our internal world by means of poetry. Of course, our poetry isn't solely concerned with ideas. We are always playing with language and with the poetic form.

GP Why did you move from poetry to the novel?

MA I felt I could express more of the rich, magical world, more of reality. Poetry is limited by rhythm and the canons that determine the way it's written. Poetry has its own express-ive world but description is easier in the novel.

GP To what extent is your fiction a way to publicize what is happening in El Salvador? Do you think of it as a form of propaganda?

MA I have thought of the novel as a way of making our reality more widely known. In a way, it is also a work of sociology or history. The novel offers you so many possibilities of portraying the way things are, and it is more accessible to the public than a scientific or academic work.

GP It's not just a matter of accessibility. A history book about El Salvador is horribly depressing, whereas you attract the reader by showing a positive side that isn't in the history books. For example, one of your characters, instead of stating that there is a very high infant mortality rate, says something like, 'We are very strong. If we reach three there is a good chance that we'll survive.'

MA Our people are optimists. The Salvadoreans have suffered so much but they still have hope. They are still fighting to find their own forms of expression and a better life, despite all the military and economic forces against them. They keep fighting, even returning to their land at the risk of their lives. The attachment to the land of our parents and grandparents is very much a part of our culture.

GP You never show the *campesinos* as pathetic or beaten. No matter what happens, they are not objects of pity and they are never looked down on; they are always on the same level as the reader.

MA This is also part of the reality of our country. It has to do with the nature of the indigenous people here, who have been integrated into a capitalist economy for a long time. The main products of El Salvador, sugar and cotton, have always been cultivated by big capital. Coffee to a lesser extent, but it has been closely linked with industry because the coffee drunk here is always processed into powder. So, the Salvadorean *campesino* has a more advanced mentality than, say the Bolivian, who often lives completely outside the cash economy. In El Salvador the *campesinos* are also integrated in the sense that everyone speaks Spanish – they are not restricted by an indigenous language.

In *Cuzcatlan* I write about the involvement of our *campesinos* in the production of fabric dyes for industry. We were the biggest producer of fabric dyes until the Germans, in the middle of the last century, discovered how to make artificial ones. We had a central role in the textile industry, which was the keystone of the formation of capitalism in Europe. We have dye works going back three hundred years. The first book published in Central America was a manual that the *campesinos* had to read in order to learn how to make dye.

GP But, as you say in the novel, they were three hundred years of poor health for those who worked in the dye factories.

MA Yes, the fumes ruined their health. According to the statistics, there was a high percentage of death by poisoning amongst the workers. There was no form of social security. In fact, there still isn't, and it is very rare, even today, to find workers wearing any sort of protective mask in a factory.

GP Is there any hope of things changing in the near future?

MA I think there is a triple crisis occurring in a number of Latin American countries. There is a social, economic and political crisis. When you have to face three crises at the same time, what can you do? The sectors that have dominated our society through force and terror are finding it difficult to cope. As well as great political turbulence there is the social crisis: the workers continue to protest, undeterred even by the terrible deaths some of them have suffered. As for the economic crisis, El Salvador currently ranks third in the world for economic aid, yet we have 50 per cent of our labour force unemployed. How are we ever going to repay two million dollars of aid per day? What's more, this aid doesn't go into economic growth: 80 per cent goes to the army, and I suppose the other 20 per cent goes to politicians who keep it in the bank. The infrastructure of the country has been destroyed by the war and there is no prospect of industrial growth or development.

The end of the war is important not only to the poor but to the industrialists, who would then have a chance to communicate with other sectors, some of whom have seen the war as a way to enrich themselves. However, even they are beginning to realize that peace is in the interests of more than one sector of society. There is now a very large group who support greater sovereignty, democratization and an end to social injustice in El Salvador. Agreement on these issues would be the basis for a national accord that would cut across class barriers.

GP Do you think that this agreement is likely to occur? Can you realistically hope for it?

MA We have to hope, otherwise this favourite child of the United States isn't going to survive. The crises we are experiencing can't be overcome by sending more arms. They have been trying that for years and, as the *New York Times* said, nothing has changed except the fact that the insurgents used to have five states and they now hold fourteen – despite all the money spent to finish them off. The basic problem grows out of years of injustice and will only be solved when the different sectors in the country realize that, for their own self-interest, they need to work together. I think that may not be too far off.

GP What are you working on at the moment?

MA I have been adapting *One Day of Life* for the theatre and I've just finished a book of poetry, *La guerra florida*, which I've been working on for five years. Now I am writing a reportage on the plight of Salvadorean refugees in the United States.

GP Will that be like *One Day of Life*?

MA No, it's non-fiction. It is the story of a woman who fled to the United States. I was teaching there at the invitation of one of the universities and I used the visit as an opportunity to gather some material about the problems refugees were facing.

I have also been working on a new novel called *Los niños del otro mundo*. It is about children and is partly autobiographical. I wanted to explore the magic of the children of the Third World. I expect to finish a draft within six months, though that depends on how much free time I have. There are all the cultural exchange projects that need to be worked on.

GP How much free time do you have to write?

MA Generally I write only at the weekends. I think about my novel during the week and then it just comes out through my fingers when I sit down at the typewriter. So, if you see me in the street and I don't notice you, it's because I have my mind on writing.

There are a lot of other pressing matters for us Central Americans. Our countries are on the margin of things, we are poor and oppressed; the work for cultural exchange and literature are both ways of working towards peace in Central America, so both deserve our time.

GUATEMALA

·

Luis Alfredo Arango

Guatemala's history is in many respects similar to El Salvador's. During the 1930s and early 1940s it was run like a family business by the dictator Jorge Ubico and his circle. The Nobel Prize-winning novelist Miguel Angel Asturias was writing at that time and had a vital literary influence; he abandoned many of the elements of the European novel and adopted the myths and folklore of the indigenous people. He influenced the style of magic realism used by Alejo Carpentier, and later by García Márquez, though myth often predominated over realism in his own work. How to treat the reality of the indigenous people was a question that continued to be important for Guatemalan writers, though important social factors also played a role in their choice of theme.

Things changed in Guatemala after 1944 when popular pressure led to Ubico's fall from power. Democratic elections resulted in a ten-year spell of democratic government until 1954, when plans to redistribute the land prompted the CIA to send in a mercenary force which deposed and shot the president. The military then took over and ran the country for the next thirty years with a firmness of grip that made all expression of opinion risky. Writers were only one of the groups who suffered. In the late 1970s the dictators were killing so many people, wiping out whole rural communities, that President Carter was moved to cease supplying them with weapons and training.

Democracy returned to Guatemala in 1986. In the nervous aftermath, with a government eager to show new openness, I spoke to Luis Alfredo Arango, Guatemala's leading poet. I was

interested in the way the heirs of a tradition forged by Asturias
had progressed and how writing could survive thirty years of
virtual isolation in a country where publication and distribution
are extremely difficult.

Though principally a poet, Arango has recently written a
fine first novel, *Después del tango vienen los moro* (1988), in which
attitudes towards the indigenous people are explored indirectly
though the reminiscences of a young man from a middle-class
home who shares much of his childhood with a poorer boy
from an indigenous family. The assimilation of Indian culture
and the difficulties faced by the Indians, who are the majority
of the population, is an important theme in contemporary
Guatemala. The technique of reminiscence allows Arango to
switch time and place with an associative freedom that brings
to mind his poetry. His personal background may also be
important, as the novel mingles social comment with a certain
nostalgia. Like many other Latin American novels, this is a
blend of autobiography, history and fiction.

GP What first aroused the interest in the indigenous peoples
that is so evident in your novel?

LA Well, for one thing my wife is Indian. She has told me
about her early childhood, about how she had to make trips
across the high plains of southern Guatemala and how she
was unjustly treated and exploited. She was badly fed; the
conditions in which she lived were very unhealthy. That was
partly because of the spraying of the plantations where she lived
and worked with insecticides, defoliants and other chemicals. It
was very damaging to the health of the local people. The
owners of the plantations didn't bother to take safety measures.
Every year there are still some workers who die after coming
into direct contact with plants that have been heavily sprayed.
I was always very affected by the stories that my wife told me
about her childhood.

GP In some respects the plight of the indigenous peoples
hasn't improved much since the conquest.

LA It is very clear that when our countries became politically independent of Spain, the independence was more symbolic than real. The structure of society remained unchanged. There had always been a dominant class and they simply stepped into the shoes of the *conquistadores* and colonizers. Society remained almost feudal in its power structures, the dominated people being the Indians, who make up the majority of the population here. For almost five hundred years they have been looked on with disdain. They've been called lazy, foolish, alcoholic and ignorant. The Indians themselves were brought up to accept this to some extent, but they had a remarkable means of surviving: they took refuge within themselves. A new culture was born, with roots in pre-Columbian times and also with Christian influences. During the first centuries of the colonization the missionaries set about converting the Indians by keeping them in settlements, as a means of control. With time, however, they came to fill the political vacuum amongst the Indians caused by the destruction of the indigenous communities. The missionary settlements became, paradoxically, places where the Indian languages and culture were kept alive. Culture was alive in secret, under the noses of the missionaries.

GP The people who have been dominant in countries like Guatemala have often been the landowners. Has the system of land ownership changed very much?

LA There have been slow, gradual changes since the revolution of 1944, when the bourgeoisie toppled Jorge Ubico, who'd been in power for fourteen years. Before and during his dictatorship the conditions for the *campesinos* were terrible. For example, all *campesinos* had to have a document that showed they were under contract to work in a certain place. If not, they were put in jail for vagrancy and set to work in road gangs. Things have improved since then, but it has been a slow process.

Eight or ten years ago the indigenous peoples had their own intelligentsia: doctors, lawyers, agronomists, teachers, social workers, nurses, accountants and so on. They have been severely persecuted. Many of them have died. Perhaps their demands, being the first expression of the indigenous peoples, were more emotional than philosophical or political, but it was valid for them to make demands.

I had the opportunity of working with an Indian agronomist on a government programme to improve conditions in one of the villages. We were giving advice on harvesting and how to improve supplies of drinking water, there was a health programme and we were teaching people how to read and write. My friend then had the chance to go to university and became a lawyer. He started to defend the rights of the Indians. One day he was in his car, going to do some shopping here in Guatemala City and he was machine-gunned. This is one example of the persecution of the indigenous peoples.

GP Things are said to have improved in Guatemala since the last elections, but I was reading in the paper that between January and March there have been over three hundred killings, mostly in Guatemala City.

LA Yes, but those killings wouldn't all have been political. There is also a great deal of common crime. Even though the press is still claiming there are a lot of political murders, I think the scale of political violence is much smaller than it was. A few years ago the number of killings was horrific. Thousands of people were dying. Whole villages would disappear. Students and professional people, priests and businessmen were being killed as well as *campesinos*. Poets and intellectuals were hit too.

Last night I was with some other writers. We were remembering the birthday of Manuel José Arce, the Guatemalan poet who had to flee the country after making himself unpopular with certain groups of people through working as a journalist. Oscar Arturo Valencia, another poet, was machine-gunned in the street, while Luis de León, Guatemala's first Indian novelist, was taken prisoner and disappeared. A few years earlier, the poet Roberto Obregón disappeared in the same way. Perhaps the most well-known case was that of René Castillo, who was not only a poet but a guerrilla; he died defending his ideas.

Though we may not share the beliefs of those who have been martyred, nor agree with their philosophical and political principles, we object to the repression used against them. Ideology shouldn't matter. A parish priest or a Marxist should be equally respected, just as landowners should when they are defending their privileges.

GP How does this atmosphere of repression affect you when you sit down to write? You must be conscious of the risks involved in writing.

LA I've worked a lot in rural areas, mostly with the Indians, and I didn't realize at the time that I was living through events I would later use in my poetry. When I returned to the city I began to digest all the traumas, all the things I'd seen while working as a teacher in the country: students suffering from malnutrition; young mothers of twenty-five or thirty who looked like old women; young, vigorous men who, five or six years later, were burnt out. In the rural areas you are considered lucky if you live past forty-five. I was deeply affected by all this and I began to write about it.

In Guatemala we've always had enormous difficulties in publishing. We could only print very limited editions, between 500 and 1,000 copies. I have always felt that poetry is a more permanent thing than fiction, but in the present situation, where there is a transition from dictatorship to democracy, I feel that poetry ought to be put to one side for a while. It is now time to narrate, to tell all the stories that we have been unable to tell in the last thirty years. That is why fiction is flourishing in Guatemala at the moment and there are few poets. It is a social and political phenomenon that is easy to understand. Of course it's still very difficult to publish. We have a Ministry of Sports and Culture that, in the two years since its foundation, has produced nothing.

The editorial difficulties are only one side of the problem. The climate of fear during the past thirty years has led to a kind of self-censorship by poets, a sort of self-defence. You end up being either very militant or using language that is so elusive that it loses authenticity. It takes a lot of guts not to disguise what you're saying. There may be things that you can't write but which stay in your mind; I hope they get into the writing somehow, because we don't write just for our contemporaries but for posterity.

GP In *Después del tango* you say people are irritated and frustrated, on the point of exploding and committing murder or suicide on the slightest pretext. Quarrels are often solved violently in Guatemala. What are the sources of this violence?

LA I think they are very evident. In Central America geopolitical forces are at work. Though the superpowers are playing chess on our territory, many people have not yet realized who our real oppressors are. They don't see that the oppressors are the United States, the Soviet Union and the multinationals who are playing hegemonic games in our countries. Not knowing who to blame, there remains only the escape valve of violence, usually amongst the poor themselves.

GP It seems that Guatemala suffers from cultural isolation. Has censorship been in operation?

LA I don't know if it operates at the moment but there certainly has been censorship. In a bookshop not far from here they used to sell a Mexican magazine called *Illustrated History*. It had analyses of important events in contemporary history; there were articles about people like the Shah of Iran, Anastasio Somoza and Mata Hari, and stories about Nazism or Trotsky. One day I found it had been banned because the government had decided it was communist. Publishing houses too were black-listed.

Last year I went to Mexico for a conference of Latin American poets. It was the first time in years that a Guatemalan poet had participated in such an event. I found that we were totally unknown, no one had heard anything about us. I also realized that poets in other countries had a very different existence to ours. We would never have dreamt that poets could give lectures and live off the money they made doing that. Nor would we have imagined that they could write articles for newspapers and live off that. They are invited to work at universities. They have jobs in publishing. They run writing workshops. Here in Guatemala we have to create these kind of opportunities.

GP Where are you working at the moment?

LA I work in publicity. I'm not ashamed of that. Alejo Carpentier did the same; lots of writers have had to use their skill with words to survive in non-literary ways. Before this job I was working for a newspaper, *El Diario de Centroamérica*. I was the first editor of their supplement 'Tolkien', the only literary publication in the country.

GP Is it very difficult to get works distributed in Guatemala, even after they've been published? You don't export them, as far as I know, and your home market must be very small.

LA Yes. The story of publication here is rather picturesque. With very few exceptions, it involves writing a manuscript, typing it up, finding a printer, correcting the proofs, finding a cover design and then going out to sell the book yourself. It's not easy.

Después del tango was, fortunately, published in a different way, by a writers' co-operative. It has published over forty-five books, mainly supported by the membership fees. I don't belong to the group but they generously offered to publish my book. This is a tremendous stimulus for a writer, a tremendous weight off your shoulders; you can forget about having to go from door to door trying to sell your book. There are still difficulties but I ought not complain. At least two of my books have sold out. Some writers are left with copies and end up giving them to their friends. Very little ever gets out of the country.

GP Could you tell me a little about the background to your novel? It reads like an autobiographical work even though you insist that it has nothing to do with your life.

LA It is autobiographical, but names and places have been changed to avoid offending people who might have recognized themselves in the book. Of course, it's not just autobiography. The real events are a background, a point of departure for saying certain things. The anecdotes merely offer a means of telling the social history of our country during recent times. That is why there are breaks in the narrative – you are reading about the two main characters one moment and the next you are reading about the 1973 earthquake in Antigua. I play these games with time because I believe that the real language of our history is paranoid and schizophrenic – it's incoherent.

GP That's an interesting statement. The Guatemalan writer whose work I know best is Asturias. He breaks time up a lot. You could say his world is paranoid.

LA Asturias is a great master; we love him very much but we are not interested in imitating him because we'd do it badly. Only Asturias is Asturias. Still, we can't help sharing certain things with him. In our literary and cultural history there is a double strand of the baroque: the indigenous and the Spanish baroque. The two have mingled and you can still find strong traces of them, even in everyday matters like excessively courteous forms of address.

GP To what extent is the re-arrangement of time indigenous? The Maya had a very different notion of time to ours: for them time was cyclical.

LA In my case the games I play with space and time are the result of the influence of Juan Rulfo. I admire him very much. I don't try to imitate him because it would be beyond me to imitate *Pedro Páramo*.

GP It is interesting that you have been influenced by a Mexican author. In *The Labyrinth of Solitude* Octavio Paz suggests that the borders between one country and another in Latin America are artificial – it can be difficult to distinguish one country from another. Are there aspects of Guatemalan culture that are very close to the Mexican culture?

LA That was certainly true in pre-Hispanic times. There are zones of Mayan influence a long way inside the Mexican border, while the culture of Teotihuacán or of the Toltecs has been influential in large parts of Guatemala. It is still rather like that. Mexico is our big brother. There are cultural roots that draw all of meso-America together.

GP One thing that makes your work very different from Juan Rulfo's is the light tone you maintain even when you are talking about very serious matters. Given the subject matter, this could have been a very sad book.

LA I think that is a very important point. There have been great humorists in Guatemala. There was a great romantic poet writing in the 1830s called José Montu; he was a satirical poet of the first rank, yet his life was tragic. Manuel José Arce, whose birthday we were celebrating, had a great sense of humour. We have a name for a writer with this quality: *el escritor chingón*. Living in the situation that we do, we either get violent or release our tension through jokes and ridicule. That is the source of our humour; it is the alternative to violence.

GP Ignácio de Loyola Brandão explained to me that he chose satire as a way of capturing the reader. If you write about tragic events in a sombre way you run the risk of losing your reader.

LA A lot of Brazilian writers use this approach; Jorge Amado is one who has influenced me.

GP You said you didn't want to follow in the footsteps of Asturias. Why is there this break between generations?

LA It springs from our different attitudes towards the Indians. The Indians were 'discovered' in Guatemala around the turn of the century. Before that they were simply ignored. It was as if they didn't exist. They were just beasts of burden or cheap labour. The people who really discovered Central America were nineteenth-century travellers such as John L. Stevens, who wrote an important book, and Baron von Humboldt, who came here with a sense of scientific curiosity. Stevens discovered the Mayan ruins. It was men like him who realized that there were other eyes in the continent besides those of the *conquistadores*. They made us see the indigenous people in a new way.

Since the beginning of this century a reappropriation of our past has been taking place. Asturias is a pioneer of this movement. Until the 1920s Guatemalan writers were producing modernist literature. Then came the generation of the 1930s, who incorporated the Indian in our literature, although the Indian was still seen from a great distance, like the subject of a postcard or a calendar. Nevertheless, the writers of the

1930s were the first to turn their attention to our reality, even though they saw it in a rather picturesque way.

After the 1944 revolution writers began to look more deeply into these things. The work of Asturias is very valuable, it is admirable, but the Indians he sees are literary ones. They are the results of his research in Paris, where he studied the codexes, the *Popol Vuh* and indigenous languages. In these studies and his childhood memories he found the elements of his approach to the novel. In contrast we have had the chance to live with the Indians. I am a country schoolteacher. I have married an indigenous woman. I have lived with them, eaten with them, shared my life with them; my acquaintance isn't literary but experiential. We couldn't keep on seeing the Indian in the poetic or heroic way that Asturias did. In my case, at least, it is a matter of writing more viscerally.

GP The town you describe in the novel doesn't seem to be very indigenous.

LA Oh, it is. Ninety-five per cent of the population are Indian. The *ladinos* are a small minority. I was one of them. Our families acted as intermediaries between the capitalist system and the indigenous economy. A North American anthropologist has defined the indigenous economic system as 'cent capitalism': it is based on a multitude of small, family businesses. The role of the *ladinos* was to sell what the Indians had grown or the handiwork that they had produced. For the most part I was writing about a *ladino* family with only flashes that revealed something of the indigenous culture. Angel makes contact with an indigenous youth and that is the only direct relation between the two worlds that you see in the novel.

GP The theme of the novel seems to be the different treatment that the natural and foster sons get. It's about inequality.

LA That's right. Because Gabriel is a mestizo, he is liable to rejection, while Angel is educated and has the chance to become a professional. In Guatemala the problem is not so much racial discrimination as social and cultural discrimination.

GP You could almost speak of personal discrimination. The characters of your novel reject things for what seem to them to be purely personal reasons.

LA That is the Spanish inheritance. These white minority groups, the *ladinos*, behave as the descendants of the Spanish. Remember that the Spaniards used to be racists: purity of blood was important to them. Think of their persecutions of the Jews and the Arabs. All these attitudes come from a colonial vision of the world.

GP What do you see happening to the indigenous culture?

LA That is something I ask myself all the time. The indigenous people have certain spiritual values that I think are important not only to Guatemala but to the rest of the world. They have a code of ethics that is very admirable. They have a deep sense of honesty. Despite the misery of their conditions, there is a marvellous equilibrium in their world, a wonderful harmony between man and the land and the cosmos. At the same time there are aspects of their culture that we would call backward. I often ask myself how we are going to be able to incorporate ourselves into the modern world. If we don't make the leap soon, it may be too late to integrate the different cultures. The native culture might be destroyed or fossilized. We have to recover our past and make a creative fusion of our country's cultural strands.

Augusto Monterroso

The Cuban writer Alejo Carpentier has described the baroque as not so much a style but an expression of a spirit that crops up again and again in the arts. It is characterized by a tumultuous outpouring of energy, a profusion of forms, and an apparent disorder. In this sense, he argues, the work of the Romantics or the plays of Shakespeare could be called baroque, whereas Cervantes' *Don Quijote* could not. He goes on to suggest that the art of Latin America is baroque, from the sacred book of the Mayans, the *Popol Vuh*, right through to the modern novel.

Carpentier quotes a letter from Hernan Cortés to Charles V in which Cortés claims that he cannot express what he has seen in this new continent because the necessary words don't exist. According to Carpentier this is no mere rhetorical flourish. The role of the writer in Latin America has been to fill up a great linguistic vacuum, giving names, constructing a verbal model of a new cosmopolitan culture that is as complex as a piece of Brazilian rainforest; in this sense the culture itself is also baroque.

Augusto Monterroso is remarkable because he stands totally opposed to the baroque. His work is not tumultuous, replete, forceful or dramatic. He writes fables or parables in which words are trimmed to an expressive minimum and his bemused irony treats culture with the same respect as shears treat a garden hedge.

The status of the author in Latin America as a figure of great social importance owes something to the Romantic notion of the writer as a visionary or seer. Augusto Monterroso portrays the writer in a very deflated state. *Lo demás es silencio* (1978) is a mock biography of an author, written rather in the spirit of

Don Quijote; the protagonist, seen through the eyes of his valet, is of thoroughly pedestrian proportions.

Despite being born in Guatemala, one of Latin America's most strongly indigenous nations, we find not a hint of a temple, a ceremonial mask or a piece of native weaving in Monterroso's stories. He sometimes avoids Latin America entirely, the animals of his fables being usually European or African, inspired by the Greek fabulists and constructors of paradoxes.

When Monterroso does write politically it is with a savagery worthy of Jonathan Swift. His parable 'Mr Taylor' (1959) investigates some of the pitfalls of economic development by tracing the progress of an export trade in nicely folkloric, shrunken human heads; demand is so great and the trade so profitable that soon the nation is without citizens. However, by focusing on the universal foibles of human nature, his stories, until you consider them carefully, often seem to turn their back on their social context. This is part of what makes Augusto Monterroso one of Latin America's most unrepentant iconoclasts.

GP Tell me about your childhood.

AM I came from a middle-class family. I am the grandson of lawyers and generals. My father was a man of letters — something of a journalist and something of a writer. He ran a number of magazines, but we were not very well off because he never made much money out of his work. His magazines always went broke; they were too good. My father moved between the two capital cities of Guatemala and Honduras. I was born in Tegucigalpa, of a Guatemalan father and a Honduran mother. I grew up mostly in Guatemala City.

My family were always involved in the arts, with the theatre, the opera and literature in general. However, I wasn't well educated. I hated school and in fact never finished primary school. I am self-taught, although I did learn a lot at primary school. In Guatemala and Honduras education was very serious and concentrated. The teachers used to care a lot about their students. Looking back now, I see five very good, productive years and I am grateful to the priests for what they taught me about literature.

GP In some interviews you have accused yourself of being lazy. Is that really true?

AM Perhaps not. I am lazy if the activity doesn't interest me. It is necessary to be very lazy if you want to dedicate yourself to literature. If you are a hard-worker, you become a businessman or a sailor or you climb mountains. Lazy people are generally dreamers. You look at the clouds, the sky, the trees, rivers and people because you simply want to look – you don't want to work or study.

GP So were you contemplative even at an early age?

AM More introspective than contemplative. From an early age I was very aware of myself, of what I saw, felt and liked.

GP What did you do when you left school?

AM I went to work in a butcher's shop. My father died when I was young so in my early teens I had to start earning my living. I never actually worked as a butcher, just as an assistant on the meat counter of a general store. On the cover of one of my books that appeared in German, they say that I've been a butcher and a diplomat!

GP Did literature begin as an escape for you? You must have read at night to forget the boredom of the day.

AM I don't know if children get bored. Also, I don't know whether you could say that reading was a form of escape. I am free; literature for me is a search for a way not to be free, to imprison myself. So it is more of a refuge than an escape. If you want to escape you go out into the country, to space and freedom. Literature took me to libraries, which was an escape in reverse.

GP That reminds me of a photographer who once told me that for him the pleasure of photography was that when he put the camera hood over his head and saw the image through the lens, he was in a different world. It is like a refuge from which to look at the world.

AM I like that comparison a lot. When I read I put a hood over my head in order to see the world through the little rectangle of the page. So in this sense you could say that literature was a way of escaping everyday reality.

My parents were very cultured people. There were always a lot of books in the house, and a lot of music. You could say that the family was bohemian: they weren't good writers or singers or artists, but art was something they took very seriously. It was their life. They even died for it, in the sense that they preferred not to do anything else, so their lives were a failure. They spent their time singing operas and operettas, going to bullfights or the theatre.

It was in this bohemian atmosphere that I grew up. It made me what I am and I couldn't be anything different even if I wanted to. When I began working I worked as much as was necessary to survive but my mind was on literature. It's always been like that. I've done many jobs.

GP How did you come to be a diplomat?

AM That is a long story. When I started to write I found friends who were also interested in literature. I was eighteen or nineteen, and after work I would see friends who were students. I wasn't a student, of course, but I read a lot. At that time, in 1944, the law students were beginning to put up some resistance to the dictatorship of the president, Jorge Ubico, whose brutal rule had lasted for fourteen years. As I was a friend of the law students I became a part of the fight against Ubico.

GP That is known as a very bloody battle. A lot of students were killed.

AM That's right; in the end we won, although at the time of the victory I was in Mexico. When Ubico fell in 1944 initially he was replaced by an even more repressive non-revolutionary government. I had started a magazine and as a result I was taken prisoner, together with a friend. We were sent to jail but managed to escape and made our way to the Mexican embassy. We asked for political asylum and the embassy got us out of the country. I have lived in Mexico ever since. It was after I'd come here that the real revolution broke out: people realized that, although Ubico had gone, there was going to be no real change. When the movement led by Jacobo Arbenz became the government it gave me a job in the Guatemalan embassy here in Mexico. Some of my friends returned to Guatemala but I wasn't able to for complicated family reasons. I spent the next nine years working in our embassy in Mexico.

GP So the government followed the long tradition of making its writers into diplomats?

AM Yes, the long Latin American tradition. I don't know if it is good or bad.

GP When you worked as a diplomat did you have problems finding time to write?

AM Nothing has ever stopped me finding time to write. Being a diplomat, in one sense, was a way to support myself. On the other hand, I'd never imagined that I'd work that way. I was only doing it because it seemed a duty, a revolutionary duty. During the nine years I worked in the Mexican embassy my other life went on as normal. I was a writer. I had friends who were writers, some of whom didn't even know that I was a diplomat. Diplomacy didn't mix with writing, though it was a job that I took seriously, especially because of the opposition we were facing from the North American government.

Work did take up my time in 1953 when the US campaign was most intense. I'd been sent to Bolivia as first secretary. It was a very difficult situation because the United States had made up its mind to depose the Guatemalan government and in 1954 the government did fall. The United States gave arms to a group of mercenaries who invaded the country. The Guatemalan army didn't resist them so the government had no way to defend itself. During 1953 and 1954 I was working day and night, fighting the enormous propaganda campaign being mounted by the US.

The accusations that Nicaragua is communist and a possible Soviet base are exactly the same as those made against the Arbenz government in 1954. Lacking imagination, this is the only story the US can come up with to fool people. Neither government wanted to be an enemy of the United States. The only thing they wanted was to change the conditions of hunger and misery that people live in. Any visitor to Central America can easily see what these revolutions are about. They have nothing to do with the Soviet Union.

GP Your story 'Mr Taylor' is a piece of black humour, but it is also an analysis of the economic strategies that have been used in Central America. It's a parable, a way of creating a model for what you saw.

AM The word 'parable' is a good one. I was going to call the story 'The Parable of Mr Taylor'.

GP Your story about the benefit concert given by the president's wife, 'Primera Dama', is another parable, this time dealing with false charity.

AM Yes, these are both stories on political themes. I have political views and I've tried to incorporate them in my writing, though my main aim is always to create a work of literature. I've always tried to avoid using politics as a way to be more widely read.

GP Do you think the writer should be openly involved in political affairs?

AM I have friends who write and also have a high political profile. They are very sincere and are quite within their rights to behave in this way. In my case I've had scruples about embracing a cause and gaining some of the popularity that goes with that. However, in my personal life I've always taken a political stand. My position has always been very clear. When I have the chance to speak outside the field of literature I do so.

GP So writing and taking political action are always separate for you?

AM When a political theme can be treated in a literary way, I think I have tried to do this. I was once asked in an interview whether I participated in politics through my literature. I answered that when I write I'm always making calls to rebellion or revolution but I do it in such a subtle way that my readers generally become reactionaries!

GP Haven't you also said that when you write a funny story your readers take you seriously, or you write a serious one and your readers think it's funny? I suppose when you use black humour this is a risk you take.

AM Yes, it's not just a political matter. It has to do with the vision people have of the world. Some critics consider me a pessimist and I think they are probably right.

GP Because of what you've seen?

AM Because man is very stupid. Man, frankly, is a pain. Human beings are generally disappointing. History shows that.

GP Jung said that we'd never see an end to war because war is part of the human make-up.

AM It is horrible to think that – that there might be a biological element in this repetition of wars and destruction. Perhaps it's not true. We may be able to overcome these tendencies.

GP You've said that, for you, literature is to a great extent a game. What sort of game is it?

AM You could say that war is a game. It is brutal and terrible but a game nevertheless. Everything can be a game. I don't have any personal definition of literature in this respect. If I said that, it was because of the context I was in. When someone wants me to take literature very seriously, because literature is going to change the world or change man, then I suggest considering literature a game. It is a fine and serious game, a beautiful game, but I don't want it to be useful. That is the real question. I say it's a game because I don't think literature ought to be considered socially useful. It is true that literature *can* be useful. It can be put at the service of many things, it can be used as propaganda.

GP Is it that you are against solemnity: you don't want to be solemn about literature?

AM No, that's not it. I just don't think literature ought to have to serve a cause. Still, this is a very vague area. If there's a cause that interests me, I might put what I write at its service.

GP In the English-speaking world the idea of a writer becoming a hero through espousing some cause seems very improbable, whereas here writing is such a political thing. In

Latin America writers are often considered good or bad not for literary reasons but because of their politics.

AM The situation here is very different compared to the US or England. Latin American writers respond to what they see around them and what they see is generally very sad. They can't avoid taking sides. In England that may not be so necessary, nor in the US, although socially the United States is a very backward country. There is a lot of misery. Writers there ought to pay more attention to it. They ought to be almost like Latin American writers because the United States is a country of great contrasts, just as Latin American nations are.

England is another matter, though it too has its contrasts. Its history means that things are different. You may be a conservative, like Chesterton, or a socialist, like Bernard Shaw, but for reasons that are much less clear than they are here. In Latin America writers go out on to the street and what they see makes them feel ashamed. In the countryside it's even worse. That is why so many of us become political figures. Of course not all writers are clear about the changes that have to be made. Some want us to be democracies but their only definition of a democracy is a country where there are elections. Some of us disagree with that. We want to see much deeper changes than instituting elections every few years. That way you might make the necessary changes within two thousand years.

When the Latin American nations became independent they modelled their constitutions on those of countries like the United States. They thought that this would automatically bring social change, that you could decree it. In 1821 we had a congress, a judicial and executive arm of government, and a separate press. There were four separate powers, just as there are in the United States, but this has never worked. According to our constitutions we are all democratic countries and, above all, liberal democracies.

GP But behind the formal façade there is an older, colonial system with an oligarchy, usually in league with the army, working against change that it finds disagreeable.

AM Yes. That means there is terrible inequality among the

citizens of Latin America, even though in the eyes of our constitutions we are equal.

GP Borges said that he sometimes carried stories with him for a long time before writing them down. He'd tell stories to friends as a way of trying them out. Do you do anything like that?

AM No, not at all. I never talk about what I'm working on.

GP But do you work on stories over a long period of time?

AM Yes, I work very slowly and with a lot of patience. Everyone has their own internal rhythm and scope. I work slowly, so I would never set out to write a 600-page novel. Still, I don't say to myself that I am going to write a very short story and write it very slowly. It just comes out that way. I write the way I can. By tradition fables tend to be short, so I have to concentrate what I want to say.

GP You touched on this matter in your story 'Leopoldo (sus trabajos)', about the writer trying to write a story about dogs. He spends months in the library reading everything he can about them, which is clearly futile because almost all the information would be useless for a fable.

AM Completely useless – it would be useless for any writing that wasn't historical or scientific. The only thing you need in writing a fable is a clear idea of some point of human behaviour. Fables are generally about human errors or weaknesses and it is a matter of finding an animal to attribute them to. Still, I haven't really worked much in this way. For one thing my intention is not a moral one. I point things out rather than draw morals.

GP Your work isn't traditional but *Lo demás es silencio* struck me as a reworking of *Don Quijote* in a different context.

AM Well, you are the first person to notice that. There may be parallels between the heroes of the two novels. My protagonist, Eduardo Torres, is an elderly man who is poorly equipped for what he wants to do, for what he dreams of doing. He throws himself into it, colliding with all sorts of things and people on his way, but he always fails because his capabilities aren't what he thinks they are. He always runs up against a reality that defeats him, but he never realizes this and keeps on writing against customs or what he considers bad in literature, trying to teach others what he doesn't know himself.

GP And as in *Don Quijote*, the errors are always humourous. When he writes a criticism of *Don Quijote* another critic criticizes him, noting various errors in his text.

AM Yes, the protagonist is trying to do battle with the other critics, the other interpreters who also consider themselves knight-errants of literature and who need to reform or explain the world. Eduardo Torres is against them. He is against the great false figures who are constantly explaining literature.

GP There is another parallel, in that the theme is honour, or honour in the sense of fame.

AM Yes, Eduardo Torres seeks fame and honour. He wants to reform society through pure and elevated behaviour. But finally, only his wife manages to understand him, to have an idea of him through her love; and even she doesn't understand him enough to agree with him in his fight. Rather, she considers him a weak man who needs to be helped.

These parallels do exist but they are very vague. I was trying to write the life of a provincial teacher who was poorly equipped for the task he had set himself. The people around him don't understand him very much and in the book we never find out if he's crazy, silly, intelligent or a joker, because the narrator never gives you any facts other than those provided by those who know him. At times the protagonist appears as they see him, at times as he sees himself, and at others as he really is. That's what makes the character complex; he hasn't been very well read. The critics haven't paid much attention to the book, probably with good reason.

GP I don't agree. I suspect that if you write a book in a joking spirit you run the risk of critics not considering it a serious work.

AM Yes. They don't take it seriously because they think it's all a joke, but in fact my intention was quite serious: I just haven't managed to get them to notice it! I suppose posterity will do me justice. In general my books don't reach a wide public. They are not for many people.

GP But they have been widely translated.

AM Yes, they've been translated into many languages, but their fate is always the same. They only reach certain groups of people, their reputation is probably spread by word of mouth. I think there are books for a wide public, books for a reasonable public and others for a very small one. I write for a very small public: I know that and don't complain.

MEXICO

.

Elena Poniatowska

Mexico has been one of the most culturally influential nations in Latin America, partly because the Mexican revolution was followed by a cultural nationalism that inspired many of its neighbours. Mexico City has been an artistic metropolis, a refuge for exiles not only from Latin America but also from Europe, notably Spain. Mexican writers have maintained an ambivalent stance towards European culture, adapting the techniques of the modern novel in a self-conscious search for a specifically Mexican point of view – an appropriate aim for a nation with a large indigenous population.

Mexico's government might best be described as a kind of benevolent authoritarianism, though that benevolence is tempered by the demands of various sectional interests. Though the country has elections every few years, it is effectively a one-party state dominated by the PRI, or Party of Institutionalized Revolution. At times the authoritarian regime has shown a much uglier face, as in 1968, when government troops opened fire on demonstrators, killing thousands. This is documented in Elena Poniatowska's *Massacre in Mexico* (1971). Written as an oral history that patches together accounts of that night, it poses many difficult questions for the PRI. *Fuerte es el silencio* (1980) is a later, similar project, based on the accounts of mothers of political prisoners. The thrust of effective reform in Mexico has always come from above and Poniatowska's documentary work is a way of giving voice to grievances from below.

Poniatowska also writes fiction. *La 'flor de lis'* (1988) is similar to Lygia Fagundes Telles' *The Marble Dance*, in that it is written from the point of view of an insecure young girl, troubled by sexuality. It deals with the relationship between European and Mexican culture, and expresses feminist concern at the destructive qualities of male charisma.

Dear Diego (1978) is a novel written in the form of letters from an abandoned mistress of Diego Rivera who gradually reconciles herself to the fact he won't be returning. Far from being maudlin, *Dear Diego* is a revealing and thought-provoking novel, thanks to Poniatowska's mental toughness and resistance to any sort of sentimentality. Once again there is a feminist angle: the heroine seems to have been crushed by some of the very qualities that made Rivera such a great artist.

Until We Meet Again (1969) explores the border between fiction and non-fiction. It is based on the account of a *campesina* and, in a rather picaresque way, traces her life of misadventure. Poniatowska does not see the life of the poor as sustained by myths or the sense of ethnic dignity, evident in the work of Manlio Argueta; that has been lost through acculturation. Though the dramas that unfold sometimes have a biblical resonance, as when a group of brothers gang up to gain vengeance on a favoured son, there is no God or omniscient narrator to right wrongs. The only real hope is offered by the heroine's resolute character and strength of will. She battles against the odds, and the reader's interest is sustained by the fascinating, apparently truthful view of an unknown and remarkable world.

GP When you write fiction is it completely different to writing non-fiction?

EP Yes. For me, there is an absolute distinction between the two forms.

GP So how would you classify *Until We Meet Again*?

EP It was based on facts that I learnt during a series of interviews with a *campesina*, but at the same time it is fiction, because I wrote the facts up the way I wanted to. When the *campesina* read the novel she complained that it had nothing to do with her real life and that I'd invented a lot. She was right.

I made things up whenever it served my purposes. I didn't write the novel as an anthropological study. Of course it might have been interesting to do what Elizabeth Debray-Burgos did when she spoke to the Guatemalan woman Rigoberta Menchu, but that was a different kind of work, faithful to the tape recordings they made in Paris.

GP When you wrote *Dear Diego*, had you had access to the real letters written to Diego Rivera?

EP No. I was reading *The Fabulous Life of Diego Rivera* and when I reached the chapter dedicated to Angelina Beloff I identified very much with her. I felt that her story had something to do with me and I wrote the book based on what I read in this chapter. Her letters were later published, but I hadn't read them at the time.

GP Is your novel *La 'flor de lis'* autobiographical?

EP The book does have autobiographical elements. I was born in France. I came here when I was very young. Later, I spent two years at a convent school in Philadelphia. Unfortunately, my education was not a good one so I am more or less self-taught. I think all literature is autobiographical. Carlos Fuentes' *A Change of Skin*, for example, is an autobiographical novel. One of the characters is a self-portrait. What you write is always based on reality.

GP *La 'flor de lis'* is about a clash of cultures: the culture of the United States, of France and of Mexico. They have influenced the main character and so she doesn't know where she belongs. Did you feel that?

EP Of course. There is also the issue of social class. At a certain social level you live in the same way whether you are in Paris, New York or Mexico – you may be in Chiapas or in Egypt but if you are staying in a certain kind of hotel, you are in the United States. Some classes have an international notion of how to live that has nothing to do with where they live. That's part of the novel too: fundamentally, money has no national loyalties. How can you love a country if what you really love is money?

GP So how can the Mexican upper class be nationalistic?

EP The upper class is never nationalistic, not in any country. They may be a little more nationalistic in the US than they are here, but that's because the US government is always very responsive to the needs of the rich. In Mexico the upper class keeps all its money abroad, generally in the United States. In San Diego there's a building called the Taco Tower, owned entirely by Mexicans. San Antonio and Houston are full of rich Mexicans. Latin America is invading the United States – not just the poor from the rest of the continent who use Mexico as a corridor, but also the rich. The reason in both cases is financial. Of course, there have always been a lot of Mexicans in the United States. As you know, half of what was once our national territory was either taken by the US army or sold by Mexico's dictator Santa Anna.

GP There are still strong class divisions in Mexico, aren't there?

EP The poor are the slaves of the rich. The most the poor can hope for is a form of paternalism and that is what Mexico usually offers. The government is a superior, paternalist one that still takes advantage of the poor; that's because in Mexico a government post is usually seen as a means of personal enrichment. Almost without exception, people leave office having made themselves wealthier. On the corner here there are two trucks belonging to the police. They are parked outside the house of the head of the senate. He's been renovating the house and all the materials have been transported in government vehicles. That is the way Mexico works: power is the source of all privileges. Obviously the politicians don't consider their actions corrupt, because they are the beneficiaries.

GP The main character in *La 'flor de lis'*, being a member of the upper class, has been forced to repress or oppress herself. When her instincts are freed she seems to undergo a sort of social liberation.

EP All social classes have their own forms of repression. How to dress, how to brush your hair, what is good or bad taste – these are the things that the upper class imposes on you. The bourgeoisie have their own set of rules. They tell you who you should marry to climb the social ladder. Even the so-called liberated sectors of society live with repression. If you go to a meeting of the Communist Party, for example, you'll see that the women do the same things they do at home. Due to either custom or inertia, they are the ones who prepare the coffee, make the cakes and sandwiches, and play only a small part in the discussions. The party leaders find it completely natural to say to the women, 'Comrade, where are the *tacos*? Would you mind bringing me one?' As usual, the women are relegated to the secondary jobs, the ones they've been doing for the last thousand years. Why? Because customs are very hard to break and, whether you look at the Communist Party or the Socialist Party or the PRI, you'll find that machismo rules. Mexico is a man's country.

GP But what you are saying is true of all societies, with the possible exception of a few tribes that are matriarchal.

EP To an extent, but when I visited Australia, for example, I felt that women there had greater freedom than in many other countries. They have many more opportunities. I was very surprised, shocked even, because I come from a country where women are always forgotten about. I thought there was great sexual liberty; I'd never seen a demonstration where the women could walk through the streets shouting, 'We demand an orgasm.' Sexual pleasure, of whatever kind, is possible for them. Women can do whatever they want with their bodies because it is all legal, from a very early age. Having or not having sex isn't their parents' decision. There are refuges, run by women, for the victims of wife-beating. There's nothing like that in Mexico.

In the United States, too, you now have banks run entirely by women, whereas in Mexico many middle-class women are not even allowed a cheque book. I remember asking the wife of President Díaz Ordaz what she did besides being wife to the president. She said, 'Well, twenty minutes after Gustavo leaves, I leave too. Half an hour before he returns, I'm there waiting, so that I am ready to look after him when he arrives.' She was at the service of her husband.

GP In your novel *Dear Diego*, Diego Rivera appears to be, if not exactly a demon, almost a supernatural force. Your heroine, on the other hand, seems to be very weak, perhaps because she lacks confidence. She finds it difficult to commit herself fully to her work. She says that before, when she saw a child in the street she'd start thinking how to draw it; now when she sees a child she can only think of the child she lost and still wants. Rivera, on other hand, has no difficulty in leaving children or women and setting himself to work again. Would you say that women tend to have greater problems in committing themselves to art?

EP Yes, you've put it very well. You've almost answered the question. Women are the ones who give birth. The great majority of women wish to have a child. They want the experience of maternity, of conceiving, of being pregnant and of giving birth. These are feelings that a man never has – or at least I've never met a man who has said to me, 'I'd like my belly to swell up and my breasts to fill with milk.'

Women have been used to the idea that maternity is the most important thing in their lives. Only now are some women willing to give it up, although, even in Mexico, a great many single women decide that, husband or no husband, they want a child. There are also a great many rapes, because men feel, deep down, that they are doing the woman a favour: at least a raped woman won't pass on to the next world as a virgin. According to men, the experience of penetration is almost as important for women as the experience of maternity.

That is one side of things. The other is that women's lack of security is something real, even for women who are very successful. Think of Frida Kahlo, for example. She tried to become pregnant many times, not simply because she wanted a child, but because she wanted to show that, despite her physical limitations, she could be a mother. She also saw it as a way of keeping Diego Rivera. In Mexico women who had no children were called 'mules'. Until recently, being called a mule was a serious insult. Not being in love with a man meant being condemned.

It was very serious for a woman to step outside the norms of social behaviour in other ways too. Her position was extremely precarious. Life can be especially difficult for a woman who wants to be an artist. If you make a list of Latin American women who have achieved something, you will find two types: spinsters or suicides. That goes right back to the seventeenth century and Sister Iñes de la Cruz, who had to retire to a convent in order to be able to write. There is Alfonsina Storni, the poet who walked into the sea and drowned herself. Antonietta Rivas Mercado shot herself in front of Nôtre-Dame cathedral in Paris. Violeta Parra was another suicide. The number of women who have committed suicide is enormous. Clarice Lispector, the Brazilian writer, suffered from terrible fits of depression, partly due to her extreme sensitivity, but also partly due to the female writer's lack of support. She killed herself too.

Women writers have to fulfil two roles, that of a mother and that of a writer. Still, at least being a writer is seen as a decent and proper profession. A woman who writes does so from her home. In Latin America it's not considered decent for a woman to be a dancer.

GP So the problems are partly social and partly biological in origin?

EP Yes. It's always been that way, and not just in Mexico. Think of Virginia Woolf, who also committed suicide, or the plight of the Brontë sisters. The fate of a woman who wants to step outside the norms of behaviour is almost always tragic.

GP Arrogance is a quality that comes much more easily to men than women; given that writing is a solitary and vulnerable activity, I suspect that a degree of arrogance is necessary for writers if they are to survive.

EP That's interesting. Thinking of the Mexican women writers I've known, Rosario Castellanos — who is dead now and in a sense could be classified amongst those who committed suicide — was never arrogant. Elena Garro, the first wife of Octavio Paz, was never arrogant either. You could say that both of them were a little emotionally disturbed, but never arrogant. Carlos Fuentes, however, is arrogant. Mario Vargas Llosa is arrogant, when he wants to be. Paz himself is arrogant. Why? Because he has the capability to be that way; it's not difficult for him.

Women aren't arrogant because they don't have faith in themselves. They always keep a low profile, which is what they have been brought up to do. They are frightened even by the goals that they set themselves and that marks their work.

GP When I was reading your work I failed to find qualities that could be called exclusively feminine. I could only come up with qualities like 'clarity' or 'intelligence'. I wondered to what extend the conception of women as being closer to the magical and intuitive side of things might not be just another male myth. Foucault argues that the legend of women as witches arose in the Middle Ages when doctors started a scare campaign against old women who were operating as midwives in competition with them. Old women were being defamed and drowned as part of an industrial demarcation dispute. Would you say that there is a literary style that is exclusively feminine? Do women have qualities that men lack and which can be expressed in literature?

EP It may be that women, being more visionary than men, can create new forms of literature. At the moment in both literature and politics women follow the same models as men do in order to be accepted. If you think of women who have gained power, like Indira Ghandi, Golda Meir or Margaret Thatcher, you'll find that by the time they reach office they are more masculine than men. They are men with skirts. In their political decisions, in their vision of the world, and in the way they run their countries, they don't act like women. Their politics is one of competition and dominance, just like the politics of any other head of state.

In the field of literature, although there have been great women writers, they have tended to adopt the models used by men. A few women have escaped this by writing books as a kind of confession or as self-justification. But, as for writing a great book based on a woman's visionary abilities, her intuition, and using a language that comes from these visionary capacities, I don't think that has ever been done. Women like Marguerite Yourcenar and Susan Sontag have written works of great erudition and creativity, yet you couldn't say that Marguerite Yourcenar is very interested in feminine intuition. Nor is she very interested in writing about herself; she is more interested in male characters. Susan Sontag has written as an intellectual, absorbed in whatever subject interested her.

GP So the language of literature remains monolithic: it can't be divided into male and female categories?

EP Certainly not on the basis of the literature that's been written up to now. We have to see if woman can transform her intuition and her nature into a new language. Perhaps you can see something like that happening in the cinema. Films by Margarethe Von Trotta portray aspects that you don't really see in the novel, like the relation of women to women, or the relation of women to power. In *Two Sisters*, for example, the relation between the two women is something new.

GP That's on the level of content, but I wonder if a clear distinction between writing by women and writing by men is possible on a formal level, because, as Lygia Fagundes Telles suggested to me, women have some masculine qualities and men have feminine ones.

EP I think that's true. We all have both masculine and feminine qualities. Even though I am a fragile woman, I feel I have many masculine characteristics, even to the extent that I sometimes feel I look at a woman the way a man does. I have the capacity to feel affection towards women or to love them like a man. I don't mean that I'm a lesbian, but I've always had a great sympathy for women and a great interest in them. That includes being interested in their bodies. I'll turn around in the street to watch a woman, to see the way she is, to look at her legs, her thighs, her shoulders. I look at men too, but not only at men.

GP But isn't this a fairly general trait among women? After all, women's magazines are full of pictures of beautiful women.

EP I'm not interested in the beauty portrayed in women's

magazines. I make my own choices. Beauty is a personal thing as far as I'm concerned. It can be a matter of a face that takes my attention. I remember my husband once saying to me that I was a billy-goat, and he wasn't really joking. I don't believe these theories about an exclusively female or male literature. I'm male or female when I want to be.

GP In your novel La 'flor de lis' Mariana thinks of her mother as a goddess. Her mother is almost poetic. She is elegant, something to imitate, but more than that, a person loved not only as a mother but as a woman. Is that the feeling you're talking about?

EP Yes, it is more or less the same thing.

GP How much has Mexico changed since you wrote Massacre in Mexico and Fuerte es el silencio? In those books you paint a picture of a very oppressive country. Mexico, at least to a visitor like myself, doesn't seem quite that bad today – and you have been able to publish these books, which are very severe criticisms.

EP I never said that the Mexican system is dictatorial. It's not like many other Latin American countries. It's oppressive because of the misery that people have to suffer here. It's oppressive because power is so hierarchical, yet it isn't absolutely oppressive. Of course, I say that sitting here, drinking tea in a house that is luxurious by Mexican standards. If you go elsewhere in the city and do a different kind of interview, you'll see just how oppressive society is for some people.

GP When I was speaking to Luis Arango, a Guatemalan writer, he mentioned a number of writers who had been shot in the street. Mexico is nothing like that.

EP No, compared to Guatemala or El Salvador, Mexico is paradise. The security services continue to operate clandestinely, but I don't think there would ever be another massacre, as in 1968. Even though they managed to keep the scale of the killings a secret in Mexico, photographs and film of what happened appeared everywhere else in the world. The photographs prompted Octavio Paz to resign from his post at the Mexican Embassy in India. I don't think the government would use a degree of repression that would lead to it being branded as fascist by the rest of the world.

GP In *Fuerte es el silencio* you speak to a group of women who have staged a sit-in in the cathedral to protest at the disappearance of their children. That was in the 1970s. Are people still disappearing?

EP President Miguel de la Madrid says that he inherited the list of the disappeared from the previous administration. Lopez Portillo blamed the president who came before him. A group from Amnesty International came to Mexico but got a very poor reception from the government, who claimed that there were no political prisoners or disappearances in Mexico. It has to be admitted that the last writer or intellectual to be taken prisoner because of his ideas was José Revueltas in 1968.

GP I find it hard not to be optimistic, despite the negative aspects of the country.

EP Mexico is a great centre of energy. Mexico City compares favourably with the very uniform cities you find in the United States. Though US cities have a high standard of living, there is no feeling of things being on the boil, which is something you always sense in Mexico. If you open the cultural pages in our newspapers, you see so many new things being tried. There are many failures, of course, but at least there are attempts. Mexico has a level of popular culture that is unknown even in a country like France. Technologically we may be backward, but we are in no way backward in our creative capacities.

GP That is certainly very clear in Mexican painting. Visiting the Palacio Nacional or the Palacio de Bellas Artes I felt dwarfed by the scale and energy of the work.

EP Mexico is a monumental country. It's a country of great, open spaces, of mountains and deserts. It is not like the small countries of Europe, and it has a tremendous capacity to transform misery.

Octavio Paz

Octavio Paz is among the greatest of Latin American poets. He is also one of the continent's most acute and controversial commentators on matters literary, social and political. The breadth of his interests, the scope and quality of his extraordinarily prolific writing, make him hard to define.

In his critical work *The Bow and the Lyre* (1956) Paz advocates an exalted notion of poetry, separating it from other types of discourse and arguing that it is prior to, not a result of, social and historical factors. Time spent in the United States provided material for contrasts in *The Labyrinth of Solitude* (1950), a meditation on the Mexican character noted for its compelling prose, written with the imaginative freedom of poetry. A stay in India not only influenced his poetry but resulted in another piece of imaginative, critical prose: *The Monkey Grammarian* (1974) is an exploration of the themes of language and poetic meaning that anticipates some of the conclusions of postmodern literary criticism.

Poetic influences in English include Ezra Pound's early style of terse, visually brilliant poetry. The poems of Octavio Paz carry this same energy. They please in the way that a painting, often a surrealist painting, pleases. Paz seems to have taken the surrealist aesthetic to heart; the striking, the illogical and the marvellous are beautiful. He finds arresting images that may spark a sense of awe and wonder, but whereas the surrealists drew inspiration from the freaks of the unconscious, Paz has a keen eye for his surroundings. A strong sense of Mexico and its landscape is always present in his poems.

A reading of modern philosophy has also been very import-

ant in Paz's work. He captures the moments when nature itself
seems to be conspiring to speak, yet he is acutely aware of the
way nature and everything else is constituted through language
and desire. Central to his poetry is the interplay of these two
opposing perceptions. His landscape breathes animism and even
when the poetry is strongly political, as in collections like *Vuelta*
(1976), the spiritual element is always dominant.

Octavio Paz, still the most stimulating of writers, spends
most of the year in Mexico City, where he continues to work.

GP In *The Bow and the Lyre* you wrote that Heidegger, Witt-
genstein and Lévi-Strauss conceive of reality as a network of
meanings, the last term of which is unsayable. What does this
imply for the poet?

OP The idea that zones of reality are inexpressible in rational
terms is not a new one for poets. All artists work to explore
and find expression for these areas.

GP Haven't you also described reality as being an invisible
network of relations that is never, in any way, sayable?

OP No, it is sayable − through allegory or analogy, for
instance, through images of all kinds. I am neither a philosopher
nor a scientist, but it seems to me that the great problem for
contemporary scientists is the breaking of the relation, or what
the physicists would call the complementarity, between the
universe on the large and the small scale: the gap between
quantum and macrocosmic physics. The old hierarchy, what
used to be called the 'great chain of being', stretching from the
inanimate world through the animal kingdom to the spiritual
life has also been broken. There is great uncertainty now but
uncertainty is something the poet has always thrived on.

GP I hadn't realized you were interested in the sciences.

OP I think the scientists are the ones asking the really important questions. When you read the modern philosophers, the
phenomenologists or the analytical philosophers for example,
you are drawn into a kind of solipsism that fails to confront
the fundamental issues. The philosophy of language touches on
none of the great themes that have led us to re-assess ourselves

and our values, while the existentialists leave you in a street with no exit. However, when I read Stephen Hawkings' *A Brief History of Time* I had the feeling of being involved in a dialogue with one of the great pre-Socratic philosophers who tell us of the beginning and end of the world.

GP Bertrand Russell wrote that over the centuries the ground covered by philosophy has become narrower and narrower.

OP Narrower, and less interesting, as the sciences have gradually taken over the area that belonged to the ancient philosophers.

GP I was very struck by these lines of your poetry: 'Unknowing I understand/ I too am written,/ and at this very moment/ someone spells me out.' Without asking you to interpret your own work, but speaking as a social critic, what would you say are the most important forces that spell us out?

OP When I said that someone was spelling me out I was thinking, in the first place, of the fraternity of life. I'd come across a poem by Ptolemy, the ancient Greek philosopher, or rather scientist. He wrote that he'd seen a star and the sight of the star had confirmed his belief in the immortality of the soul. I may not agree with him on that, but I believe there is a fraternity of life that carries on, with or without the individual. The star is a kind of writing in the sky that I try to decipher. I don't understand it, of course. If I did, I would be God. Still, I try to spell it out and at the same time someone else is doing the same thing, whether on this planet or on another. The poem is really about the brotherhood of man and a kind of communion with everything living.

GP I'd been reading *The Bow and the Lyre* and so interpreted the poem in a different way. I thought you were implying that we were spelt out by religion, by social forces, by the state and by history.

OP That is one interpretation, though not what I had in mind. I was thinking of a much older and simpler idea, based on a feeling of being in communication. I see the star, and someone is there, trying to decipher me, probably without success. I don't understand the star but there is a kind of call and answer; that is part of the network of relations you were referring to.

GP So your critical and poetic preoccupations are different?

OP That is true for everyone. I'd say the deeper concern is the poetic one, which is instinctive and expresses itself more completely. Ideas are forgotten more quickly than the fundamental attitudes that come out through poetry. It is Dante's poetry that people remember, not his philosophy or his political ideas. Who cares now if he was a Guelph or a Ghibelline?

GP You wrote in another poem 'Tomorrow it will be necessary to re-invent the reality of this world.' Is this need to constantly remake ourselves a counterweight to those forces that spell us out?

OP No, not at all. I was talking about the way the world can appear unreal. The poem is about the beginning of a new year, when the Aztecs believed that time would finish and the world would begin again. Really, the world is born every day, with or without us, of course, but we do collaborate in its reinvention by watching, deciphering and speaking. We are the invention of the sun just as, every day, we invent the sun as we perceive it.

GP In the same poem you speak of going from a visual reality to a deeper one, which puts you in a philosophical line . . .

OP No, don't ask me philosophical questions. Linguistic ones would be better. The lines you quoted are fine if they have the right number of syllables and express the feeling I have of rebirth.

GP But I feel your philosophical reading is very evident in your poetry.

OP Possibly, but all poets have been similarly influenced. It is true that the poets I've taken as models have been thinkers and have wanted to find a certain unity of thought and feeling. That is why T. S. Eliot interested me, for instance, or Antonio Machado. Still, I have great admiration for very instinctive poets such as Pablo Neruda.

GP In your critical works you've written a great deal about language as a system of metaphors. However, metaphor is only one kind of symbol. You don't use allegory very much in your poetry. Why is that?

OP Allegory is the only kind of symbolism I tend not to use, though I have resorted to it occasionally. Allegory belongs to another age. To use it you need to have the kind of ideas they had in the Middle Ages.

GP You have said that the act of writing is like throwing yourself into an abyss.

OP I'd say that all writers feel this way when they sit down at the table. Being faced with a blank page is a terrible experience. It is almost like facing up to death.

GP Perhaps in other times writers could use allegory because they didn't have to face up to this complete emptiness. They already had a system of symbols given, such as that provided by the 'great chain of being'.

OP Which we don't have now. When Dante wrote allegorically he had the sacred scriptures to stand as a book behind his book. When the poet reaches heaven in the *Divine Comedy* the divinity speaks to him of a great book, the kind of book we no longer possess. We are without a key or a code of meanings. When you look at the modern novel you find not allegory but irony. Instead of Dante's regularity you find a humour and irregularity that breaks down analogies. As Baudelaire said, the beauty of ancient times is an allegorical beauty made up of correspondences, while modern beauty is one of rupture and irregularity. Irony is a way to name death or emptiness.

GP Your poems have translated very well, haven't they?

OP I've had excellent translators. Eliot Weinberger, and the English poet Charles Tomlinson, among others.

GP Does the success also have something to do with the nature of the poems, which are often like chains of images? Image and concept translate well.

OP That is possible, though there is always a verbal element that doesn't appear in the translations: rhyme, alliteration and any play on words is naturally lost. The translation of a poem is like a black and white reproduction of a painting.

GP In a sense your poetry has a photographic aspect anyway. Reading one of your poems is like walking through an exhibition of photographs.

OP That's interesting, because it would mean I've succeeded in being concrete. The important thing, as Ezra Pound saw, is for the poet to write strikingly and concretely, presenting not ideas but images, visions and moments.

GP Pound had difficulty in writing at length. For my taste, his best poems are his short ones.

OP I agree. The *Cantos* are a bit of a disaster, though they are rescued by some wonderful moments. The great modern poems in English are *The Waste Land* and *Four Quartets*, don't you think?

GP Yes. Perhaps Pound was hindered by his unwillingness to use the techniques that usually make a long poem possible, such as narrative or allegory. Would you have difficulty in writing an extremely long poem for the same reason?

OP I have written relatively long poems, such as *Pasado en claro*, which is 600 lines long. It came out in an unplanned way. It has a little narrative − broken narrative but narrative nevertheless. One of the most important characteristics of modern poetry is the attempt to write the long poem, not only in English but in Spanish and French.

GP In *Four Quartets* Eliot permits himself the use of argument and logic, rather as the metaphysical poets did. You use the same resource at times.

OP Yes, though whereas Eliot borrowed from the metaphysical poets, I looked to the Spanish baroque poets.

GP You've said that the language of poetry is closer than prose to our everyday speech.

OP I feel that what we call prose is a late genre. It was born with history and philosophy. The first philosophical and religious texts are in verse. That wasn't only because it made them easier to remember but because verse was closer to natural language. Prose is rational; it is the language of philosophy, history and the sciences, which are abstract; poetry is concrete. It is interesting that the most characteristic modern genre, the novel, participates in the language of both poetry and history. The novel is a hybrid genre, as is the essay.

GP You have described the poem as self-sufficient and circular, while the artificial character of prose is demonstrated each time prose writers abandon the natural flow of their language. You expounded this view in 1956, about ten years before the publication of *One Hundred Years of Solitude*, a novel which is mythical, circular, self-sufficient and written in the language of everyday life, being modelled on the speech of the author's grandmother – all the qualities you value in poetry. How do you see the progress of the Latin American novel over the last thirty years?

OP That is a difficult question. Coming from an earlier generation, my primary interest has been poetry, which in many ways prepared the way for the novel. There were the great poets, such as Rubén Darío, Vicente Huidobro, and so on. Then there was the most famous prose writer of our language, Jorge Luis Borges, who was really a poet. His prose owes a lot to symbolist poetry and to his sense of the fantastic. Then you have the great power of myth and realism used together in the Latin American novel, which constitutes, I think, one of the most important developments in contemporary fiction. At the moment they seem to have taken this line as far as they can. It is necessary to explore other paths now, as Vargas Llosa is doing in some of his recent novels.

GP The labyrinth has been a very important motif, not only for Borges but for you as well. Why does it hold such fascination for Latin American writers?

OP The labyrinth is an emblem for human consciousness. We are all born enclosed in a bewildering network of relations. The labyrinth is the form in which the enigma of existence presents itself. For Latin Americans it has not only a psychological but a historical dimension, because we are from countries that have not yet managed to decipher their own features. You Australians must find yourselves in the same situation. In one sense we are a product of Europe and in another we are clearly not. In Mexico the contrasts are very clear, while I suppose Australia would be closer to Argentina, where the differences are not so pronounced. Borges fell in love with the south of the United States because he saw a reflection of European Argentina, above all in Texas. There was the physical similarity of the plains and the same evident problem: how to create a civilization that has its root in European culture but which must inevitably be different.

In Mexico the matter is much more complicated. It is a country of mountains and valleys, with many ancient civilizations and different races. When the Spanish arrived Mexico was a Babel, full of different gods and languages. The Spanish only added to the complexity, so in Mexico this human enigma is much more mystifying.

GP The labyrinth is the baroque symbol *par excellence*, isn't it?

OP Yes, and of course the seventeenth century, the century of baroque art, is the century of labyrinths.

GP Two important aspects of the Latin American labyrinth are cruelty (which fits in well with the minotaur who lurked in the classical labyrinth, waiting to kill those who entered), and solitude.

OP The interesting question is whether we ourselves aren't the minotaurs. We are not just the victims. That is a question for Mexico, when you think of our civil wars and the oppression we have sometimes inflicted on ourselves.

GP In the first essay of *The Labyrinth of Solitude* you describe Mexicans as alienated and dismayed in the face of their natural surroundings. In one paragraph you suggest that solitude is the reason Mexicans are the way they are, the reason the Mexican cries out or keeps silent, fights or prays or sleeps for a hundred years. I wondered whether the title of *One Hundred Years of Solitude* is a reference to this paragraph. You speak of a race closed in on itself, alienated, which is one of the principle themes of the novel.

OP I wouldn't want to comment on that interpretation, but

if it were true, it would be another example of the way literature is a network of relations.

GP You've said a number of times that you don't see yourself as a Mexican writer, in that you write for everyone. To what extent has Mexico's past, with its indigenous civilizations, influenced you?

OP It has been very influential. I do aspire to write for everyone, but of course I am a Mexican, and more and more I realize how important that has been.

GP You've written of Marxism as a philosophy that sees time as linear, dialectical and heading towards a goal. In meso-America the notion of time has been quite different. For example, the Mayans saw time as going in great cycles, with periodic deluges where the world was destroyed and remade, and in modern Latin American literature time is often cyclical.

OP I don't know if time is cyclical or unrepeatable. Being a modern man, I'd say it is unrepeatable (though having read *A Brief History of Time* I couldn't be sure about that). But what I find really interesting is the instant. Though the instant is unrepeatable, there is a sense in which all instants reproduce the instant. For example, all men have felt the sensation of waking in the morning. They have all felt erotic passion. They have felt awe in the face of nature. This has been true from primitive to modern times. So while the instant never repeats itself, at the same time it is always repeating itself.

GP When André Breton came to Mexico he said that Mexico didn't need a surrealist movement because it was already surreal. Your anecdote of a man emptying his pistol into the head of a compatriot who complained of a headache makes me see what Breton meant. Would you say that Mexico is surreal?

OP No, not particularly, though there are certain things you could call surreal: Mexican humour, for example, and fantasy; but these are elements that you could find in all cultures.

GP A line like 'Time, stretched out to dry on the rooftops' implies that your notion of beauty has been strongly influenced by the surrealists.

OP Yes, but for me they were more of a moral than an aesthetic influence. I found all my repugnance for the modern world there in the surrealist poets.

GP That repugnance has surfaced in your political and social criticism. How do you feel about the current political situation in Mexico?

OP I think that the PRI has completed its task. We're really in a period of transition. Let's hope it's a gradual and peaceful one and that we arrive at a pluralist democracy.

CUBA

.

Guillermo Cabrera Infante

Cuba, like Mexico, has been one of the strongest literary nations in Latin America. Despite widespread poverty, in the early part of the century Cuba had a middle class large enough to support a thriving literary community. Cuban writing drew on many influences, including the French avant-garde and the African culture that has left such strong traces in the Caribbean.

The Cuban revolution of 1959 brought about very basic changes in the condition of the writer. Guillermo Cabrera Infante would contend that it was easier to write even under the corrupt dictatorship of Fulgencio Batista than under communism, yet he, like most of the Cuban writers now living abroad, was initially supportive of the revolution.

Cabrera Infante's early work *Así en la paz como en la guerra* (1960) is politically committed, tracing the ramifications of poverty and state-sponsored violence in the years that led up to the fall of Batista. It also reveals a concern with the gratuitous and accidental. A fascination with the anarchic, which Cabrera Infante was later to explore through humour, leads him to focus on apparently irrelevant details with a cinematic clarity, as when an ant crawls across a wall where a man is to be shot.

Cabrera Infante's interest in humour and the cinema is evident in *Un oficio del siglo veinte* (1963), a collection of mock film reviews. The visual element is very important in *View of Dawn in the Tropics* (1974), a series of glimpses of history. Eduardo Galeano used this technique some years later, but whereas Galeano writes in an attempt to revivify history, Cabrera Infante sees history as a series of tragic accidents, of lost, sad

and now unknowable moments; implicit in this is his rejection
of Marxism.

His last book written before going into exile was *Three
Trapped Tigers* (1967), which moves away from cinematic
economy to verbal abundance, play and sensuousness. In a
welter of anecdote, parody and verbal wizardry a complex
social portrait of a sad and hedonistic city begins to emerge.
Three Trapped Tigers is one of the great achievements of modern
Latin American writing.

Infante's Inferno (1979) is a pseudo-autobiography that has
moved a long way from the very socially responsible attitudes
of *Así en la paz como en la guerra*. In fact it focuses on areas that
a committed writer would find most unworthy: the narrator
chronicles his sexual adventures from an early age to maturity.
The book is so close to a simply literal account that it verges
on both pornography and non-fiction; it seems to have no
larger theme. On this level it is a literary thumbing of the nose.
On another, it is a sort of picaresque novel, the narrator slowly
climbing out of poverty and frustrating meanness, the inferno
of the title. The hero grows gradually in status and self-esteem
as he finds a purely personal escape, one without solidarity. He
says bitterly of two people, who have let him down, one a
communist: they are not his brothers, never his equals.

Infante's Inferno may owe something to radical French realism
of the 1950s, in that it excludes metaphor or any sort of imagery;
it is a refusal to make literature an analogy for anything larger
than itself. Austerity of intent, however, gives rise to indulgence
in a wealth of sensory and sensual detail. The world is as it is
perceived, not as it is supposed or idealized.

Holy Smoke (1985), which Cabrera Infante wrote in English,
is a return to the audacious game playing of *Three Trapped
Tigers*. It retells Cuban history in terms of the history of the
cigar, with the implied exaltation of Groucho over Karl Marx.
This is flippancy with a purpose. Cabrera Infante continues to
be one of the great innovators and provocative practical jokers
of fiction.

GP Since the 1930s there has been quite an advanced literary culture in Cuba, hasn't there, with an interesting mixture of influences from France, Spain and Africa?

GCI In terms of poetry, I feel that the nineteenth century was more important than the twentieth. For example, there was José María de Heredia and his nephew of the same name, author of *Les Trophées*. Heredia was the first to write romantic poetry in Spanish, a remarkable feat, though the only place you'll find him commemorated is on a plaque on the Canadian side of Niagara Falls. (He wrote a famous ode to Niagara.) Heredia was a model even for modern writers. He was a man without a country. You could call him an early exile.

Another important poet called Zenea also went into exile; he didn't follow the path of poetry but became disastrously involved in politics. He became rather a megalomaniac and decided that he could change the course of the Ten Years' War Cuba fought with Spain in the 1890s. He felt he could be a mediator between the rebels and the Spanish government. Zenea obtained a safe conduct from the Spanish embassy in Washington and came back to Havana. Then he went on to the rebel camp where he asked for an interview with the commander-in-chief of the rebels, Carlos Manuel de Céspedes, Cuba's first president in arms. Céspedes wrote memorably of their encounter: 'This poet came by who turned out to be rather a rare bird. He didn't dare tell me one word about his project.' Fidel Castro, another guerrilla chief, had the same attitude some years later: with similar machismo, he sees poets as rare birds. Zenea, without discussing his plans with Céspedes, went back to Havana, where the Spanish governor had him arrested as a spy. They kept him prisoner for six months and then shot him. He wrote a pathetic poem before he died.

There is also the case of José Martí, who I consider to be the greatest nineteenth-century prose writer in Spanish and whose poetry even influenced Rubén Darío. He wrote lines such as, 'I have two loves, Cuba and the night,' and some very mysterious poetic reflections on death. At seventeen he was sent into exile over matters that in many countries would have been considered trifling misdemeanours. The Spanish government only allowed him to return to Cuba for a brief three months in 1878, then in 1895 he returned for nineteen days as the president elect of the republic in arms and head of the insurgent forces. Without doubt, he committed suicide. He was very unpopular with some of the other leaders of the insurrection abroad. In the first skirmish with the Spaniards one of the commanders-in-chief, Máximo Gómez, said to him, 'Get out of the way, President.' Martí then mounted his horse and rode directly towards the Spanish troops, who shot him dead. Martí, like Zenea and Heredia, was a romantic poet but clearly too concerned with politics.

Another poet whose case is interesting, Julio del Casal, spent all his life in Havana and lived in poverty. Like many Cubans in the late nineteenth century his family had been ruined by the wars. He was a great admirer of Verlaine and other con-temporary French poets, but unlike the other Cuban poets he wasn't at all interested in politics. He had tuberculosis and one night when he was in a café in Havana someone made a joke and he began to laugh. The laughter turned into a vomit of blood. He'd burst one of the arteries of his lung and he died instantly. He was only thirty-five.

Yes, I believe that the last century was more interesting than the present one.

GP Even though this century has Cuban writers such as Alejo Carpentier?

GCI That is different. He is a prose writer. I was really talking only about the poets. I would rank Virgilio Piñera and Lino Novás Calvo as peers of Carpentier. Many would also add José Lezama Lima, but I've always felt that the praise given to his novel *Paradiso* meant his work as a poet was overlooked, yet his really important achievement was his poetry, not his prose. In my opinion he is the greatest Spanish-speaking poet Latin America has seen this century. He is largely unappreciated because his poetry is not exactly difficult but truly hermetic. He is a cross between Góngora and Mallarmé and has explored areas where normally only fools rush in and all the well-known literary angels fear to tread. He's been much praised by other writers, people like Vargas Llosa and Julio Cortázar, but they have been interested in his only novel, not in his profuse poetry.

Piñera was a novelist, a short-story writer and a playwright; Novás Calvo was a master of the short story who could easily be placed next to Jorge Luis Borges and Juan Rulfo. Because Piñera was a homosexual, he suffered much indignity from people like Che Guevara and was even sent to prison for 'improper conduct', which consisted of wearing sandals and shorts – he lived on the beach. Novás Calvo, who was born in Galicia, died in exile in New York in a hideous old people's home. Lezama Lima, after being denied an exit permit, died of neglect in Havana. Obviously, the life of the exiled writer is Lot's lot: never look back.

GP Poetry doesn't seem to have had a great influence on your prose style. You began writing in a very simple, concrete and rather cinematic way.

GCI I was influenced by a certain kind of poetry, what you'd call popular poetry, such as songs – the lyrics of *boleros*, various kinds of Cuban music – and, above all, that other form of popular poetry, the cinema. The dialogue of the movies made a great impression on me when I was very young, before it occurred to me to become a writer.

At the age of eight or nine I was already a movie fan. Bits and pieces of movie dialogue naturally stayed in my mind. For example, I remember going to see *Scarface* in 1936, starring Paul Muni and George Raft. The Paul Muni character had an obvious obsession with luxury. When he was hired as a bodyguard, he looked at his boss's suit and touched it, saying, 'Expensive, eh?' Those words were like a leitmotif in the film; when he found himself with the boss's moll he touched her silk dress and said, 'Expensive, eh?' This was clearly a way to imply that he wanted to have not only the boss's suit but his moll and whatever else he saw as belonging to his employer. At the time I had no idea what the words meant, but that didn't stop me from going around repeating this phrase, 'Expensive, eh?' My friends in my home town did this too, though none of us had any idea what we were saying.

There is this element of popular poetry in everything I've written, but it is true that I haven't shown a tendency to assimilate more difficult forms of poetry. All the same, in *Three Trapped Tigers* you can see the influence not only of Joyce and Lewis Carroll but of Mallarmé, who has always interested me a great deal. My next book, to be called *Cuerpos divinos*, begins with a quote from Mallarmé disguised as one of the narrator's thoughts. The quote comes from the beginning of 'Prélude à l'après-midi d'un faune': 'I want to make these nymphs live for ever.' I like that line very much and it fits in well with the subject of the book, which is women. This book could be called *L'après-midi d'Infante*.

GP Your early work *Así en la paz como en la guerra* is written in the style of realism. Were you influenced by the French realists?

GCI No, all the influences were American: William Faulkner, primarily, then Ernest Hemingway and J. D. Salinger. Other American writers interested me at the time, like Erskine Caldwell and Sherwood Anderson. The French influences are evident in another book of mine, *Un oficio del siglo veinte*, which purports to be a collection of cinema criticism, though it is a work of fiction. Raymond Queneau and the critics of Cahiers du Cinéma were influential here, but the book is really about the interplay between criticism considered as a form of fiction and fiction become friction. Interplay means to play a game – just like tennis with two balls!

GP You began with very politically committed works, didn't you?

GCI Only *Así en la paz como en la guerra* can be considered political – not the stories themselves, but the organization of the book, which was hideously Sartrean. I've disowned this book, but it keeps creeping back.

GP What about *View of Dawn in the Tropics*?

GCI The aim there was to debunk history.

GP *Holy Smoke* is also concerned with debunking history, isn't it?

GCI I'd say that *View of Dawn in the Tropics* was a sad song, whereas *Holy Smoke* wants to treat whimsy as though it were something very important and decisive. I tried not to worry that the book might seem to offer frivolous and fancy phrases or be facetious. It was enough that it should carry a certain form that interested me.

GP I have the impression that humour is for you, as it was for Oscar Wilde, a means of self-defence. It offers a way for a member of a minority to defend himself against the majority.

GCI That's possible. I like the comparison with Wilde. Like Borges, I think of Wilde as a great writer. Humour for me is often a game, just a game. I can't resist using *salidas de tono* to extricate myself from a catch phrase. Wilde didn't really do that. He was more interested in the epigram. His humour was based on something that the Victorians were the first to see as a source of literature, inversion. Lewis Carroll is the great writer that he is, not because of his use of the pun but because of his reversals of logic. Wilde did the same. He is a great inventor of reversed sentences, some of them really masterful. Unfortunately one of his poses was to adopt a moral stance when he was only a humorist. That's why Beerbohm or Lear, both homosexuals, escaped Wilde's nights of wrath.

GP Doesn't it worry you that some people won't take books such as *Holy Smoke* seriously?

GCI Absolutely not! The book was very poorly understood in the United States but it was well understood where understanding was important to me: in England. It was written simply to outdo two English writers: Compton Mackenzie and his book *Sublime Tobacco*, and J. M. Barrie's *My Lady Nicotine*. I began with the aim of writing a book about tobacco and specifically about the cigar. I wanted it to be lighter than Barrie's book and to have more information than Mackenzie's. I don't think Compton Mackenzie is a great writer but he has written one of the best books about smoking. Barrie's book is, like the man himself, very light, very elegant and very

Edwardian. Every time I read his book I wear a velvet smoking jacket and a paisley scarf I treasure. I envy Barrie's title but in these Jacobean times the Surgeon General thinks otherwise.

GP But wasn't the most important impulse in writing the book the wish to compare Karl Marx with Groucho Marx?

GCI No, not exactly. I've made that comparison in other works, for example in a long short story called 'Delito por bailar el chachachá', which appeared in 1967 or 1968 in Paris, in the magazine *Mundo Nuevo*. This story had the express purpose of combining the levity of Groucho with the gravity of Karl. Of course, the story is all ironic. Irony was also very important in *View of Dawn in the Tropics*, where a heroic story is told but the ending tends to undercut heroism.

I believe there are two great illnesses – not just in Cuba but affecting mankind in general – namely, the love of heroes and patriotism. I see both as ways of fooling the majority of the people. Heroes are heroes only when they are allowed to be so. There were heroes in the fight against Batista because the dictatorship created heroes. The dictatorship was cruel but discontinuously so. It was menacing and also careless. In contrast Castro's dictatorship hasn't permitted heroes.

I knew heroes who fought against Batista. Many of them even became martyrs. One was a friend of mine, named Enrique Hart. He was the brother of the present Cuban minister for culture, Armando Hart. When I knew Enrique Hart he was a very intelligent young man. He wasn't an extremist, he wasn't even political, but he died in a house in Havana because he was making bombs. One of them exploded and he was torn to pieces. This upset me a lot because I felt that Enrique ought not to have died in this way. The other hero I knew at that time was Commandante Alberto Mora, who was an intimate friend. He spent six months hidden in my house but finally ended up in jail. He managed to survive until the revolution succeeded and they made him minister for foreign trade. However, he fell into disgrace with Castro, such disgrace that Fidel planned to send him to work as a rural labourer. The night before he was to be sent away he shot himself.

So, the hero under Batista becomes a weakling under Castro. It seems that under Castro a man as brave as Alberto Mora wasn't allowed to be the hero he was under Batista. It wasn't because he'd changed with age. He can't have been thirty when he killed himself. There were other eponymous heroes under Batista who became cowed under Castro and mere minions. One wonders if they were really heroes.

GP There are heroes in *View of Dawn*, though they are unknown. You seem to be mocking the sort of heroism commemorated in statues in public places.

GCI There are also useless martyrs.

GP The bravest people in the book seem to be those who die alone or with just a friend.

GCI That's true up to a point. There is one character that the social realists or the Stalinists would call a positive hero, who appears in a verbal snapshot in front of a house, dressed as a commandant, but he later dies in a banal accident. But in general what you say is true.

GP You seem to have a liking for characters who aren't approved of. In *Infante's Inferno* there is a passage where a neighbour asks the narrator 'Did you wake up a lunatic today?' In the book waking up a lunatic seems to be rather a good thing. I wonder if you'd like more people to be such lunatics – or at least less serious.

GCI Less serious, yes. More playful, yes. But not crazier, because madness is something that, unfortunately, I've suffered here in London and it is a state of extreme anguish and disorder. Madness is not a state which permits play. It is certainly not a state that you could recommend as a magnificent protection against society. The idea that lunatics are created by the system or their surroundings is absolutely false. Madness is like other illnesses, such as cancer, where the symptoms are clear but the causes are unknown. I wouldn't wish what I went through on anybody. I certainly wouldn't recommend that any of my readers solve any of their problems by going crazy. You can't say that the great madman of literature, Hamlet, did very well out of his madness. No, I don't recommend waking up a lunatic.

GP Rather than talking about madness perhaps we could talk about humour?

GCI There is a connection between humour and madness, no doubt about it. I like moments in literature where the humour has no cause, where it is a little gratuitous. This brings it very close to madness. You can see that in the case of a great French humorist Alfonse Allais. At the end of the last century he wrote a series of short stories that are exemplary, though he didn't feel they were at all important. Writing was just a job for him. He lived on the outskirts of Paris. In the afternoon he would sit in a popular café drinking absinthe, a drink that later killed him. After a while the owner of the café would come and say, 'Monsieur Allais, your messenger is about to arrive.' He would then set to work writing his five pages at the table and just as the five o'clock train was about to leave for Paris his messenger would arrive to take the completed work to the newspaper.

This extraordinary writer was very much appreciated by the surrealists. For instance, he wrote a short story called 'The Umbrellas of the Squad' and then explained that the title had umbrellas but the story had none! Coincidentally (and this shows that if there is an *esprit de corps*, there is also a *corps d'esprit*) Erik Satie composed a piece which he called 'Trois morceaux en forme de poire'. The music was about everything but pears or the number three! Even at high school in Havana I knew of Satie and his exploits. But I discovered Allais only many years later, when I was editing *Lunes de revolución* and commissioned a translation of three of his stories – none, by the way, in the shape of a pear. Allais had a vein of humour that was close to madness.

You could say the same of the work of Mark Twain, Raymond Queneau or the English humorists like Lear and Carroll, where logic loses control of the text. The text itself takes the reins and the result is very close to the reasoning of a lunatic. This is the point where the link between madness and humour interests me. Above all when the humour is completely gratuitous and unexplained. Neither of the two great analysts of humour, Freud and Bergson, really understood their subject, because they weren't humorists, they were explainers of humour. One must laugh at Bergson's *Le Rire*. Then again, where is Freud's umbrella? The two things are very different.

GP Very committed people and those very firm in their convictions seldom have a sense of humour. I imagine that Karl Marx had no sense of humour, for instance.

GCI No, I think he did. The disagreeable thing about Marx is not his relationship with what he wrote but rather the implications his writings have. The fact is that if he woke up today he would realize that he had been completely wrong in his economic analysis. But in *Das Kapital* – which I haven't read but looked through once – there is this sentence: 'As goods cannot go unaccompanied to market there have to be intermediaries.' That is a very funny statement and also a statement of economic analysis. A number of phrases like that appear in his writing, so you have to presume he had a sense of humour. The one who had no sense of humour was Engels. He was an industrialist and very worried about money matters – including Marx's financial situation. Marx was really a bohemian.

GP However, his thought was clear, systematic and definite, while humour is naturally subversive.

GCI Nevertheless, I think humour is not absent in Marx. It is absent in his followers. Lenin was humourless. Stalin was sinister. Khrushchev, whom I met along with Brezhnev in the USSR, had a peasant's sense of humour. After all, he came from rural Russia. Brezhnev, on the other hand, had no sense of humour at all. That seems to be a characteristic of those who have a Marxist education. Fidel Castro, of course, came to Marxism late in life, but he doesn't have a sense of humour either. That is not Marx's fault, because Castro never had any sense of humour other than a sense of scorn, a kind of disdainful irony.

I think that humour, in a sense, is always gratuitous. Humour doesn't wait for anything to happen, not even laughter. Laughter comes after humour but that is not because humour has an end or a purpose. In fact there is no direct link between humour and laughter.

GP Humour works against the creation of heroes. In your book *Holy Smoke*, you tell an alternative history of Cuba, an unheroic one. You tell the history of trivial things, which are important despite this appearance of triviality.

GCI It's not only the history of Cuba that is treated with humour. The book also looks humorously at the planting, cultivation, harvesting and processing of cigars. The reason for the humour was that I was dealing with material that had been written about before. Books had been written about the cultivation and processing of tobacco. I would have been bored simply copying this. So, introducing the disruptive element of humour was a way of avoiding the boredom, mine and the reader's. Don't you think starting a book about the cigar with a quotation referring to *The Bride of Frankenstein* is funny? From the very first sentence I'm laying my cards on the table, letting the reader know that this can't be a serious book. It is a fictitious history. The name of the game is not fact but facetiae.

GP In *The War at the End of the World* Mario Vargas Llosa has one of his characters say that men always see a logic or a pattern in circumstances that isn't really there. Reality is always much more complex and mysterious and unreachable than our schematic theories. Does your idea of writing about apparently trivial things support this?

GCI No, it's just that humour has always been a part of my character. When I was a student, for example, I was known as a joker. At that time I hadn't even thought of being a writer. I wanted to be a baseball player. Later I wanted to be a bongo player. Never a writer. Humour is really a character trait. No matter how much Thomas Mann or Tolstoy or Dostoyevsky wrote, they'd never be humourous writers. With Chekhov or Gogol, on the other hand, humour is essential. Even when they are writing about serious matters you can always detect, if not laughter, then at least a smile on their sealed lips. Or just a crack.

GP Does the English sense of humour have anything to do with your settling in England?

GCI In my experience, having lived here for twenty-three years, the English don't have a sense of humour. They've never had one. The reputation they enjoy for it is due to two or three extraordinary writers. Shakespeare, for example, had a great sense of humour, but Marlowe didn't. The other Elizabethan poets had less humour than Marlowe. Ben Jonson had an understanding of satire and irony but he didn't have a sense of humour. Over the centuries you find that the English have shown less of a sense of humour than the Spanish. The witty Englishman is just one of those stereotypes that are built up over time. The French, for example, are supposed to be avaricious, but that's not true at all.

There have been English writers with an exceptional sense of humour, such as Sterne, Wodehouse or Waugh, but the majority of English writers are stern and not swift enough. In fact the English are always complaining that this or that novel is not serious, that it's whimsical or facetious. For example, one of the things that otherwise generous English critics have criticized in my work is the abundance of puns. This is a direct attack on humour because the pun is vital to humour. I think that writing that uses the pun is closer to poetry than to prose. I don't believe that the books considered important here show a sense of humour – with the exception of Anthony Burgess. The most recent generation of English writers has been very serious indeed. Peter Ackroyd is really serious, as is Martin Amis.

GP I wasn't only thinking of literary humour. The English have a reputation for being very witty in everyday life.

GCI They also have a reputation for being very civilized and law-abiding, yet they also produce some of the biggest riots when it comes to something as peaceful as going to a football match.

No, my reason for living here had nothing to do with either

humour or the English. In fact, I went to Spain initially, because my wife, who was an actress, could work in Madrid. When, after nine months, I went to apply for a resident's permit, the police asked me political questions about Cuba. I refused to answer – quite reasonably, because I couldn't be expected to know about current Cuban politics after nine months in Spain. Finally I was told, 'We'd better keep this resident's permit for some other Cuban, more in need than you are. You travel a lot. You can find shelter somewhere else.' There was a film director here in London who wanted me to work on a script with him. So I came here.

It wasn't humour that tempted me to stay, it was the fact that I arrived in June. There was wonderful sunshine. It never rained. I thought that the English climate must be similar to the Cuban. This was 1966 and the era of 'Swinging London' had arrived, with girls wearing see-through blouses or very short skirts. As Renfield says in Dracula, they looked very inviting. I presumed that these things would remain unchanged, so I settled here. But the sun disappeared behind autumn clouds and the girls covered their limbs for the winter.

At the beginning it was difficult. I had a stamp in my passport saying that I was forbidden to work, whether paid or not. An English lawyer helped me in my predicament, pointing out that I didn't need to look for work. I was my own employer and I produced a product for sale, my writing, so I didn't have to worry any more. I stayed, having really arrived at my destination by chance, as Einstein would say.

GP Do you think your difficulties in Franco's Spain were due to Spanish suspicion about Cubans?

GCI Not suspicion, rather the certain knowledge that I had been the editor of a magazine called *Lunes de Revolución*, which had published six issues on Spain and its suffering under Franco, on the Spanish writers in exile and so on. One issue even began with a series of drawings that Franco was known to hate, a sequence by Picasso called 'Misery and Fear under Franco'. In a bureaucratic fashion they had their pound of flesh.

GP When I spoke to Mario Benedetti about exile from

Cuba he said that it was a question of self-exile. No one had expelled the Cuban writers. Did you leave because you wanted to?

GCI No one flees their country just because it takes their fancy. In my case, living had become unbearable. At one time I thought that, while you perhaps couldn't write in Cuba, you could at least live there! When I returned from my diplomatic post in Brussels I realized that you couldn't even live there. Just being alive was deadly. Laws weren't respected. Something you did innocently today might turn out to be a crime tomorrow and the police were creating laws as they went to wake you early in the morning. That is a characteristic of all police states. If conditions weren't bad, how do you explain the one and a half million Cuban exiles? Why didn't they flee before, when there were difficult times under Batista?

GP You are very much aware of the evils of Batista's Cuba, aren't you?

GCI More than a little aware. I have the misfortune to be the son of one of the founders of the Cuban Communist Party. My parents were taken prisoner in 1936 by Batista. They were released after six months due to lack of evidence. Yet in 1937 my parents were canvassing for Batista as president because there had been an agreement between Batista and the Communist Party, which had been legalized.

So I have seen all the changes in Cuba. It is not as if I arrived one day from Uruguay and left when I wished to. Remember that there are many people who want to leave Cuba but can't. Asking for a permit to leave is looked on very unfavourably. You automatically lose your job. They cut off your telephone. Your belongings (if not your days) are numbered and later confiscated. It is very difficult indeed to leave the Cuban paradise.

GP Do you think that life for today's Cuban is better than in the 1930s or 1940s? Haven't the standards of living improved?

GCI No, not at all. How can you expect a totalitarian regime to improve things? Why not ask about the 1950s? I'd say that Batista's Cuba was totally corrupt but there were at least pockets of life where you could live without being part of that corruption. For example, the magazine *Bohemia*, or *Carteles*, where I worked. You could enter or leave the country when you wanted. You could evade the sporadic censorship to an extent. At least there were laws, even though they could be circumvented. Today in Cuba you have no human rights. No one can enter or leave the country freely. Life is extremely difficult for the average citizen. People have lived with ration cards for twenty-seven years. Even in Poland, when there is scarcity, you don't need ration cards. The list of grievances is long, but the queues are longer. Life is really terrible. All they've done in Cuba is to socialize poverty.

GP Returning to literature, do you see a line of development running through your novels?

GCI In the first place, I wouldn't refer to my books as novels. They are just books. They're not really novels if you look closely. In *Infante's Inferno* there is a certain tension between fiction and autobiography. At one point the narrator says, 'I have decided to be faithful to my memory even though it deceives me.' Contradictions of fact run like a seam throughout the book. Life is more deceptive than fiction.

I've had many debates with publishers who want to call my books novels; they argue that if the bookshops don't put them amongst the novels, where else will they put them? The Englishman who designed the cover for *Holy Smoke* objected to the cover photograph that I had provided – the picture is of Groucho Marx lying down, feigning sleep with an unlit cigar in his mouth – because he said the book might be misplaced and put into the cinema section. I retorted (I always retort) that I couldn't think of a nicer place for it to be.

GP *Infante's Inferno* is rather like one of those 'continuous showing' movies – you could pick it up at any point and read through until you returned to the same point.

GCI That is why the epilogue is called '*función continua*' in the Spanish edition. I also feel that each chapter could be read separately. In fact, a chapter previously omitted from the

English and American editions has recently appeared as a short story in an American magazine.

GP The picaresque aspects of writing are clearly important to you. It's not just that your characters are often *pícaros* but that your books have the same, very linear structure.

GCI The picaresque novel first appeared in Spain around the end of the Middle Ages, when there were new social conditions. It featured social climbers taking advantage of their disadvantages. The last truly picaresque novel was *Don Quijote*. There is the *pícaro*, Sancho, but also the opposite extreme, the innocent hero. Don Quijote is dragged along by the times but he is really a reactionary and belongs to a different social class than the *pícaros*. The dreams of the night are the facts of fiction. You can see a similar pattern in certain American novels, whether from North or South America. *Huckleberry Finn*, for example, is a picaresque novel. There is the same two-character pattern. Huckleberry Finn is very astute, while the Negro is very loyal. To an extent *Huckleberry Finn* is derived from *Don Quijote*. You could say the same of *Tristram Shandy*. Even Sterne, a shifty character, acknowledged this.

GP Milan Kundera said that Sterne opened up paths for the novel which, up to now, have not really been explored. I noticed that you included a black page in *Three Trapped Tigers*.

GCI The path was opened up somewhat earlier, when *Don Quijote* was published. Modern role models forbid seeing this clearly. I've been very much influenced by Sterne but the black page was also a homage to Raymond Chandler. That part of the book refers to an occurrence very common in Chandler: the hero appears to be bumped off. He claims to fall dead into a black hole, only to awaken some time later. I've always been an avid reader of Chandler, ever since I was very young. Chandler introduces the element of humour into the detective novel. He is not a hard-boiled writer. He is really a humorist who adopted the genre for his hero to be the smiler with his gun under a cloak.

GP Both the detective and the picaresque novels are alternatives to the sort of novel that emphasizes the development of character and ethical and moral issues. You don't seem to be interested in deep character analysis in your novels. Why is that?

GCI I've wanted to avoid writing psychological narratives. My characters generally don't have any family. There is friendship in *Three Trapped Tigers*, but it's a doubtful sort of friendship. *Infante's Inferno*, on the other hand, has an immediate relation to the family, always there in the background. Of course the suppression of the family is not my invention. It's common to a lot of literature this century. But you are right: I'm not interested in characters or in plot development or in narrative display.

GP At the beginning of *Three Trapped Tigers* there is the story of a country girl who has left her parents.

GCI It really begins with a false narrator, who introduces you to characters you think are going to be the protagonists, but of course they never appear. That is something I adopted from Pirandello. It is a way of pointing out that nothing that happens in a book is ever real. Rather, you have to read and gradually understand what it's all about. The book begins with a master of ceremonies at the Tropicana cabaret introducing all these characters and incidentally shedding some light on Havana. A little later you find the characters rebelling rather than revealing, having come to life, or rather having arrived in the big city. That is the beginning of the section called 'The Debutantes'.

A French critic saw very clearly the relation of this kind of writing to detective fiction. He claimed that *Three Trapped Tigers* is where semiology meets the detective novel. The whole book is a kind of *cherchez la femme*. Everyone is looking for the woman who goes to the psychiatrist and who turns out to be Laura. She is in love with Silvestre and is at the root of the great betrayal in the book, namely the betrayal of Arsenio Cué by his bosom pal Silvestre. These are the connotations that interest me most.

I was also interested in introducing Cuban music into a novel as a kind of popular poetry. The fact that there is a 'suite' called

'She Sang *Boleros*' is central to the novel. The constant mention of music is of course important, as is the fact that one of the characters is a bongo player. This is much more interesting to me than the introduction of literary elements in the book.

GP One character in *Infante's Inferno* says, 'Love has no morality.' Is that linked to your comparative lack of interest in moral or ethical issues?

GCI It's not just that love has no morality. More importantly, humour has no morality. Words have no morality. True literature, as Chekhov said, is amoral.

Select Bibliography

(This is a list of some relevant titles available in English translation. Editions in Spanish have been listed for some works not in translation.)

Mario Benedetti

Inventario, Editorial Nueva Imagen (rev. edn), 1978
Pedro y el Capitán: pieza en cuatro partes, Editorial Nueva Imagen, 1979
Primavera con una esquina rota, Editorial Nueva Imagen, 1982
The Treaty, Harper & Row, 1969

Eduardo Galeano

Days and Nights of Love and War, Monthly Review, 1983; Pluto Press, 1983
Memory of Fire (3 volumes), Pantheon, 1986–8; Quartet Books, 1986–9
The Open Veins of Latin America: Five Centuries of the Pillage of a Continent, Monthly Review, 1983

Mario Vargas Llosa

Aunt Julia and the Scriptwriter, Farrar, Straus & Giroux, 1982; Faber & Faber, 1983

Conversation in the Cathedral, Harper & Row, 1975

The Green House, Harper & Row, 1968; Cape, 1969

The Perpetual Orgy, Farrar, Straus & Giroux, 1986; Faber & Faber, 1987

The Real Life of Alejandro Mayta, Farrar, Straus & Giroux, 1986; Faber & Faber, 1986

The Storyteller, Faber & Faber, 1990

The Time of the Hero, Grove Press, 1966; Penguin Books, 1966

The War at the End of the World, Farrar, Straus & Giroux, 1984; Faber & Faber, 1985

Who Killed Palomino Molero?, Farrar, Straus & Giroux, 1987; Faber & Faber, 1988

José Donoso

The Boom in Spanish American Literature: A Personal History, University of Columbia Press, 1977

Curfew (La Desesperanza), Weidenfeld & Nicolson, 1988

A House in the Country, Knopf, 1983; Allen Lane, 1984

The Obscene Bird of Night, Knopf, 1973; Cape, 1974

This Sunday, Knopf, 1967; Bodley Head, 1968

Isabel Allende

Eva Luna, Knopf, 1988; Hamish Hamilton, 1989

The House of Spirits, Knopf, 1985; Cape, 1985

Of Love and Shadows, Knopf, 1987; Cape, 1987

Ernesto Sábato

On Heroes and Tombs, Godine, 1981; Cape, 1982

The Tunnel, Random House, 1988; Cape, 1988

Manuel Puig

Betrayed by Rita Hayworth, Dutton, 1971; Arena, 1984

Blood of Requited Love, Aventura, 1984; Faber & Faber, 1984

The Buenos Aires Affair: A Detective Story, Dutton, 1976; Faber & Faber, 1989

Eternal Curse on the Reader of These Pages, Random House, 1982; Arena, 1985

Heartbreak Tango: A Serial, Dutton, 1976; Faber & Faber, 1989

The Kiss of the Spider Woman, Knopf, 1979; Arena, 1984

Pubis Angelical, Random House, 1986; Faber & Faber, 1987

Under a Mantle of Stars, Lumen, 1983

Luisa Valenzuela

Clara: Thirteen Short Stories and a Novel, Harcourt Brace Jovanovich, 1976

He Who Searches, Dalkey Arch, 1987

The Lizard's Tale, Farrar, Straus & Giroux, 1983; Serpent's Tail, 1987

Open Door, North Point Press, 1988

Other Weapons, Ediciones del Norte, 1985

Augusto Roa Bastos

I the Supreme, Knopf, 1986; Faber & Faber, 1987

Son of Man, Gollancz, 1965

Márcio Souza

The Emperor of the Amazon, Avon, 1977; Sphere, 1982

Mad Maria, Avon, 1985

The Order of the Day: An Unidentified Flying Opus, Avon, 1986

Ignácio de Loyola Brandão

And Still the Earth, Avon, 1985

Zero, Avon, 1984

Lygia Fagundes Telles

The Girl in the Photograph, Avon, 1982
The Marble Dance, Avon, 1986
Tigrela and Other Stories, Avon, 1986

João Ubaldo Ribeiro

An Invincible Memory, Harper and Row, 1989; Faber & Faber,
 1989
Sergeant Getúlio, Houghton Mifflin, 1978; Faber & Faber, 1986

Jorge Amado

Captains of the Sand, Avon, 1988
Dona Flor and Her Two Husbands, Knopf, 1969; Weidenfeld &
 Nicolson, 1969
Gabriela, Clove and Cinnamon, Knopf, 1962; Chatto & Windus,
 1963
Home is the Sailor, Knopf, 1964; Chatto & Windus, 1964
Jubiabá, Avon, 1984
Pen, Sword and Camisole: A Fable to Kindle a Hope, Godine,
 1985
Sea of Death, Avon, 1984
Shepherds of the Night, Knopf, 1967; Collins Harvill, 1989
Showdown, Bantam, 1988
Tent of Miracles, Knopf, 1971; Collins Harvill, 1989
Tereza Batista: Home from the Wars, Knopf, 1975; Souvenir
 Press, 1982
Tieta, Knopf, 1979; Souvenir Press, 1981
The Two Deaths of Quincas Wateryell: A Tall Tale, Avon, 1965
The Violent Land, Knopf, 1945; Collins Harvill, 1989

Ana Miranda

Boca do Inferno, Companhia Das Letras, 1989

Manlio Argueta

Cuzcatlan, Chatto & Windus, 1987
One Day of Life, Chatto & Windus, 1984

Luis Alfredo Arango

Después del tango vienen los moros, Grupo Literario Editorial RIN-78, 1988

The Black Sheep and Other Fables, Doubleday, 1971
Lo demás es silencio, Joaquín Mortiz, 1978; Seix Barral, 1982
Movimiento perpetuo, Joaquín Mortiz, 1972; Seix Barral, 1981
Obras completas (y otros cuentos), Universidad Nacional Autónoma de México, 1959; Seix Barral, 1981
Viaje al centro de la fábula, Universidad Nacional Autónoma de México, 1981; Martin Casillas Editores, 1982

Elena Poniatowska

Dear Diego, Pantheon, 1986
Massacre in Mexico, Viking, 1975
Until We Meet Again, Pantheon, 1987

Octavio Paz

The Bow and the Lyre: The Poem. The Poetic Revelation. Poetry and History, University of Texas Press, 1973

The Collected Poems, 1957–1987, New Directions, 1987; Carcanet, 1988 ·

The Labyrinth of Solitude: Life and Thought in Mexico, Grove, 1961; Allen Lane, 1967

The Monkey Grammarian, Seaver, 1981; Peter Owen, 1989

Guillermo Cabrera Infante

Holy Smoke, Faber & Faber, 1985

Infante's Inferno, Harper & Row, 1984; Faber & Faber, 1984

Three Trapped Tigers, Harper & Row, 1971; Faber & Faber, 1989

View of the Dawn in the Tropics, Harper & Row, 1978; Faber & Faber, 1988